PRAISE FOR K.M. COLLEY

"All-consuming and totally arresting, The Roaring Ridleys is a party of a read. Colley's world-building will make you want to sit down with a bottle of champagne, and her edge-of-your-seat plotting will make you want to finish the book (and the bottle!) in one night. Colley loves the 1920s so much, and it's clear in her writing. This debut author is one to watch!"

—Nekesa Afia, author of *As Long as You're Mine*

THE ROARING RIDLEYS

THE ROARING RIDLEYS

A Novel

K.M. COLLEY

This is a work of fiction. Names, characters, organizations, places, events, and incidents are either products of the author's imagination or are used fictitiously.

Published by Thomas & Mercer, Seattle

www.apub.com

EU product safety contact:
Amazon Media EU S. à r.l.
38, avenue John F. Kennedy, L-1855 Luxembourg
amazonpublishing-gpsr@amazon.com

ISBN-13: 9781662536113 (paperback)
ISBN-13: 9781662536106 (digital)

Cover design by Logan Matthews
Cover image: © edwardolive, © Purebo, © Wachiwit, © VicW, © InnaFelker, © NatliZ / Shutterstock; © Annie Spratt / Unsplash

Printed in the United States of America

To the wonders who have fought to create spaces where they've always belonged

LONG ISLAND
The Garden of Eden
Speakeasy
The Ridley Estate
and Maze

THE RIDLEY ESTATE
Dock
Path
Beach
Garden Maze
Estate
Stables

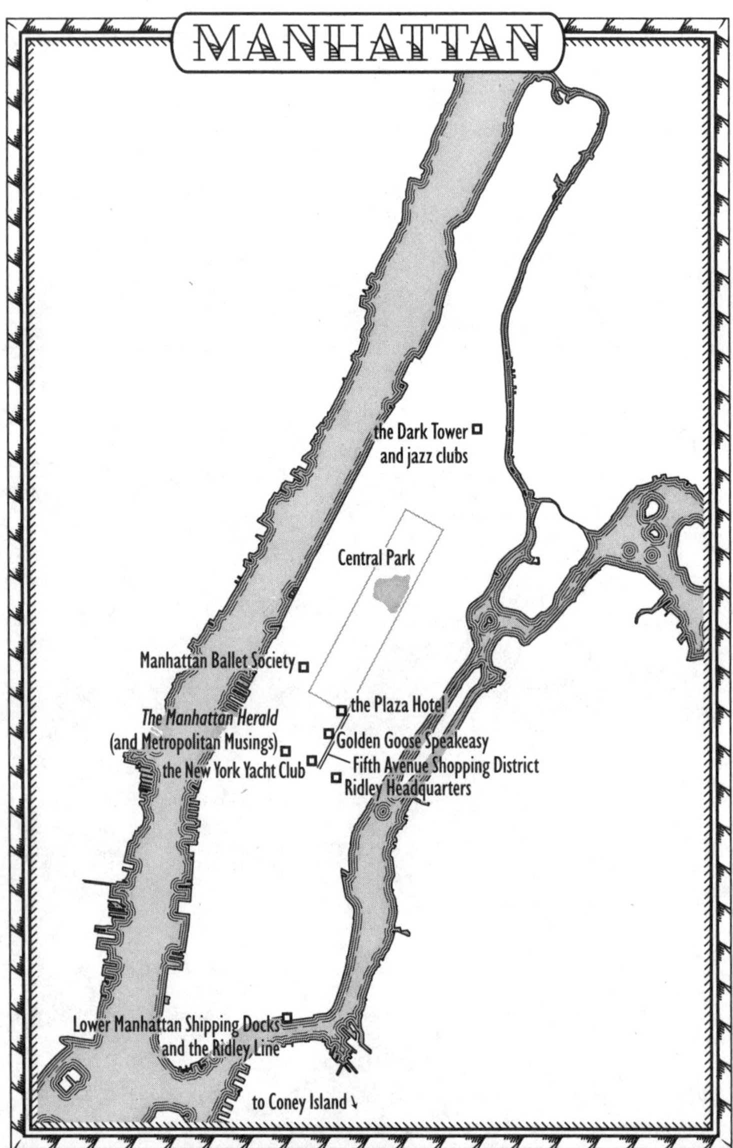
MANHATTAN
the Dark Tower
and jazz clubs
Central Park
Manhattan Ballet Society
the Plaza Hotel
The Manhattan Herald
(and Metropolitan Musings)
Golden Goose Speakeasy
the New York Yacht Club
Fifth Avenue Shopping District
Ridley Headquarters
Lower Manhattan Shipping Docks
and the Ridley Line
to Coney Island

Prologue

A gold envelope, the symbol of the most exclusive thing in New York City, was what everyone who was *anyone* eagerly awaited in the mail as summer approached. And what might the little envelope contain? An invitation, of course, to the most prestigious party in New York and perhaps even the entire United States. Gossip about who would be lucky enough to attend was rampant in cafés, hotel lobbies, and on the subway. Reporters scoured every available source for information about the family hosting the event. It was a spectacle, to say the least.

> *The Manhattan Herald*
> July 1, 1915
> Metropolitan Musings
> MR. AND MRS. RIDLEY ADOPT 7 CHILDREN!
>
> Mr. Edward Ridley and Mrs. Caroline Ridley of the Ridley Line are not only taking over the industry but also the hearts of the city. They have now adopted seven children from diverse backgrounds worldwide. Their little Seven Wonders, each with a unique story, are the new talk of the town. Amelia comes from Paris, Adesua from Illinois, and the youngest daughter, Kavita, is from India. Now for the handsome boys: Omar is from Egypt, Diego is from Argentina, Wei is from China, and

Henrik is from the United Kingdom. The Ridleys have put them in the most prestigious private schools and are finally happy that their family is complete.

To celebrate their big, new family, they will host what they are calling an inaugural annual party this summer—the first of many, they say. We at *The Manhattan Herald* are one of the fortunate few to have received a golden invitation early. Be on the lookout for one special invite, fellow New Yorkers!

So much time had passed since that grand momentous occasion. This set a precedent of what the Ridley family would soon be known for. Now, after twelve years, the Ridley family's philanthropic ways, from supporting education in underprivileged communities to funding medical research, had risen to a level that surpassed even the esteemed Astor and Vanderbilt families. Every year, Edward Ridley's favorite printmaker had to assemble a team of twenty to cope with the overwhelming demand for invites. The phones rang incessantly for weeks. Socialites and aspiring socialites alike went through hell and back to secure an invite, from sweet-talking anyone who'd listen to offering substantial sums to friends of friends who knew the Ridleys.

Was it all a little much? Maybe, but you'd be forgiven for going to exorbitant lengths. After all, the Ridleys' Annual Summer Party had evolved into a mecca of sorts, where the most influential gathered to discuss their new business ventures and make connections, and the wealthy gave back to the less fortunate communities through hefty donations. On the Gold Coast of Long Island, this party offered more than just decadent food, loud luxury, and dancing; it had become an opportunity for social climbing and finding a suitable partner to maintain your place in society's good graces.

It was where you could seize the attention of someone capable of changing your world. A rising young professional plucked from oblivion could arrive at the Ridleys' party as a nobody and leave as a star.

To attend was to have a shot at becoming like Edward Ridley himself: the embodiment of rags to riches. Whatever it took to get to 17 South Hampton Lane in East Meadow, Huntington, people did it *every* single year, using trains, ferries, vehicles, and for some local Long Islanders, even horses. Luxury cars filled the impeccable elm-tree-lined driveway and front lawn.

This year was a little different, but all the same nonetheless. All because the youngest Ridley daughter, Kavita, had recently gotten engaged. So of course, Mr. Ridley had to make this year's party a grand occasion. He strived for perfection in every last touch, and that included his seven children being the centerpieces that caught the guests' eyes. And the three Ridley daughters, now of age, had *everyone's* attention.

Chapter 1

Amelia Ridley

The grandfather clock's gold hands struck half past four. Yet, at 4:37 p.m., it was the *seven* that stood out in that time more than anything to Amelia. It had been seven years since the public had seen her, the Ridleys' eldest daughter, and the rest of her siblings together in one room. Still, that seven wasn't even the worst of it. It was now seven minutes and counting. Her insufferable youngest sister, Kavita, was late for their solo press interviews.

The garden room was stuffy that evening, with a heavy cloud forming in the room—not from the summer heat, but the hovering words that each might say. The members of the press cleared their throats, some coughing, trying to break the silence that kept aimlessly dragging on.

Father had insisted that each of them do an interview with the press in their sacred place—their *home*. This confused Amelia to no end, and she wondered why their father had invited the vultures into their safe haven, ready to tear into her and her siblings' flesh, regurgitating and twisting each word they said for every gaping mouth, widened eye, and listening ear in New York. Nonetheless, they never argued with Father. What he said went, no matter how they felt.

The Ridley Annual Summer Gala was now also an engagement party for Kavita. No one knew this but the family. Well, her siblings had had no idea Kavita was even engaged until, as of five hours ago, Father made a mandatory announcement, gloating that, finally, one of his children would be out of the estate. Father and Mother had raised them—especially Amelia and her sisters—to wed to make their family more powerful. That was the name of the game.

This changed *everything* for Amelia. Not only was she the eldest sister, and still unwed, in the most illustrious family in the city, but now her youngest sister—who was completely reckless, with scandals to boot—was getting married before she was. If she didn't seem unworthy of marriage before, she definitely took the cake now. It wasn't because of her looks either. Amelia Rose Ridley was nothing short of stunning by the highest degree.

Her chestnut-brown locks, olive skin tone, and piercing jade-green eyes that seemed to stare into your soul made her a sight to look at. The problem was the words that escaped her mouth, which made her seem like one of *those*. Too bold and brash to be told anything because she always had everything under control, or too blunt when she wasn't interested in a suitor, scaring them away. That was the way she liked it, anyway. Her on-again, off-again boyfriend since childhood, Jamison Grant, was the only man she would tolerate, but chatter had spread: If he wouldn't marry her, then who in the world would?

Amelia bit the tip of her tongue while rolling her eyes with annoyance as each of her siblings waited for her to do something. That didn't last long, though, because only one of the interviewers didn't seem to be taken aback. If anything, his creepy upside-down smile and prominent missing tooth made it clear that he took joy in the infamous Ridleys' disarray.

Dale Caimen, the sleazy head journalist of the famed gossip column Metropolitan Musings in *The Manhattan Herald*, with a smile as wide as a preying wolf, prowled for any weak moments to report back to his greedy coworkers at the paper. Amelia insisted on calling them the hyenas of New York. His mere presence was an eyesore, especially his face, weathered from two decades of taunting citizens, but not as much as his daunting burgundy leather briefcase. It was abnormally large compared to the others' belongings, as they had small journals, fountain pens, and cigarettes hanging from their dry mouths, thirsting for dirt. Dale took notice of Amelia's face, which was now twisted in disgust.

"So are we supposed to wait all day for the future, miss, or can we get to know more of what each of you has done these last seven years? Other than perfecting your poker faces," Dale said snarkily.

"Mr. Caimen, since you have so much haste, why don't you give your counterparts a chance to interview my eager siblings. A gentle reminder that they have done quite a few worthy things in their lives. Perhaps you can observe their talents to write about *us*, not you."

Amelia took a side glance of her sister Adesua, who shot her eyes to the door. With that, Amelia bolted out into the hallway, her footsteps echoing louder and louder. She wasn't sure whether her heels were making the sound or it was the constant strumming of her ever-raised heartbeat.

Mr. Caimen's laugh echoed from the garden room through the hallways, almost devilish. Amelia wondered whether he was mocking Adesua or her brother Wei, but now was not the time to think about them. Kavita, the most important detail, was missing. Usually, her insistence on showing up fashionably late wouldn't worry anyone, but this party was all about her. Amelia's palms glistened with beaded sweat. She tightened her fists, hoping the staff and early-comers passing by would see her forced smile. Mr. Caimen had been as ready for them as he would have been for the most prized possessions at an auction.

Amelia peered through every door, hoping to catch a glimpse of Kavita hiding somewhere like she had as a child, but to her dismay, her youngest sister was nowhere to be seen. She made a swift turn toward the garden, needing a chance to breathe even though the thick air felt trapped inside her. The water fountains sprawled throughout the garden maze and by the lake drowned out the incessant noise of the busy grounds.

Amelia found herself in a trance, watching the water trickle from the fountain's tiny lion's mouth. She chuckled slightly as she looked down the path that led to their perfect private beach that sat along Huntington Bay. She vividly remembered seeing Kavi's and Dusie's faces light up when they first moved here. They didn't get peculiar looks from strangers wondering why they were so happy together. It was like being in their own little world where they could just be themselves. Amelia didn't realize how long she had been out there, but she knew someone would be calling for her soon. Amelia always thought it was a gift given to the eldest daughter of every family: When a sibling needed her without saying her name, she was there as if it was magic. As she turned around to head back into the garden room, Dale stood there, blocking her path.

"Tell me, Amelia: How on earth does Kavita get involved with a man like Franklin?" he asked before setting down his briefcase and lighting a cigarette.

Amelia wanted so badly to kick that briefcase over and rip up any piece of paper she found in there, sabotaging anything he was working on, just like he had destroyed the reputation of people like her and the rest of high society. But she exhaled every pent-up feeling of wrath, biting her bottom lip.

"She must have found a way, like you find yours snooping into our everyday lives." She chuckled before continuing. "I guess you do have one thing in common with people like us."

Dale nodded, squinting his left eye before clicking his tongue. "Hmm, I suppose so. But we all know how your father raves about his daughters marrying the finest of New York—not the gutter class like Franklin. Unless your father and Kavita have something to hide?"

Amelia felt the knot in her throat grow thicker as she stared right through his beady black eyes. She swallowed her fear of the what-ifs surrounding her missing sister and her father, who had more secrets to bear. If she'd learned anything from him, it was to never let a pawn think he knew your next move.

"Actually, if you did better research with that ostentatious briefcase of yours, you would know my father started from those so-called 'gutters' you speak of. So yes, Franklin is more than acceptable to my sister Kavita, and has more class than you will ever have," she said with a pleasing head tilt, hoping he would try her once more.

Dale cocked his eyebrow, twisting his mouth in near defeat. "If you say so, darling. I must admit, I have other plans for you Ridleys that are far more entertaining than what any of you could say, but I am rather curious who your father shall name his successor." He winked at her while she took a shuttered look at his briefcase.

Amelia felt her heart stop in that moment. What could be more entertaining than this party? One thing Amelia Ridley didn't like was not knowing about a scandal. In this case, she knew Mr. Caimen had nothing to speak of them but pure ragged gossip, which he would twist to make sure the city's elite would remain humbled. At this moment, she refused to let him do that.

"Oh, I am quite sure our family keeps food on your table at night," Amelia said calmly, turning to walk away. "Also, I'll have you know, if you think you are going to make another headline, tearing down my siblings again, you are surely mistaken, Dale—I mean, Mr. Caimen." She brushed by the journalist, shoving into his shoulder as she did.

An hour had passed when Amelia and Adesua heard the sudden blaring of a loud car horn, coming closer to their winding driveway.

"Mellie, I think our little mischievous sister has returned," Adesua sighed as she pinned a loose curl.

Amelia scrambled toward the window, almost bumping into Adesua to see. There she was, like a stream of sunrays, smiling and giggling: Kavita Marie Ridley, pulling up in her blue Rolls-Royce. Her amber-bronzed skin stood out in her signature warm glow as she excitedly waved to everyone as she parked at the estate entrance. She was nearly hanging from the window.

Usually, this would have excited or relieved the two sisters, but not when they had less than two hours until the party started.

"Never mind her, Dusie. I have no time to deal with her games today. Let Mrs. Darla and Mother deal with her. Let's try on our dresses to see which looks better."

Amelia tried on dress options as Adesua slipped on her shoes. Amelia zipped up her sister's dress and marveled at her look. Adesua was a timeless beauty, with her coiled black hair adorned with pearls and crystals. Her onyx skin glistened as the falling sun shone through the window. But as soon as Amelia glanced at the clock, her nerves began to set back in.

Downstairs, the staff and lead maid, Mrs. Darla, rushed to Kavita to help her as she stumbled out of the car. Amelia caught the side-eye Adesua gave her, knowing they should go check on their wild-card sister. They opened up the French doors to the balcony to hear the commotion. Adesua caught a glance and could not contain her laughter.

"My God, she is falling over like a bull in a china shop," she said, while Amelia seethed. All four Ridley brothers—Wei, Omar, Diego, and Henrik—stood on the porch beneath them, sighing as their irresponsible younger sister failed to climb the steps.

"Dammit, Kavi. How many times do I have to carry you up the stairs? You aren't a kid anymore!" Omar said as he swooped her up.

She waved one hand at her brother and dragged ten shopping bags with the other. "Oh, my Mellie! My sweet, sweet Mellie. I got one helluva dress for ya tonight, hon!"

Omar was annoyed at her antics. "Why don't you be quiet before Mother and Father find out about this?"

The other brothers had a hoot, sipping their old-fashioneds.

"Did you see what she was wearing? I'm certain that was a lampshade on her head!" Henrik, the youngest brother, exclaimed before gulping his drink.

Amelia rolled her eyes, listening to the ongoing foolishness her siblings were causing.

"Well, now the party has officially started with Kavi here," Wei said.

"You know, Omar always says this is the last time he's helping Kavita—but here he goes helping her again," Diego remarked.

Wei raised his glass in a toast. "To our dear baby sis, Kavi, the life of the party, for better or for worse."

Amelia met Omar at the top of the steps and brought Kavita to her room. He looked at her, lifting his eyebrows like she wasn't his issue anymore.

"I don't understand how Father and Mother let her leave the house after all these stunts she pulls," Adesua said in amusement.

Wei chuckled with her. "Well, she sure knows how to keep everything lively. You know Father loves to argue with us about watching her."

Kavita reached behind her back, struggling to unzip her dress, stumbling. Amelia, exasperated at her attempts, swatted her hand away. Kavita was then handed off to Adesua as she helped her into the tub. They had a specific order of things even Kavita knew by heart, an order they had performed many times like a well-oiled machine. The maids and Amelia frantically scrubbed Kavita down. The aroma of alcohol permeated the whole room, prompting Adesua to pour rose and jasmine oils into the water. Kavita started laughing like a madman, her speech slurred.

"Oh, my sisters, if you coulda seen those dashing men last night. The music was truly electrifying!"

Amelia scoffed. "Kavita, at every event, you do this. Do you realize you're not just affecting yourself, but us too? Dusie and I are over this. You are about to be a married woman, supposedly, so act like it."

Kavita was in another world, making a bubble beard. "Well, shucks. I hear ya, Mellie. But I wish you could see how I feel." Her eyes sparkled lazily as she smiled and started to speak, almost singing, "You know, on a beautiful night like this, I wish I could be a puddle of water from the rain being stepped on because I am invisible. No one would care to bother me . . ." Her voice trailed off. "A nice night of rain will make me feel cleansed." Her words hung empty in the air.

"Honey, what on earth are you going on about?" asked an apprehensive Adesua with a smirk of disbelief.

The maids scurried over with Kavita's scented towel and gold robe as she clumsily jumped out of the bath. Amelia stepped over to her bed and held out a cup of coffee for her sister.

"Yuck, you know I hate black coffee, Mellie! Are you trying to kill me?"

Amelia pressed on with the hot coffee with a downward look. "Kavita, at this point, you have no room to talk. You need to wake up and get it together. We will not have you stumbling around the party like a fool."

Amelia pulled out the black crystal gown with tulle trim for Kavita to wear.

"And you know what's crazy, Adesua? You or I would be the ones to get in trouble for letting her come out acting wild like that. Isn't that right, baby sis? Now, why on earth would you miss our family interview today? You know the press is going to have a field day over the fact that we couldn't even come together for one hour."

Kavita closed her eyes, hoping it would make her vanish. When it didn't, she took a few gulps of the bitter black coffee and revolted at the taste. "Oh, did I say how lovely you two look right now?"

"Oh, nuh-uh, you will not get—"

Wei walked in with Omar, following as the eldest brother would, and interrupted Amelia before another ruckus broke out. "Kavita, you need to get in line. I'm tired of Mother nearly having an aneurysm over you every day. If you don't cut it out with your silly antics, your silly fiancé—and every man in New York—will run away from you."

Kavita let out a scream as if she were a toddler. "And what exactly do you know about getting a partner, huh, Wei? You are always so serious. No one knows how to have fun other than Henrik."

Henrik and Diego, listening from the next room, began to chuckle. Kavita heard them and slammed her fist on the wall twice.

"Well, since everyone is listening, I might as well make a show out of it. Fine, I will sober up for you all. You want me to tap-dance for you too?"

Kavita stood up, waving her hands like a showgirl, and toppled over her feet.

"All you boys need to leave," Amelia said with a steady authoritative voice. "Kavita is in no state to entertain your company. Leave this instant, before Father and Mother hear."

The boys left, though Wei hesitated before finally relenting and leaving the room. Amelia closed the door and locked it for fear of any more shenanigans. She turned to see Adesua rubbing Kavita's head, as she had fallen fast asleep.

"Okay, we can let her have a catnap. Oh, Dusie, what are we going to do with her?"

"I don't know, but we need to find Mr. Jenkins to see if he has your—"

There was a light knock on the door. "It's Mrs. Darla. I was able to take your dress to a local designer earlier to get it fixed. Her name is Ann Lowe, and I think you will be surprised."

Amelia turned to Adesua with the biggest grin and jumped up and down. The door opened to a dazzling dark-blue silk dress covered in crystals and sequins. Amelia raised her eyebrows, taking in the intricate beading that traced the lines of the dress. She could tell that Ann had sewn on every crystal with love and care.

The girls gushed over their outfits and then struggled to dress Kavita. Somehow Kavita had mustered enough energy to apply a small red dot of kumkum in the middle of her forehead, creating the perfect bindi. She still practiced Hinduism, although Father and Mother had them attend the Catholic church. Kavita liked a mixture of both, but she held her peace.

The Ridley sisters strode to one of the rooms near the ballroom. The moon ascended as if it were a spotlight on the Ridley estate. Tonight would be an evening of escape, wealth, and the city's finest. The final preparations had been completed, and everyone in New York held their breath, ready to witness a show that only the royal family of the grandest city in the world could deliver. Amelia had a feeling that tonight's party would be one for the books, unforgettable in every way.

She just didn't know it'd be for all the wrong reasons.

Chapter 2

Adesua Ridley

Adesua's chest tightened with each breath. Her emerald gown with flickers of gold specks felt as if it were about to pop off as she waited with her siblings in the private foyer for their father. The staff swung open the double white French doors with gold trimming for Father, who was adjusting his coat and cuff links while clearing his throat. As a child, Adesua had always found him quite intimidating, with his coy demeanor and constant smirk as if he knew everything under the sun, but she remained grateful because she could have been homeless or left at the orphanage, forgotten.

"My children, we have done this far too often not to know how important this night is. Not only for our family but also for your future families as well. This celebration of success is a prime opportunity for some of you to find a suitable partner. You are all of age now, and I expect each of you to be involved tonight. We must uphold the prestige of the Ridley name through business and the company we keep." He shot an aggravated look at Kavita, who rolled her eyes and began picking her nails.

She groaned a silent huff that only Amelia could hear. Adesua found it comical that Kavita was the engaged one, as unruly as she was. She knew exactly what her father meant by the "company" he'd mentioned. Adesua and Amelia knew it would be their fault once again if they couldn't keep Kavita and her hellish flapper friends in order. It felt like they were pieces of prime rib on a platter being served to the people of New York.

Adesua made her way behind her brothers to the grand double doors cascading with red roses. The moment had arrived. She heard the trumpet players alarm the crowd with nine notes. Everyone knew what it meant: The Ridley siblings would be making their first appearance at the ball in less than five minutes.

An announcer's voice brought the room into a roar. "I hope you all have your best dresses on. The Ridley siblings are in this very room right behind me! Can we make some loud noises for the illustrious Ridleys? We have the king of the keys, Duke Ellington—make some noise for us, Mr. Ellington!"

Hundreds yelled at the tops of their lungs while the piano harmonized with the violinist, briefly getting the crowd louder.

"All right, quiet down, you're all going to make me lose my job. Save your vigor for when the real feast is served, if you know what I mean!"

Mr. Jenkins, the head butler, shot the announcer a stern look as he approached him.

"Right you are, right you are! Back in a flash, folks!"

Just on the other side of the grand double doors, the siblings waited as the jazz band played their iconic entrance song. Adesua tried to resist the urge to tap on the side of her leg along with the beat. It wasn't that the tune wasn't catchy, more so that it all felt rather performative to her.

"Oh, this is about to be one helluva night." Wei smiled like a wolf in the moonlight while jabbing his younger brothers Diego and Henrik in their sides.

Adesua's gaze shifted to Amelia, her hand firmly gripping her arm. Kavita, ever the bold one, took the lead, striding confidently to the front of the line, passing each of her siblings with an assured nod.

"Well, it's no secret who the star of the family is," she declared, her voice dripping with confidence. "And it's only fitting that I lead the way."

Mr. Ridley shot a look at Kavita, tilting his head so she would know to go behind her brothers. Instead of turning around directly, Kavita dramatically circled around her siblings to show her annoyance. Adesua grabbed Kavita's arm to get her in line.

"I am the *only* one getting married, and here I am still being treated like the spare."

"Oh, be quiet, Kavi, you know you're Father's favorite. You get away with everything, so just try to keep your little friends in line," Wei said, annoyed.

A hush fell over the room after the last note played. It was time to shine. Adesua's eyes darted from one sibling's face to the next; she understood what this meant. It was time to put on the most incredible show of their lives. The room felt heavy amid the sea of delicate silks, diamonds, and tuxedos, and they all seemed to exhale simultaneously.

Suddenly, the ballroom doors swung wide.

The announcer's voice rang out ferociously, clearly astonished at the sight before his eyes. "Ladies and gents, I give you the immaculate Seven Wonders of our beloved New York City: the Ridley siblings!"

As the siblings lined up one by one in the small foyer room near the balcony overlooking the crowd, they felt like royalty, peering through the tiny slits in the windows at everyone laughing, filled with fellowship. The crowd screamed vigorously, those gathered almost salivating at the mere sight of them. Adesua had always known what it was to live in the public eye. Before, she might've gotten innocent looks of awe and admiration. But today was different. She scratched behind her ear, her face, and the tops of her knuckles. She noticed Amelia looking at her with somber eyes; she was the only one of her siblings who could usually spot her sign of distress.

"Hey, we are going to be okay," Amelia whispered to Adesua. "A few smiles and nods, and the night will be over before we know it, just like usual."

Adesua knew that was a lie, but it made her feel better. Out of all the sisters, she was considered the soft-spoken one. She'd never made a headline in Metropolitan Musings, which she didn't care about, but she never felt seen—not in the way she would have liked to be. It was always assumed that she was one of the lucky ones, that people like her rarely reached this caliber.

Tonight, it was about the sisters, especially Kavita, even though Adesua knew she was worried. While the brothers were a part of it, everyone wanted a chance to marry into the city's royal family. She looked at her four brothers, each of whom looked at ease compared to her and Amelia. They had contrasting waistcoats, cuff links, and pocket watches. Adesua often noticed how women would fall to their feet over her brothers, especially the older ones.

Although none of them shared blood, they all had the same swagger. Omar and Wei were the golden ones of the Ridley brothers, whereas the younger two, Diego and Henrik, were still very young and not as confident, having just graduated from high school. It was written in stone that her older brothers would help lead the family business. The real question among the whispering voices of the city was, Which one was going to take it all? There was Omar, with his stoic, firm demeanor, who preferred strategy over small talk. Then Wei, with his impeccable social skills, who could convince a lion to be his friend. From the moment she'd met him, Adesua was sure it would be Wei who would take over the business. Simply because his ego was so grand that he spoke as if the business was already his. It was a rite of passage for the Ridley children to attend the best universities, regardless of the circumstances. Everyone knew they would take on the highest roles in their family's company.

The announcer warmed up his voice to continue. Wei knew he'd be introduced first, as he always was. "All right, boys, I don't know about you three, but I know I'm feeling good enough to snag a few ladies tonight," Wei said.

Henrik, the shy one, but keen to be very observant with his remarks, chuckled. "Well, isn't tonight about finding only *one* woman to wed, brother? Not that you can keep any around."

Wei laughed so hard that the guests heard him. "In due time you'll understand, little brother, why that is."

As the eldest brother at twenty-five, Wei had a demeanor that was both brooding and alluring, drawing everyone in. He combed his silky ebony hair and gave a pearly white smile in the gold mirror before he walked toward the double doors. Wei was most like Adesua in certain ways, such as the signature scent that followed him everywhere he went; he wrapped everyone in the room with the subtle blend of peppermint and cedarwood. Wei, always wanting to create a scene, waved his hands to the attendants to back off. Instead of letting them open the doors per usual, after each sibling's entrance, he pushed them open himself.

The announcer took his place after swigging some alcohol to clear his throat behind the podium. "Now, for the eldest boy—" Wei cut his eyes to the announcer, and his gaze felt like knives heading for his head. "I mean, the eldest *brother*, a man who has brought the Ridley Line to new heights ever since graduating from his class at Columbia. Everyone, Wei Dimitri Ridley."

Wei paused at the top of the stairs to look down at the crowd with a smile. Adesua knew he loved this feeling of power. She and he both knew he was in a world where people who looked like him were villainized just because they came from China. Some of the people here tonight probably agreed with the Chinese Exclusion Act, but now he was on top of the world, and Adesua nodded with approval.

Because he should feel ever so worthy, the crowd cheered for him, desiring his wealth and the swagger that no one could buy. Wei could give a simple wink to a group of ladies while walking in Central Park, and they would all fuss about which one of them he was winking at. He walked down, his every step matching the beat.

Kavita turned to Adesua and slowly clapped when he made it down. "And I thought I was the dramatic one."

Wei gave a smug, approving smile, turning around to look at his siblings above him, knowing they had a hard act to follow.

Now for Omar. Adesua loved him the most for his stoic and observant demeanor, which was the complete opposite of Wei's. He was more introspective, though he still retained that steady inner confidence. He had a muscular build and a certain strength about him from his championship-winning rowing days. Omar had a razor-sharp jawline on par with the Grecian gods. His thick dark hair fell into his golden-hued face if he looked down too much. Everything about him made him seem mysterious, and women wouldn't dare look him in the eye.

Adesua called him the mediator and peacemaker. Every time Kavita went into Adesua's room to use her lipstick and left it open to dry, he was there to stop the screaming match. He was there if his younger brother Henrik cried because he didn't know what he wanted to do after high school. Omar knew most women were too intimidated when he approached them, but this didn't bother him. He was not one for a party, as he would seemingly vanish after saying brief hellos, only to approach bold women who wanted a chance with him. He was always the one to make a beeline for any potential business partners or owners who had no connection to his family.

"Omar Idris Ridley—this twenty-four-year-old man warms all of our hearts here in the city, and he's a Columbia grad as well and everything you'd want in a businessman."

Adesua never understood why her younger brothers were announced ahead of the girls, even though she and Amelia were older. Nonetheless, Diego and Henrik were next. Yes, the youngest boys were often forgotten, because what good were eighteen- and nineteen-year-olds in business? They were still seen as mere children, while their sisters were considered of age as soon as they'd graduated from high school. Young and old men frolicked and waited for a chance to see Adesua and her sisters.

But now it was Diego's turn. He stood out from all his siblings. He was shorter, around five foot six, but was still as handsome as ever with a charming face. He had a noticeable rich and warm tan, along with effortless wavy chestnut-colored hair. The confidence was still there despite his more diminutive stature. Diego had a passion for cooking; it was his way of showing love. Girls at his school swooned every time he called them "darling." Diego was never one to be involved in the Ridley Line, just like his brother Henrik. They would nod at family meetings to feign interest.

"Our next brother is Diego Rafael Ridley, our favorite chef since he was a little boy. He has been attending Columbia since last fall and will also be working with the Ridley Line after his studies, hoping for a great career playing polo. One can dream!" the announcer said with joyful glee, just as instructed by Mr. Ridley.

That was a lie. Diego had repeatedly told his father that he wanted nothing to do with the Ridley Line and that he was planning to quit polo. He played with great aggression, and his jaw-dropping swing set him apart, like Henrik with baseball. He was met only with laughter and his father's signature line: "You'll learn in due time. Sacrifices are far more important than our little needs." Diego wanted more than cold buildings and studying endlessly for . . . what? To be marked for a life that was premade for him? A life where he had no choice? He only found happiness in the kitchen, with the smell of his favorite cranberry bread. Diego loved how his food made his sisters, especially Adesua, smile. He loved bringing happiness in unconventional ways that money couldn't buy.

"Hey, don't get cold feet now," Henrik whispered to him, worried.

Diego snapped out of it and quickly galloped down the stairs. He stood next to his staggeringly tall brothers, gripping his hands together to appear as confident as they were. His hazel eyes were clearly inviting to women, as they began to edge closer to the siblings. They hadn't noticed Diego until this year. Perhaps because his hair was gelled in a certain way, and now, one year older, he had better potential than his playboy brother, Wei, and the observer, Omar. Diego liked the feeling. For the first time, some of the younger ladies saw him as a man, not as the little boy who wanted to serve cookies to guests.

The announcer had grown exasperated, but he was quite pleased when he got to the last brother. Henrik stood next to Adesua and Kavita outside the room. Unlike his siblings, Henrik was the easygoing golden boy who lit up the room when he decided to show up for family events. He had fair skin, bright-blue eyes, and flat blond hair. Even at five foot ten, he appeared to be a very small-framed young man to most. The only thing grand about him was a voice that could bring a room to tears. He'd only discovered this power as a young teenager, when Adesua asked him to sing "Happy Birthday" to their mother, Caroline.

Everyone had been silent when he sang the last "you" in the song. The only thing that could be heard was his mother whimpering through her tears as she hugged him. There'd been a constant hum of music in Henrik's mind from that moment. Soon after, he made little ditties in the grand music room. He wanted his voice heard, but his father wanted only to hear him talk about where he wanted to go to college for baseball since he had one hell of a swing, if Columbia was out of the question. Henrik wanted to do everything his brothers didn't, and that started with not attending Columbia after high school.

"And now we have the baby boy, Henrik Joseph Ridley, currently at Collegiate School, with a voice to boot."

Adesua waited patiently, as she knew Amelia would be announced next, so this gave her some time to catch her breath—in a dress that felt like it was getting tighter and tighter with every moment that passed.

Mr. Jenkins approached her with a downward smile. "Mr. Ridley has informed me you will be announced next." He turned away before Adesua could interject with her usual stream of questions.

She turned around to Amelia in confusion. "What is that all about?"

Amelia shrugged. "You know how Father is always changing plans on us. I am not sure, Dusie."

Adesua didn't like not knowing things, even something as simple as this.

The announcer stirred up his papers, wiping the sweat from his brow and looking back, ensuring he was announcing the right name next.

"And now we have our lovely jewel, Adesua Louise Ridley, a soft-spoken connoisseur of fine art, a ballerina, and a recent graduate of Spelman College."

Adesua walked out the double doors with her head bowed and brought her hands together in prayer, in awe of the roaring crowd. Her smile drooped a little when she saw Dale talking to people from her Harlem circle, which added to the list of confusing happenings tonight. Dale had never spoken to them before, so why now? Her boyfriend, Joseph, shook his head. She gripped the sides of her dress, probably making a few of the stones pop off. She smiled as she came down the other side of the stairs. Her emerald gown shimmered on her deep-mahogany skin like magic. Everyone was entranced by Adesua, even if they didn't want to admit it. She trailed a vanilla-oud-and-honey scent anywhere she went; it made men and women look at her with a sense of envy or admiration. Adesua glided like a princess with soft poise.

She looked up at Amelia and Kavita, now the only siblings left standing. She thought maybe her father wanted Mellie, as the eldest sister, to make the announcement. The look on Amelia's face said otherwise. Strangely enough, Father approached Kavita and grabbed her hand, bringing her up to the podium.

"I wanted to tell the finest of New York some amazing news before all the columns get word of it tomorrow. My youngest daughter, Kavita, is now engaged," he said with vigor. A round of applause and whistles flooded the room. Adesua noticed that Kavita looked down with a smile that didn't match her usual self. Father gestured for Kavita's fiancé, Franklin, to come up the stairs to be formally introduced. Franklin took large steps, almost flying up the stairs in happiness to get next to Kavita. Adesua had never met him before this, and for a stranger to be invited into their family so easily was concerning to say the least. He had never been in their scene or attended their events, so seeing Father so eager for Kavita to settle down was peculiar.

"I am grateful to my father for blessing this union between me and my fiancé. We are excited that, finally, the world knows of our love," Kavita responded almost mechanically while grabbing Franklin's hand.

Father had a way of making them all talk to the crowd in a certain way. Even Kavita knew she had to feed his ego to stay in his good graces, no matter what. Father then continued his speech, which felt almost never-ending.

"So now only two of my beautiful daughters are in need of an eligible husband," he said, chuckling, ending his sentiments and gesturing for Franklin to walk Kavita to the front, in the center of the siblings. Adesua was upset by this because she wanted to see what the fuss was about over having Amelia announced last.

Father cleared his throat while fumbling with his gold ring.

"I had to save this for last, because for a long time, I wanted this moment to be spontaneous. So, Amelia, please come closer to your old man," he said with a gleeful smile.

Amelia didn't react in any way. In Adesua's eyes, it almost seemed like she knew what would happen next.

"My daughter has been around the Ridley Line since she was a young girl: picking colors of rugs in our ships; sitting in the captain's chair pretending to steer; delivering handwritten notes to the crew; and now negotiating international deals with France, handling port contracts, and so much more." He started to get teary-eyed. Mother rubbed his shoulder in support.

She interrupted Father, which was out of the ordinary. "And let us not forget, she's also a great daughter, always there for all her sisters and brothers."

Now, this was strange, very strange indeed. Adesua furrowed her brow as she looked back at Father. Wei turned toward her, shaking his head in confusion. She shrugged.

"It is my great pleasure to announce Amelia, our Mellie, will be the future owner of the Ridley Line," he said, raising his glass.

Adesua nearly blacked out hearing those words, not because she cared whether she would run the company, but because she was concerned for her brothers. She knew how much the business meant to Wei and Omar. She was supposed to be Amelia's confidante, but now she wasn't even seen as important enough to be told this groundbreaking news. What hurt the most was that Amelia had kept this from her, making her feel like they were the odd ones out for not settling down, or even just secretly mocking Father. Now, all of a sudden, she was his right-hand woman? What else was Amelia hiding?

Everything became a blur when Amelia walked down the stairs. She must have known Adesua wouldn't be able to hold back from saying how she felt, because she made sure to get far away from her sister. She took the coward's way out and stood next to Henrik, making him and Diego move apart to make room for her. Adesua felt like she was a mere memory compared to her sisters. Nothing that she had done so far had been notable enough for the press to even bat their eyes her way. As the announcer made his final remarks, encouraging everyone to enjoy the night's festivities, Adesua made a beeline straight for Amelia.

Before she knew it, though, the siblings broke apart after hors d'oeuvres started flowing and the music was amped up again by Duke Ellington. She shot a look that could cut glass at Amelia, shaking her head to insinuate she better not move. She walked toward Amelia quickly, until her footsteps came to a screeching halt when a man got in her way.

"Oh, our lovely Dusie. How we missed you at the Manhattan Ballet." He hugged her with such force she didn't get a chance to realize who he was.

When he released his grip, a rush of emotions flooded over her. It was Iman Gerielli, one of the board members from the ballet society she was involved in until she left for college.

"Oh, Iman, you look so much younger," Adesua said gleefully. He, in fact, did not look younger. He had gone completely bald. Iman used to have hair that flew down his back like a princess in folklore. Anytime he was dismayed by a performance, he'd sling his hair back and forth.

"We at the society would love to showcase your artwork at our next ballet performance, where we're featuring what our alumni are doing after leaving the ballet world."

She was shocked because she remembered how much trouble they'd given her for being the eyesore of the group. Never blending in, as even with her bright-pink tights, her dark skin shone brighter than everyone else's. Painting was her quiet escape, and no one could tell her that it was considered inappropriate. For Adesua, after leaving the orphanage, having a paintbrush in her hand always felt like her escape. She remembered when Mother asked her what she wanted to be when she was older. Adesua went from saying "ballerina" to "painter," and to her surprise, Mother wanted her to do it all, and that was exactly what she did.

"I would love that, Iman. Please send me any information to our estate, and I will make sure to accommodate it."

He clapped his hands together with such excitement. "Oh perfect, darling. We will be in touch soon."

With that, Iman disappeared from her view—and so had Amelia.

Chapter 3

Kavita Ridley

The party seemed to have gone on for hours, but it had only been twenty minutes since the announcement of her engagement. A parade of guests streamed in, running late. Kavita noticed there were over thirty men in deep-burgundy suits standing guard at every entrance, ensuring only those with proper invitations touched a sole upon the marble floor. Even the back area, where the guesthouse and kitchen were located, was a spectacle.

All this, for her and Franklin, didn't even feel real for a moment. With how combative Father had been about Franklin's background, his introducing the two to society made her feel seen, for the most part. However, she still felt like she needed to prove something to her father, even now that she was engaged. She wanted her father to be happy no matter how many scandals she'd found her way into.

Yes, she loved Franklin, but she needed a way out from under Father's overbearing control. Every choice she made was in line with his demanding orders. Marriage was her way of removing herself from under his wing, and especially from under her older sister Amelia's. Kavita knew how terrible this sounded in her thoughts, but it was true. Father didn't even care for Franklin, but Kavita had run through so many eligible bachelors, tainting her name in society, that the ones who were worthy in her father's eyes were men she wouldn't take a second glance at. Everyone married for something in their life to be improved—or rather, *removed.*

Kavita was pleased to see the entertainment: four troupes of fire-breathers, bodies painted gold and clad in daring crimson; women walking around with lampshades and crystals on their heads, greeting the guests; and one stilt walker towering over her, giving her a red rose as the guests watched in awe.

"Hey, I am the only one to give my girl roses, you sly fox," Franklin yelled, in amusement, to the stilt walker, who raised his hands and faked running away from them.

Franklin sat down in the chair next to Kavita, giving her a kiss on the temple.

"What's wrong, dollface? You look a little down."

Kavita wore her emotions on her sleeve. Everyone could see how she felt, no matter how hard she tried to hide it. She couldn't keep a poker face like Wei, Amelia, or Omar. She didn't want Franklin to pester her. Deep down, Kavita was frustrated that Amelia had, once again, taken her shine. She had always been aware of the comparison to Amelia, and tonight made that slight twinge of envy seep through onto her face. Yes, Kavita was happy that her father was finally acknowledging her and Franklin as a couple, but he always found a way to make it about *Amelia.* She loved her sister, but slick moves like this made her question her actions.

As the siblings dispersed into the crowd, Kavita, the family's wild card, knew Adesua and Amelia would seize any opportunity to escape the party after a little time went by. Kavita knew they wouldn't leave if she were still running around. The only way to make them stay longer was to stir up a little chaos. Kavita relished this role, knowing that her antics were the glue that held her family together, even if it meant causing them constant worry over her whereabouts.

Every night since the age of fifteen, Kavita had been sneaking out of her bedroom and climbing down her balcony with the convenience of a winding staircase. Amelia and Adesua silently prayed their sister would return every night. She would, but the next morning would be everything but silent because of the screams of everyone saying how silly and reckless she was. After two years, everyone was tired of protecting her and simply pretended she wasn't doing it anymore. The only person who would stay and wait at the door was their family driver, Mr. Pierre. He was a staple at this house, along with their cook, Chef Laurent, and Mr. Jenkins and his wife, Darla, the head maid.

Tonight was more of the same, with Mr. Pierre watching from afar, waiting to see if he and Mrs. Darla needed to escort Kavita to her room to avoid a big scene as usual. Kavita was momentarily still, which put everyone at ease as the evening's much-anticipated performer arrived. Bessie Smith took the stage dressed in a red satin dress that hugged every accentuated curve she had. The room was so silent you couldn't hear one heel click. It was something to see a bodacious Black woman commanding the stage. Even Adesua smiled, knowing that this could be the new normal for talent who looked like them, instead of just being seen at the run-down speakeasy or a family member's backyard party.

Every moment Bessie Smith was on that stage, the voice within her somehow synced with the water fountains rising behind her, as if her voice had some majestic power over each drop of water. When she sang "I Ain't Got Nobody," everyone was in awe.

Amelia knew this was her time to leave. She knew no man would interest her. She gave Adesua a firm side hug before she began to walk away. That was, until Kavita stood in her way.

"Kavi, move. I have no time for your games tonight."

Kavita was taken aback by Amelia's audacity to challenge her. She saw it as a playful jest. "You think I'd let you leave while the iconic Bessie Smith is performing? That's disrespectful, even for you. The only way to earn forgiveness is to dance with me."

It was as if the band had heard her. The music's tempo increased, and soon enough, people began to swing and twirl the night away while doing the Charleston. Kavita grabbed Amelia's hand, and they began kicking their feet in unison while they spun each other around. Amelia secretly loved the sound of music on the dance floor, but she would never let Kavita know this, even if she were on her deathbed.

Kavita hopped on the stage and grabbed the mic from the singer as she was about to hit a high note. Everyone was at attention while she tapped the mic multiple times. The guests were all looking, but that wasn't enough for Kavita. She grabbed a champagne glass and hit it with a fork, and the glass shattered. She covered her mouth apologetically while blushing.

"Hello, my lovely ladies and gents," Kavita said in a drunken voice. "Tonight has been one of the grandest nights of my life, but I wouldn't be here if it weren't for my beautiful brothers and sisters. Which is why I'd love to dedicate a song to them right now at this *very* moment." Kavita squealed between hiccups, trying to get her words out. "Did you know my youngest brother, Henrik, and I have our own little band? As a matter of fact, where is my darling baby brother? Henrik, get up here!"

Henrik shook his head while mouthing, "No." He never let anyone see him play instruments or sing, because he was embarrassed. Henrik was always perceived as soft and not like his older brothers by his peers at high school. If he started singing with his intoxicated sister, he would never hear the last of it.

"Aww, my baby brother is a little shy. Maybe a round of applause would do it for him? What do ya say, everybody? Can we get some claps for my baby brother, Henrik?"

A few muffled claps were heard around the ballroom as everyone's high was brought down when the music stopped. Adesua stormed the stage and grabbed Kavita by her wrist while snatching the mic from her.

"My best apologies, everyone. Kavi here has enjoyed our punch and a lack of sleep from party preparation. I hope you all have a good time! Band, strike a beat for this lovely crowd." Adesua's save was good enough until Kavita was in Amelia's presence.

Amelia's eyes darted to Kavita. "Oh, I promise the moment I talk to Father and Mother in the morning, you will never be able to leave their sight again."

Kavita laughed in a way that someone who was insane would. "Why? So Mother and Father can yell at you for not watching over me? Aren't you tired of always being on your best behavior, huh, Mellie? No one cares tonight. Everyone wants this as badly as I do, and not one of these people will want to remember the night, as they'll feel foolish by their actions."

Adesua looked her in the eyes. They both knew Kavita was right. Amelia would be the only one yelled at, while Kavita would walk away unscathed, as she was the youngest daughter and didn't know any better. Once again, she found herself looking at Kavita and promising herself to have fun tonight, just this one night. She walked over to the crystal punch bowl and poured herself and Adesua a glass. They knew what was in the drink, but it was already done. Amelia didn't notice any difference. That was, until Kavita's smile looked more expansive and the stars looked like they were falling from the sky. She could see Kavita shimmy her way out of hand's reach. Kavita ushered her mischievous and closest best friend Lila and her other friend Pam to sit by Amelia on the chaise longues near the pool. By the time she laid her head down, Amelia was fast asleep.

Kavita laughed heartily, pacing back and forth while stumbling to the garden for peace in a place where no one would go. It was a nice trail, with cobblestones that led to a little maze, rosebushes, and an immense pond with koi fish, ducks, and swans. The cobblestones were cold as her hands touched them when she tripped. She heard footsteps behind her but couldn't tell who it was through the winding maze. This confused Kavita, because not too many people came out here unless it was staff trying to get away from work briefly or a couple of lovers who were being scandalous. Kavita felt a slight chill as the wind made its way through the rosebushes.

A waiter approached from behind her, a cigarette in one hand and a plate of hors d'oeuvres in the other. He set it down on the nearby bench. He raised one eyebrow, lighting a cigarette and then offering her one. Kavita waved him off because in that moment, she wasn't in the mood to chitchat with the staff. He tiptoed around her, going deeper into the garden's maze. Kavita loved being alone, but she could sense something was lingering near the bushes—or maybe *someone*.

"It's funny, truly. With an engagement, you'd think you would be your father's prized child," a sleazy voice said, coming from none other than the journalist Dale, who sported a devilish smile.

Kavita raised her hand up to Dale's face. She was about to strike him out of the rage she had built up against the man.

"I am starting to grow annoyed by your presence in my home at *my* engagement party. If my father hasn't ruined this for me already, it will be a cold day in hell before I let you do it, Dale," she spat.

"Well, sweetheart, better get a nice fur coat, because it's coming sooner than later. You and your family make it so easy for me. It's quite comical." He shook his head in near amazement.

She brought the palm of her hand to his rough bearded cheek, hitting so hard, her fingertips tingled with heat. He grabbed the side of his face, cocking his head, which made his smile even wider than before.

"Oh, you are going to regret doing that," Dale said, wiping the grin from his face.

The waiter from earlier caught Kavita's eyes as she pushed Dale.

"Is everything okay, Miss Kavita," the waiter said sternly.

"I am fine. You may go back to work and not speak a word of this, if you would like to keep your job with my family. Understood?"

He quickly put his head down and walked away to show he was respecting their space. It just had to be Dale, taunting her once again. She knew he was baiting her—better yet, luring her—into a splashy headline about a monstrous bride-to-be ready to attack anyone who disagreed with her. The Ridleys had brought the devil into their home, and Kavita wanted him gone.

Chapter 4

Amelia Ridley

Amelia hadn't had one moment to think when her father made the unexpected announcement. Now, still feeling disoriented from her unexpected slumber, she walked through the grounds as fast as she could, trying to find her siblings, who seemingly were avoiding her. Amelia almost tripped on her blue silk dress in the trouble of it all. She whipped her head around when the crowd gasped as if a king and queen had arrived. She moved past the guests to make a beeline for her mother to see what the fuss was about.

"I hope no one fell off their stilts again this year. What is everyone going on about?" Amelia asked, feeling confused.

Mother pointed to the far right of the stairs, beyond the dancers. It was none other than the Grant family, each dressed in the finest gold-and-cream attire. They were the Ridley family's rival when it came to fame and wealth. Respectfully, they were on the same playing field, with a young son named Elion, reminiscent of Kavita, with scandals that even Kavita couldn't hold a candle to. The one thing they didn't have was a summer party.

Not that they hadn't tried, but their attempts were met with failure the year their eldest son, Jamison, had to grab Elion from off the stage when he started calling everyone at the party frauds who lived to see each other's failure. Everyone in the city knew about it because of the unfortunate timing of Metropolitan Musings' report of him peeing near the entrance of the Plaza Hotel after a wild night at the Cotton Club. Some argued that he was trying to be like F. Scott Fitzgerald after that stunt.

"Why must they show up as if this were their party?" Mother scoffed, exasperated, while pacing near the bottom of the staircase by the bushes. "Mellie, go over there and thank them for coming. They shall not see us fold. Why didn't we think of having you all dress like that in some way?"

Amelia chimed in, "Well, Mother, you have the finest-looking children in all of New York. We don't need to be overzealous with outrageous attire."

Mother chuckled, then whispered, "I am guessing you and Jamison aren't back together yet."

Jamison was the love of Amelia's life. Even when they weren't together. The only reason they weren't at the moment was because of their families' damning rules. For years, they would meet secretly, and if it showed up in Metropolitan Musings, they would say that they had to meet for school-related things. Now, with Father's desire to make history and have Amelia be the future owner of the Ridley Line, she was taken so many steps back in even having a sliver of a life with Jamison.

Mother walked hand in hand with Amelia in a slow but sultry way up to the Grant family, rolling her eyes at the same time at the nerve of them.

"Well, it looks like a flock of angels decided to join us this evening," Mother said when she reached them.

The mother, Ella Grant, looked like a vision in the bold choice of a gold gown with cream appliqué details that shimmered, spiraling down the sides. Ella smiled when she saw her. She had always been fond of Amelia, as she was the Ridley sister who stood out to her the most. Amelia could hold her own next to Jamison, while other girls would falter trying to get his attention.

Her skin was ice cold when she grabbed Amelia's hand. "Amelia Rose, you are a star in my eyes, as always, my dear. What must a mother do to get you and my son married so I can have perfect little grandchildren walking around?" She glanced over to Jamison as her cheeks began to quiver.

Jamison was beautiful in a way that made Amelia feel that God had to mold men after him. His skin was the perfect shade of honey tan, slightly lighter than hers. The Grant family's hair was their signature trait. It was a chestnut blond with hints of earthy-brown hues. He had two distinct dimples that made you want to poke them, like popping a little bubble. Jamison's eyes were a goldish brown, similar to Amelia's mother, Caroline's, which made her think that's why she loved them so much.

When the Grant family went into the shipping industry, they became the Ridleys' prime rivals, not for who could have the most sought-after family but for legacy and who had the empire to die for. The Ridleys had a luxury liner for passengers, whereas the Grants did not, but they also had to compete with them in running cargo and for trade routes. Metropolitan Musings added even more fuel to the fire with headlines: Which child would get into what college? Who would marry off all their children first? Which family would have the most heirs and heiresses running their family business?

It was always a battle, as it felt that—at least on the Ridley family side—they were never to court or marry anyone *from* the Grant family. This was the catalyst for Amelia, as she had been fond of Jamison since they were children. Her ache for love had spilled into her diary entries for years until love was no longer a priority for her. Father had a lot of rules for Amelia, but not being with Jamison was the only one she had wanted to break for as long as she could remember.

Jamison, uncomfortable in his cream suit, adjusted his gold bow tie as if it were choking him. He dared not look into Amelia's eyes as she talked to his mother. She could tell that everything about her made him nervous. Their on-and-off relationship since grade school had never gone further than a simple kiss or a modest date to the movies.

Jamison was skilled at defusing awkward moments. "We know Mellie is always off on her horses, reading, or on a plane with her brothers. No one can keep up with her," he said with slight amusement, ending with a tight smile.

Amelia felt the heat surrounding her neck. She wasn't sure whether she should be offended or amused by his statement. She gave a brief handshake to each Grant family member.

Of course, the father, Garrison, held on for a moment too long. "Tell your father to contact me. I have a great business plan. I would love for him to participate."

This shocked Amelia, because everyone knew her father was a hothead when it came to taking advice from other people, especially his competitors. "I will surely let him know, Mr. Grant."

Jamison grabbed her hand as she walked away.

"Me. You. Stables. Now."

Mother flinched her eyebrows, giving Amelia the *You better go or else* look. Amelia wanted to fight back, but what use would that be? It would create a scene and, furthermore, play into the narrative that she was unmarriageable. His hand was heavy as he wrapped it around her wrist. They'd walked this walk many times before. Just not this exact route.

When Amelia and Jamison were no older than eleven, he was constantly getting her out of trouble, dragging her away from conflict. She would fling herself, fist moving left and then right, at a boy's face, all because he'd kicked a stray cat and she wanted him to feel the same wrath. Jamison always chuckled at this as he would drag her off him. Not because he didn't think she could hold her own, but for the sake of the other's well-being.

"Unhand me. You act like I don't know how to get to my own stables, Jamison."

He sat on the bench with his head in the palms of his hands. She didn't know why he looked so damn stressed. She was the one who had been left with no word from him for months. She'd even gone as far as scouring Metropolitan Musings for any word of him. She felt undesired, believing what the gossip columns said about her being unlovable. Even if it was due to their families' rules of keeping them apart. No one else even dared to try to compete with Jamison, who wasn't showing effort in the first place.

He looked up at her with the purest smile in his gaze. The golden hues in his brown eyes shone bright in the moonlight.

"You know how much I love you, Mellie. Whether you believe it or not. You know how our families are, and my father has been . . . You know how he is," Jamison said pleadingly.

Amelia wanted to roll her eyes but forced herself to look at him straight on. "Love doesn't leave. Love listens and responds. Love would leave a letter to make sure the other person wouldn't worry."

He nodded, taking his time answering.

"My family has been going through a lot, and it's something I can't tell you about yet. I will always protect you. Hopefully, when you do take over the company, if your crazy father doesn't change his mind, you can make your own rules, and maybe my father won't see you as another spoiled heiress who he would have to provide for as well. I love you, for whatever it's worth," he said solemnly.

Jamison stood up, adjusting his suit before walking up to Amelia, leaving a kiss on her forehead.

"I will see you soon, Mellie."

Before she could reply, Jamison left her. She was all alone with her horse, Mya. And a yell. A voice so loud that it had to be none other than Kavita's. From the stables, Amelia had a perfect view of the opening to the garden maze. She dragged herself from the stables, running for the maze. As she got closer, Amelia plummeted to the ground. Her heel had gotten caught in a twisty vine near the rosebush, causing her to nick her hand. There was blood dripping down her finger as she pulled her shoe free.

"Kavita!" Amelia yelled out into the maze.

Kavita and Dale Caimen had disappeared so quickly. Amelia was confused about how they'd managed to get out of her eyesight. Her vision began to blur slightly. The fall couldn't have made her head feel like this. Amelia stood, and her steps slowed down drastically as she looked left and right, wondering which way to go. She had been through this maze thousands of times. What was wrong with her? She dropped down slowly to the cold cobblestone ground. Heavy, slow footsteps approached.

A laugh broke out that startled her. Dale Caimen stood over Amelia with a cigarette and his gaudy briefcase.

"I see ya little trainwreck of a sister's concoction got to you," he said with a smug face.

Amelia had had enough of him and this party.

"Did you get your next big headline, Dale? I saw you got my sister riled up. Hope it's enough for your readers and for you to keep a job."

He stubbed out his cigarette.

"That's the problem with you Ridleys—you forget where you all came from and act like you're better than the rest of us. At least I make an honest living not surviving off Daddy's money."

Amelia scoffed, "You call humiliating and tormenting innocent families by putting their lives on paper 'an honest living'? It is laughable, truly, Dale. One of these days, you are going to upset the wrong person, and it won't be me or my siblings. We know your games."

Dale came a step closer to Amelia. She realized this was probably why she'd heard Kavita getting upset. His whole presence was overwhelming.

"I think the truth will set everyone free, and maybe even you too. Little Miss Paris Sweetheart has been hiding more than your little promotion with the Ridley Line."

Amelia interjected, "I did not hi—"

"Oh, spare me, Amelia. You are a liar just like your father. Don't worry, though. Kavita gave me something special enough by accident. I wouldn't trust that family of yours, who holds you in such high regard.

Looks like you aren't the only Ridley with a damning secret." He winked at her, hitting her shoulder as he passed by.

Amelia bit her lip so hard that it began to bleed. Another mark for the night, along with her finger. She had kept her siblings together all this time. Now it looked like they all had their own dealings with a devil named Dale, and they had to cover it up. But first, what was it that he had on her?

Chapter 5

Adesua Ridley

Adesua shoved nearly anyone who got in her way to get to Joseph, since Amelia had made it a mission to be out of sight and out of mind. So Adesua had to deal with her boyfriend instead. Joseph stood out, not because of his smooth, dark-hued skin, but because of his extremely tall stature, which towered over everyone, including Omar and Wei. He had full lips; the bottom was the shade of dark-pink tulips and the top, a beautiful espresso brown that she couldn't stop staring at. She had to tilt her head to take in his staggering height. Adesua waved, catching his attention so he wouldn't move.

Joseph held the tip of her chin, lifting it before she could speak. "Baby doll, you looked like a queen up there." He came down to her level, kissing her gently.

The feeling of his plush pursed lips on hers made her almost forget what she'd come to him for. He had a way of doing that to her. She shook herself out of the trance.

"Don't you do that," she said with defiance.

"Do what, my little Dusie?" Joseph smirked as he pushed her hair behind her ear.

Adesua was usually the timid one, but tonight she was giving it to everyone straight.

"Why were you talking to Dale?"

Joseph flared his nostrils, rubbing his nose while sniffling. She knew instantly this was his way of getting his story straight. Little motions he did before telling her a grand lie or hiding something. She had become adept at identifying those cues.

"Dale is a man of many words and wonders, and one of those wonders is us, my dear."

Adesua furrowed her brows.

"'Us.' What do you mean by 'us'?"

He wiped a trickling bead of sweat from his eyes, which more than likely could have formed because of the dreadful summer heat or the lies dripping from him. She didn't break eye contact.

"Me, you, our friends. He wants to do a piece on Harlem and its growing community. Especially us and all that you have done for Harlem since you have gotten back from Atlanta."

Adesua was apprehensive. It was a good answer—a great answer, at that. But the way he worded it seemed predictable. One thing Adesua had never done was doubt her intuition. She clicked her tongue because she knew better than to make a ruckus in front of everyone on the dance floor. That was what they expected from someone like *her*.

"Very well, Joseph. I have to find my sisters. Enjoy yourself."

She grabbed an hors d'oeuvre from a nearby platter, stuffed it in her face, and downed a juice cocktail, turning her back on Joseph. He knew not to stop her. She walked past the sea of men who tried to get her attention. Adesua knew far too well that the league of handsome men who would usually approach her were as sour as the milk they looked like. Even though Joseph had his fair share of problems, Adesua was okay settling on him for now.

She ran toward the back of the estate, getting away from everyone. Her body felt heavy as she found herself sitting near the steps. A group of young boys came up to her, staring.

"Hey, toots, go grab us another beer. You have some very thirsty guests," one of the boys called out.

She ignored them, as she knew from their informal attire that they had not been invited.

"I know you heard me. Go fetch us a beer."

"Clearly, you all don't know this is my home, and I'm not the damn help. So why don't you go on about your business."

The boy snatched her arm, squeezing it tightly and bringing her closer. Adesua cried out.

"I ain't ever gone let a nigger, rich or poor, talk to me any kind of way." He pushed her toward the fountain.

Adesua caught sight of Wei, Omar, and Diego walking toward them.

"Wei! Help me!"

Her brothers came running, swinging blows at each of the other boys' faces.

One of the boys tried to speak up between each hit, trying to justify his actions. "It was an honest mistake, man. I thought she was the help back-talking!"

Wei's eyes turned black. "I wouldn't even let you boys lick my boot clean. Don't you ever come back to this property again! I remember faces."

Adesua sat on the fountain's edge, crying as her brothers started to crowd her, consoling her. She had never liked causing a scene, so she ushered them all away. They wouldn't see her cry. She stood up and headed through the maze she knew too well. The garden maze was the only place she loved besides the art room. She never felt alone here, and the rows of roses seemed to reach out to her. After having some minutes to herself she saw Kavita through the tall bushes, pacing back and forth. Nothing out of the ordinary other than her cursing at the night sky.

"This is all wrong. None of this. Why would I?"

Kavita gripped her own wrist, seemingly holding herself back.

"Kavi, what in the heavens is wrong with you?"

Adesua grabbed hold of her shoulders. Kavita's eyes glazed back. Adesua started to feel like Kavita too. Her stomach and body felt heavy, like the world was pulling her down. Everything seemed brighter. The moon seemed to be edging closer to them. Stars were twinkling bright in her flashing eyes.

"Dusie, are you even listening to me?"

Adesua didn't know how long she had zoned out of the current situation, but she could tell she needed to contain this before Dale could get this breakdown on Metropolitan Musings. With almost perfect timing, she saw Amelia walking out the kitchen's back door, heading for the maze, and they made eye contact.

"Amelia, over here, now!" Adesua yelled for her to hurry, hoping she would run faster.

Amelia stumbled over to them. Adesua clocked that there wasn't something wrong with just Kavita, but all of them.

"I think something was put in the food or drinks," Adesua struggled to get out.

Kavita looked left and right, at both Adesua and Amelia, then let out a laugh so loud that guests quickly turned toward them. To Adesua, it was better they hear that than a cry.

"What did you do, Kavita? I s-swear, if you—" Amelia stammered.

"We all needed to let loose a little, don't ya think, Mellie?"

Kavita plopped to the ground once again. Adesua tried to bring her to standing, but to no avail. She found herself on the ground with Amelia, and was now laying her head on her lap. Fingers tickled the side of her head, but they weren't hers. She turned back quickly, which shook Amelia up.

"Henri! Oh, how I missed you the whole night, my baby brother," Kavita slurred.

"You ladies are wrecked. See, this is why I never drink. Kavita is always up to something. Get up, we need to move before Mother and Father see us like this," Henrik said with authority.

They all headed toward the maze, where most guests never ventured.

Although the maze wasn't used for parties, it did have a few aged stone benches that were covered in ivy. Henrik struggled with having Kavita's and Adesua's arms wrapped around him. He wasn't the strongest person, but he gathered enough strength to accompany them to a bench in the maze to sit down. Their shoes created a crunchy noise as they walked down the pathway. It didn't mean much to them until Henrik stopped dead in his tracks, making them nearly fall.

Adesua kept her head down. "Henrik, at least warn us if we are making a deto—"

She heard Amelia's gut-wrenching scream, words she couldn't make out, followed by a loud splash in the pond. Adesua's eyes were struggling to stay open. All the commotion made her body feel as if it were being dragged down. Dreadful exhaustion overwhelmed her. Everything was out of focus and out of reach when Henrik let go of her and Kavita. She rubbed her eyes, trying to get hold of herself. Adesua saw Henrik and Amelia in the deep pond, but she realized something else was in there with them. Adesua's vision blurred. All she could make out was a white suit and a full head of black hair. Was it Wei? What if the boys they'd kicked out earlier had done this to him? Her eyes began to well with tears as Kavita looked on in horror.

"He's dead! He's dead!"

Amelia struggled, pulling the body to the edge of the pond as Henrik waded into the water, grabbing the poor unfortunate soul . . .

"It's Dale!" Henrik screamed.

Adesua's rising heart rate began to slow down once she realized it wasn't her brother. As Henrik dragged the body out of the neck-high water, Dale's eyes were wide open with terror and blood slowly seeped out of his head. Adesua looked at the pointy sculptures in the pond. Maybe he had fallen and hit one? The endless possibilities made her stomach turn, but as long as it wasn't Wei, she could try to calm herself. Her spine tingled as chills went across. Someone was screaming for her to move, but she felt as if her feet were stuck to the ground.

"Adesua, help us!" Amelia said, exhausted.

Adesua mustered the little energy she had left, but even Henrik couldn't pull deadweight, even with Amelia's help. Kavita fell to the ground, looking at the moon. Adesua didn't have time to coddle her.

She took off her heels and walked as fast as she could without also falling in the pond. Henrik jumped out of the water to help Adesua pull Dale's body out. Amelia made her way out, her blue dress drenched.

"Henrik, go get Omar, Wei, and Diego. We need them now," Adesua said.

A few minutes went by before Mr. Pierre arrived. He looked over Dale's body as if it wasn't the first dead body he'd seen.

"Henrik told me to come to the pond. I told Mr. Jenkins and Mrs. Darla to inform staff to stay away from this side of the grounds and block the exits from the back of the estate," he said with ease.

Adesua felt clarity rush over her. This was indeed not a dream but very much real. It had been a struggle for Dale. All his belongings were scattered around the pond. She noticed his large briefcase from earlier, the lock broken. Adesua didn't know why that stuck out to her the most, but it did. It had been dented. The files that had been carefully placed inside were now scattered around the path like streams of confetti. Oh, how she wished it *were* confetti. The pieces of paper had different names on each of them: the Vanderbilts, the Grants, others from high society, some names she'd never heard before.

Then she saw one name she hadn't noticed at first. *The Ridleys.* She, along with a now more coherent Kavita, who was more silent than she had been all night, snatched up the file.

"Does that say our name?" Kavita asked. She look petrified as she stared at Adesua's hand.

Amelia and Henrik rushed over to her. Henrik immediately shook his head.

"No . . . no, we don't need to look at this. This isn't right," he said.

Adesua sent Kavita a devilish glare. Because why wouldn't they look at papers that had their name on it? Unless there was something of Henrik's in there that he didn't want them to see. Adesua furrowed her brow, trying to understand the meaning of why they should respect the privacy of a now-dead man like Dale. When he'd never hesitated to taunt them.

Kavita snapped her eyes to Henrik. "What isn't right? Him stalking our lives and doing think pieces on all of us and how we are horrible people?"

Adesua held on to the file tightly, not wanting to let go. Her eyes landed on a shattered champagne bottle that dripped with blood. To the naked eye, this was not an accident but a murder. She wondered whether anyone thought the same as her, or was she once again overthinking, as she did with everything? Amelia grabbed the file from Adesua's hands so firmly, it made Adesua jump.

"Henrik is right. We should at least wait until Wei, Omar, and Diego get here," said Amelia.

Just as Amelia said their names, Wei ran to them with Omar and Diego following behind.

"Are you all okay?"

Wei's instincts instantly had him panicked as he checked Adesua, then Kavita, who pushed him away as he got closer and grabbed their faces. Adesua found it peculiar how quickly they'd all gotten here. Why was everyone so eerily close to the maze? The grounds of the party extended far, but all seven of them had been near the maze at the same time. Wei stopped at Amelia.

"Mellie, why the hell are you wet?"

Adesua saw Amelia looking down at her soiled dress and pointed to the body without saying a word. Adesua took a look at her, not even realizing what a mess the scene was. The glass champagne bottle covered in blood near the edge of the pond surely didn't help. It could be seen as a murder weapon that someone had carelessly left behind. To Adesua, Amelia looked unbothered that she was the one who had just helped pull Dale's body out. At least Kavita looked as if she were entranced by a spell.

"Did anyone touch that?" Wei asked.

They all looked at the bottle. Henrik twitched nervously.

"I did . . . I tried to move it out of the way when I was getting out of the pond with Amelia. I didn't realize there was blood on it," Henrik said apologetically.

Omar and Wei shook their heads in disbelief. Of course their younger brother would make a foolish decision like that. Without hesitating, Adesua went to the bottle and smashed it with her heel, then kicked the shards to the bottom of the pond. She wasn't going to let her younger brother be seen as part of something she knew deep down in her heart he wouldn't do. She had a quick passing thought that maybe someone would try to blame it on her, as she'd been seen outside the maze first. Henrik's eagerness to touch a potential murder weapon was cause for concern.

No one said a word about what she did. They all knew what the implications would be if his fingerprints were found on the bottle. Especially with Wei getting into altercations with guests earlier. They had all looked angry, all night. From Adesua feeling that twinge of jealousy toward Amelia to Kavita taking the spotlight on a night that was supposed to be about all of them. From Omar always making calculating moves to get out from under Father's wing to Diego and Henrik despising how Father had forced them to work at the Ridley Line. They all looked guilty, and Adesua knew they all had a motive to get rid of Dale, no matter how much she denied it. She could tell her siblings did, too, from the looks on their faces.

Amelia took this as a chance to open the file with their name on it. *The Ridleys* was written in bold. Adesua's heart sank when she saw it. What did he have on them?

Omar walked up to Amelia, taking the file just as she'd done with Adesua. Omar was never one to say things in tense situations; he usually let the fire burn itself out. Adesua could see him gripping the folder as if he wanted to rip it to shreds.

"I, for one, feel like we need to burn it now. No one needs to know our dirt—not even ourselves," he said smoothly.

One by one, they all nodded in agreement. Adesua knew she wasn't the only one with something to hide.

"We need to get Tom immediately and call the authorities. The longer we wait, the more guilty we all look," she said apprehensively.

"Wei and Omar should leave with Diego," Amelia added. "We can't all be caught standing around a dead body when the cops come. It needs to be us girls and Henrik, as we were the ones to find him."

The boys each looked ready to give their two cents, but after further thought, they knew she was right. They were all standing there like lambs waiting to be slaughtered. "I will watch over the file in the meantime while you three go," Adesua said firmly.

"All right, you're right. Let's go, boys," Omar said reluctantly.

Adesua knew there would be a power struggle between the boys and Amelia. They wouldn't argue with her for taking it. Omar placed the file folder down on the bench between them. Footsteps and laughter drifted across the garden. Adesua looked at Wei, knowing they had run out of time, and they all seemingly fell into line: Amelia and Henrik stood over Dale's body in shock. The others were panicking as if they'd just discovered it.

The sounds of laughter suddenly turned to screams. A group of girls pointed at the dead body frantically, covering their faces at the horror of it. Suddenly, Mrs. Darla came along with Mr. Jenkins, and people were now gathering handfuls of their clothes around their chests as if they were clutching pearls. Elion and then Jamison ran through the growing bustling crowd, trying to get to them. A woman fainted, and people were now huddling around her. Adesua knew something must be done.

"Everyone, we must remain calm as we wait for help for Dale," Adesua yelled in a reassuring tone.

Adesua knew there was no help that could bring Dale back to life. Mrs. Darla saw it too. Jamison, Elion, Wei, and Omar took advantage of their statures, ushering the crowd back. Adesua went to retrieve towels for Amelia and Henrik, still soaking wet from getting Dale's body out of the pond. She couldn't stand being in the same area as a dead body. Just then, as if the staff already knew what was going on, they came running with towels. Adesua grabbed two. She knew they needed to inform the police. Even though they'd said the situation was under control, it was not.

As Adesua threw the towels to Amelia and Henrik, her body froze as she looked down at the bench. The file. How could she have forgotten it? She looked under the now very empty bench. She widened her eyes, trying to catch the gazes of her siblings, then looked back toward the bench. The file was gone. All their faces were as stone cold as Dale's. There was most definitely a need to be concerned about it being gone. The way all her siblings seemed unfazed by him lying there, lifeless, made her wonder: What daunting things had they each done? And who on earth had taken the file?

Chapter 6

Kavita Ridley

Kavita stared out the window as long as she could, watching the morning sun rise. The way these so-called men looked her up and down made Kavita feel like her skin was about to molt. She didn't care for authorities in any form or fashion. Especially now, as they tried to flaunt their power over her family. Police Chief Hank Johnson swished his toothpick back and forth in his mouth, to her annoyance. She was happy that at least they'd had the decency to move them from the maze to inside the estate to question them. He knelt down next to Kavita, looking at her dress, then got close to her face.

"What's with the mark on ya face, girl?"

Kavita touched her cheek, not realizing there was a deep scratch with blood showing.

"It must have been when I ran into the rosebush—they are all overgrown. I nicked my face trying to turn away from seeing Dale. I have never seen a dead body before."

The chief looked down while scribbling her answers on his notepad.

"Some of your staff said he was last seen alive a little before midnight. When you all discovered him, was he warm or cold?" the chief said, deepening his gaze at her.

Kavita's eyes started to twitch. She didn't like this stream of questions. It almost felt like she was being set up as a suspect.

"I don't know. This whole night has been a blur, and so overwhelming," she said, looking heartbroken.

Kavita tried her best to show some sort of remorse. No matter how hard she tried, her face wouldn't evoke even the slightest compassion for Dale. Especially given how awful he had been. Kavita knew the rest of her siblings had the same feelings toward Dale. They were all feigning some type of remorse for a man they'd wanted long gone. She wanted to chuckle because she was glad the bastard was dead. He'd tormented her on an important day of her life—the announcement of her engagement—and then had still somehow made it about him by dying. This made her think: Where the hell was her doting fiancé? He'd run off with his friends and hadn't checked on her the whole night. This put a bad taste in her mouth, which the officers seemed to notice. She looked over to Wei, who stood with his arms crossed as the police checked him out, looking for anything suspicious.

Chief Hank flipped some papers around while looking at the brothers. "We got a complaint earlier saying that you, Omar, and Diego were getting hostile with some guests. This doesn't pertain to Dale, does it? Maybe he got a photo of you all that you didn't want to be . . . let's say, released to the press?"

Tom, their family lawyer, raised his hand toward Wei to stop him from speaking. But as Kavita knew too well, Wei was never one to be silenced.

"Yeah, I knocked the lights out of uninvited guests who were terrorizing my sister. So if he did take a photo, I would hope the world would see not to mess with my family again. It would be rather noble of him, I would like to think. A nice parting gift," Wei said with a smug smile.

"Wei, that's enough," Amelia said, narrowing her eyes at him.

The police chief then turned his attention to Amelia. Kavita shook her head, as Amelia and Wei always had something to say. She felt nervous. What if her sister slipped up and said something she shouldn't?

"Tell me how you found the body again?" he asked.

Amelia grazed her tongue across her lip, holding her restraint.

"We needed some fresh air and to get away from the herd of people. The maze is our place of retreat when we need to be alone, and my younger brother, Henrik, and I saw someone in the pond. So of course our first instinct was to try to save them."

The chief nodded before continuing. "Yes, and we do see the sculptures in the pond did have blood on them, along with shattered glass. Was that glass there when you found him?"

Amelia nodded. "It was a mess by the time we got there. I didn't notice much until after we got him out."

He placed his finger to his beard, stroking through it as if he was calculating his next question, as if he wanted to box them in.

"Guests and staff said they saw all seven of you at the maze as they approached. Which caused an uproar, as you being the last people to see him alive, from all accounts, is rather odd, you see. Which, to the ordinary person, would make all of you suspects. Do you follow me?"

Amelia looked at Kavita, almost as a plea for help. This took Kavita by surprise, as Amelia was the one always helping others, not needing it. One thing Kavita knew how to do best was come up with something on the spot, and that she did.

"I'd find it rather odd if we weren't. I mean, is this not our party? Dale had a way of always snooping around—and not just in the city. So him crossing paths with us last night is not that shocking. That was his job. Whether we were aware of it or not is the real question. Which, clearly, we weren't. Why else would we all put ourselves in danger and remain at the scene of the crime, Chief?" She said it all in one breath, which took even her by surprise. Amelia looked over, slightly raising her eyebrows in pleasure at her answer, which was indeed a very rare moment for her. Kavita felt like her chest was tightening. The never-ending questions made it feel as if the air were being vacuumed from the room. Kavita needed more than air.

She'd wanted Dale Caimen out of her way. He'd been prying into her happiness. She had finally done something to get the public off her every move. A married woman was a bland woman in their eyes. Tiny bumps raised across Kavita's delicate skin. It wasn't cold by any means. Not as cold as his dead body. Dale's horrified face began to seep into her memory.

"Since you're so eager to speak, Kavita," the police chief said, "was Dale really here to interview you on your upcoming engagement? Dale was usually seen with a briefcase, and yet somehow nothing is inside the briefcase. Which makes me even more curious after some young gentleman saw you yelling at him very rowdily sometime before his death. What was all the fuss about?"

Kavita looked to Adesua, then to Amelia, for help, but this time they couldn't speak up for her. Her throat began to go dry as she tried her best to evoke a word. Her vocal cords tightened. She held her hand across her neck, trying to catch her breath. She gripped the side of her dress, digging her fingers in her thigh to get a hold of herself.

The police chief stepped up, cocking his head to the left. "Young lady, I asked you a—"

"Can't you just leave us alone! We have been prodded and shredded our whole lives. I wanted one night to go right. I pleaded with Dale to please let us be. I am sad and tired because I am pregnant. Is that what you wanted to hear? This has put me all in distress. So yes, I yelled at him, just as I yelled at my younger brother for giving me the wrong pair of shoes," Kavita said in one breath.

Wei cocked his eyebrow in fury as the rest of them gasped.

"You're what?"

The chief's mouth was agape. He clearly didn't know where to go from there.

"That'll be all for now, young lady. We are sorry, miss. We assure you that what you have told us doesn't leave this room. Mr. Ridley is a fine man. We just have to do our duty. We will piece all of this together, but since you all so happened to need fresh air at the same time near the maze, which is the scene of the deceased, this had to be done."

Father walked into the room, looking at them all in disgust. It was his job to clean up their messes, after all. Kavita had made a choice that surely couldn't be undone. Was she lying? Maybe, but she surely hadn't bled this month. She would do *anything* to get these pansy men out of her face.

She looked out the window as the morning sun now blared in their faces, as massive as the truth Kavita had just told. Reporters gathered around the gates, hitting each iron rod. Snapping the same pics of the estate they had taken before, but this time, a murder had made its way onto the property.

Chapter 7

Adesua Ridley

The moments before brunch were Adesua's favorite part of the day. But not today. Today, she sat in the tearoom, waiting for the investigators, while a breeze from the window caressed her cheek. She beamed as she brushed her canvas with her paintbrush. A variety of emotions flowed through her heart to her fingertips. Adesua rarely ever left the estate. She'd just started to do so more recently with her newfound love, Joseph.

Adesua felt fear when she left without her siblings. She always felt she needed her brothers Wei and Omar to escort her everywhere. Adesua wasn't like Amelia and Kavita in many ways. Amelia would gallivant around the city, going to bookstores, exploring deep into the nature trails of their family's property, and even flying with their brothers. Kavita had been leaving the house at night since she was fifteen, and somehow would be back before school started. Adesua sometimes felt like she didn't know how to live life without the safety net of her family.

Deep in thought, her stomach grumbled as the smell of orange-cranberry muffins, eggs Benedict, and maple-chicken sausage roamed through the hallways. It was now a quarter after nine, and none of them had eaten since before dinner yesterday. How could they have an appetite, when the only thing that was served to them late last night was Dale's cold dead body on the ground? Mrs. Darla and Chef Laurent knew better than to cook her favorite breakfast when they were in the middle of an interrogation. Diego and Omar tapped their feet impatiently, out of sync. It was like they could feel their impatience. The officers approached the door, motioning them to come back in, as this circus of unending questions wasn't done. Even the smell of breakfast didn't budge them.

This drove her mad. What drove her madder still was how the insistent police officers hadn't let up when Kavita had her outburst. Furthermore, she wondered how in the world Kavita was engaged and pregnant. The fact that none of them had known bothered her. Was this why Kavita felt she shouldn't get married? Because of this growing baby inside her womb? Maybe Dale had found out and was ready to leak the story of her being unwed and pregnant. Adesua's head swayed with the never-ending thoughts. Never mind that she had more problems on the rise as the investigators hammered down on poor Henrik.

"They say you and Kavita are glued at the hip. Maybe you tried to protect her from something, or maybe someone?"

Henrik couldn't stop his plump cheeks from turning as maroon as the roses in the garden maze. Whether he was lying or telling the truth, his emotions showed all over him like a red balloon ready to pop. He picked at his nails, which were nearly nubs since he kept peeling them when he was nervous.

"Sir, me and my sister arrived here together when we were children, so with all due respect, yes, I am always with her. She's home for me. As protection goes, Kavita is the one to protect me. I am sure you saw on Musings how she came to my all-boys school just to give each of them a piece of her mind when they weren't being nice to me. Kavita fights with words, and I am there by her side, just as she was for me."

He'd said his piece sure enough, and each of the investigators and cops started to soften somewhat. Because, after all, they were truly poor children who'd been thrown into this. Adesua knew how peculiar it was to everyone when they walked together to the Plaza for brunch. The world didn't know what to make of them. So they were indeed each other's homes and safe places. They couldn't argue with that even if they tried. One thing she did know was that they couldn't fully trust each other. Dale had had something on each of them for a reason.

Now, Adesua, on the other hand, was an entirely different story. She was quite literally the black sheep. She and Omar both were, and they knew they had "special" treatment coming for them. They would get blamed first simply based on the color of their skin. Diego got away with everything just because his eyes were the perfect shade of green and he had a light-olive skin tone.

He was one of them no matter how curly his head of hair was. Henrik was just the same. This bothered Adesua to no end because what if they had done it? No one would ever suspect them. It angered Adesua that Amelia, Wei, and even Kavita got away with everything with a slap on the wrist.

When the officers came face-to-face with Adesua once again, she inhaled, trying to prevent an outburst. With perfect timing, Mrs. Darla knocked on the door, moving past the officers with a few maids behind her carrying plates of food for everyone.

"Now, I reckon no one here can think on an empty stomach," she said as she shoved a plate of delectable food in one of the officer's hands.

"Of course, I can't forget my other babies. Omar, I got you two helpings of everything." Mrs. Darla glided out of the foyer before the officers could say "thank you."

It worked. Adesua could see the men diving into their plates like they hadn't eaten in days. Mrs. Darla had always protected the siblings the best way she could. For her, that was through food, kindness, and love. One of the officers spoke with his mouth full of her brown sugar–cinnamon pancakes.

"Where were you during the hours Dale was last seen?" he asked Adesua. "A staff member said they saw you and Wei arguing before disappearing in the maze, where shortly after, Dale was found."

Who from their staff was running their mouth? She couldn't believe it. Adesua always made sure to treat the staff with extreme care and kindness. Even by helping with chores she didn't have to do. Now this was how they repaid her. She felt a gradual heat rise up the back of her neck. Her tight dress wasn't helping. Oh, how she couldn't wait to rip the damn thing off and never wear it again.

"Officer, to answer your question, I was with my boyfriend, Joseph, most of the night. I then caught up with a donor for the ballet society I danced at. Then Wei and I did, in fact, run into some trouble with some uninvited guests, as mentioned before. Rest assured, I was getting my older brother to calm down by the maze away from everyone. As you see, the maze is a central place for guests and family alike to find peace and quiet."

Adesua knew that was a lie, but it was important the narrative never change. She wasn't risking anything to make them look like suspects. They all had the same alibi. The maze, the maze, it was just so peaceful and quiet, the maze. She was sure the officers had had enough of hearing the word "maze." She surely had, but that was the plan. They hadn't all murdered Dale. Or had he been murdered? Adesua may have jumped to conclusions in her head. A bloody champagne bottle could have ended up there in a variety of ways. Clearly no one had been in their right mind.

The detective came in with Tom Smith, their family lawyer, and Father trailing behind.

"That's enough today, boys. You all are free to continue your lives the best you can as we try to find the suspect. Dale had plenty of enemies, as we all know, but we also have gotten accounts from guests and staff that Dale was acting very belligerent, which checks out with the champagne bottle near the pond. It's looking like an accident due to the sharp edges of the fountain. So we have covered most of our bases. Have a great rest of your day." The detective nodded as the rest of the men followed him out the door.

"Thank you, gentlemen, for your due diligence," Father said with admiration.

The police, investigators, and detective made their way off the estate, going down the long driveway. Adesua knew her father was waiting for the moment they were out of sight. Diego was still chomping on his food as loudly as he could. He was enjoying every bite of it. Until Father swiped the table full of plates onto the floor.

"Seven of you. Seven of you interrogated for murder. After all the work I have done to build our family up. After all the years I tirelessly tried to work with the press. We had a redemption with Kavita. Giving them something good to talk about. Not only do we have the damn dead body of a man who hates us on our property. But we also have Wei hosting parties with women running these halls like they own the place. Omar over here trying to do business behind my back. Oh yes, I know, son! My eldest, Amelia, can't even—"

He stopped as if someone had taken the breath out of his chest. Mother consoled him, as his rage was something like no other. Adesua hadn't seen it in a long time. Father made sure they knew each one of them was at fault. If it was the last thing he did.

"Let us all get some rest. Too much has happened today, and we all need some time," Mother said tenderly.

Father was right about one thing, though: Seven of them, herself included, had been questioned for murder. Because, of course, they each had their own reason to kill Dale—at least, that's what she would think. No other guests were around the maze at the time. It had to have been one of them. Adesua pondered which one had the most to lose. It couldn't have been her, though. Right?

Chapter 8

Amelia Ridley

Amelia looked over to Adesua with a knowing glance. They knew Father's tantrum was just the beginning of a long, drawn-out discussion. At least Father didn't know about Kavita possibly expecting. That was another whole ordeal for her and Adesua to go through another time. Amelia held on to Kavita and Adesua as they were dismissed to go about their day.

"Amelia, come to my office after dinner," Father said abruptly before she could make her way out the door.

"Yes, Father."

Who was she to argue at this moment? The only thing she wanted more than anything was to get out of the house. Away from the stifling air of remorse and regret. She couldn't go too far, as dinner was a few hours away. She grabbed Adesua's and Kavita's hands and kissed them both. This was her little signal that it would be okay.

"I'll see you both soon for dinner. Going to the stables to check on Mya."

She did, in fact, check on Mya, but that wasn't the reason Amelia went to the stables. Her horse was the closest thing she had to a friend that wasn't human. She saddled and hopped on Mya, then headed next door to the Grants'. She needed to see Jamison, even though she had been trying to avoid her deep feelings for him. He was the only person who gave her a feeling of normalcy, and she needed that at this very moment.

The summer sun was still glaring even though dinner was quickly approaching. When Jamison was home, he had a certain schedule that only Amelia knew. He consistently checked on all his horses before nightfall. She stopped Mya in her tracks when she saw him. Every part of him was glistening, the muscles of his chiseled chest expanding as he stretched his hands out to loudly yell to the sky. Jamison was a man who truly loved doing the unexpected. That was what appealed to her the most—him not giving a care what high society saw him as. Amelia saw his pecs tightening. She shamed herself for noticing. Jamison turned, and now his bare back caused Amelia to blush and roll her neck in disbelief. She dismounted and approached him from behind. She craved the sacred love that he could offer.

The sweat beaded down his back as he patted himself dry with a ripped shirt, which he then placed back on a wooden post. Amelia didn't know whether she should spook him or speak up, but seeing him quietly petting his horses gave her a soothing feeling, until the crack of a branch underneath her foot alerted him to her presence. Jamison whipped his head around and slowly smiled.

"I thought my horse would be more loyal and warn me." He kissed his steed while rubbing the top of her head, then fed her a carrot. "What are ya doing here, Ridley?"

"You didn't hear what happened?" Amelia said, confused, as she moved closer.

"No, Mellie. You know I don't keep up with whatever gossip is going on," he said as he slipped on a white shirt that clung to every crevice.

Surely he had to have heard something from someone. Especially his father, who took pride in recounting any Ridley mishap.

"Let's go to the beach. I'll tell you what happened."

Jamison nodded. Anytime he could get away with little words, he insisted on doing so. Amelia turned away, heading back to her horse.

"Where do you think you're going now, Mellie?" Jamison yelled as he mounted his Clydesdale.

"Well, I thought you wanted me to meet you there?"

Jamison laughed. "Well, you thought wrong, now, didn't you? Get up here."

Amelia parted her lips and let out a brief gasp. She couldn't remember the last time she'd ridden on the same horse as someone. She hesitated before approaching.

"Don't worry, she doesn't bite unless I tell her to," Jamison said with a touch of playfulness.

She approached the box to get on, but instead, he grabbed her with one arm, and she swung her leg over the back of his horse. Amelia had never been this close to a man before. Even after the many years of her and Jamison's so-called dating. They were merely confidants who had exchanged a kiss here and there. Jamison had never even tried to get with her in that way. She knew during his time galivanting around the world, he'd had other women on his lap. Of course, Metropolitan Musings journalists didn't hold back whenever they saw him taking a woman who was not Amelia on a date.

It was one of the smaller reasons why they could probably never be together. With the rumors of Dale dying on the Ridley estate already traveling through the streets of New York, she knew scandal would always chase them. The public would soon suspect each of them, because such an act would make their American dream seem like a sham. Amelia knew the announcement that she would take over the Ridley Line had ruffled some feathers. Dale dying the day of the announcement could make it look like she was the aggressor, making sure no one was getting in her way.

Her chest pressed against Jamison's back, making the sides of her hips tingle in ways she hadn't felt before. As they picked up speed through the fields, the breeze cooled her rosy cheeks. Their bodies swayed in motion as she held on to his waist. Jamison dismounted, and Amelia immediately wished the pressure would return, but now she felt it in her heart. This was the feeling of lonesome love that she'd never cared for. Now she wanted it all with Jamison. He helped her down.

His horse immediately jumped into the water, splashing. Amelia laughed and then quickly straightened her face as Jamison stripped down to his undergarments. She turned away.

"Don't tell me you have never seen your brothers run around the house with drawers on, now, Mellie," he said in a low tone.

Amelia was sure no one would be there but them as she slipped her riding breeches down. After all, she rationalized, the swimsuit she had at home looked just like her bloomers. She waded into the water next to him. The horse splashed water in their faces as they laughed at their scandalous behavior in that moment.

This was the peace she needed. Amelia almost forgot about all the incessant issues at home, from her siblings giving her side glances when it was announced that she would be the future owner of the Ridley Line to Dale's murder, Kavita's possible pregnancy, and all the lies and secrets her siblings had gotten caught up in. For once, she didn't have to fix anything. Even if it was just for this brief moment.

She looked at the sky, with the daytime moon shining bright through the baby blue hues. Maybe they would get married, but she remembered Jamison's abruptness the other day at the Plaza, as if he hadn't wanted a thing to do with her.

"Jamison, are you embarrassed of my family and me?"

He looked astonished, as if she had asked him to murder someone.

"Don't ever ask me a silly question like that again. Now, tell me what happened yesterday." He rose out of the water, returning to the shore.

Amelia pursed her lips in defiance. She knew something was off. If he hadn't been embarrassed before, he might run now and never look back at her drama-stricken family.

"Dale is dead. We found him murdered in the maze—"

"Who is 'we'?" Jamison interrupted. "And what do you mean 'murdered'?"

The way he said the word "we" took Amelia aback. It was as if he was disgusted by even the thought of a possible connection between her and a murder. Amelia regretted her words, because no one had confirmed that Dale was murdered. Even the chief hadn't said so. But to her, the timing of his death was rather odd. He'd targeted all her siblings in some way that night, along with a list of notable people, from politicians to celebrities. Most of his coverage was damning. So murder was the only way for a devil like Dale to die. Amelia's face was now even redder than when she'd seen him undress. She bit her lip in frustration over ruining such a peaceful moment.

"It was me and my siblings. I am not sure *murdered* is the right term, but it was horrible seeing his body like that. We found him at the pond in the maze," she said, flustered.

Amelia saw Jamison clench his jaw. His face showed disappointment at this revelation, which she'd expected. The Ridleys having a scandal of this magnitude was something even Jamison couldn't overlook, and she knew that.

"I mean, the police have already questioned us twice and let us be . . . I am sorry. I thought it would be okay to talk about this, but we must head back." She stormed from the shore, slipping her breeches on.

Jamison ran after her.

"Mellie, come on, I was just curious. I didn't mean to upset you."

She turned, her face filled with regret.

"Just forget I came here. I have to go back to my family. I don't know, I just thought I would feel something different seeing you. Now I am even more confused than before I got here."

Amelia didn't have her horse, but that didn't stop her from running as fast as she could toward home until Jamison was no longer in sight. Every time she looked back, she noticed how he stayed in the same spot, looking as if he were waiting for her to turn back, but she didn't. She felt unclean as she returned to her room. Maybe it was only her thoughts that needed cleansing, but she knew what usually cured her and her sisters in a moment of sadness: a long, relaxing bath with the finest oils and flowers.

Kavita knocked on the door and then proceeded to sit, in a daze, on the pink velvet ottoman.

"Mellie, do you feel that Father has paid off the newspaper and the county so they won't report on Dale dying here?"

Amelia rubbed water over her face. She couldn't escape the nightmare slowly becoming their life. Deep down, she did want to deny the thought of her father doing something so immoral. Then again, Kavita wouldn't be asking if she felt as if Father weren't capable. He had gotten rid of—or better yet, silenced—many scandals before this. Having wealth like Father's had given him power that came with both enemies and protection that many people would never get to experience. A dead body on the Ridley grounds. Now the detectives felt that she and her siblings could be potential suspects? Yes, they had all had their fair share of scandals. But murder? That was an insult, even from the rabid voices of New York.

"Kavita, you have nothing to worry about. Yes, our family is powerful, but I feel the press didn't want the city up in arms with pitchforks over people like *us*. They need people to want to follow in our footsteps. We bring business to local restaurants, clubs, and even clothing designers. Look at Adesua with Ann! People will have nothing to look forward to with us out of the picture. The American dream would be a lie for so many," Amelia said with a slight sternness.

Kavita nodded in relief.

"Also, Mellie . . . I wanted to tell you and Adesua at the same time, but I bled last night. I thought maybe Franklin and I were with child, which is why Father was insistent on us getting married. He knew already. He made me swear to keep it a secret. Now it looks like I don't have a secret anymore. I am sorry for not telling you," Kavita said somberly, before kissing her sister on the forehead.

"Love you, Kavi. You can always tell me everything. I don't know if I should be happy or sad for you, but you know Adesua and I will always be there for you. If this was the only reason you were getting married to Franklin, hopefully you can wait a little longer to see if he is truly the love of your life."

She could see Kavita light up inside with the possibility of a second chance even through life and death.

"I love you, too, Mellie. Hurry up before Father yells at us for being late to dinner."

Kavita slowly closed the door while Amelia was in deep thought. Amelia knew what she'd said was a lie. Father would indeed pay off anyone who would get in their way. But the last thing she needed was Kavita screaming down the hallways in anger, asking who killed Dale.

Amelia knew Kavita was the emotional sister of the family; she was a *Do now, think later* sort of person. That was always her motto. Which made Amelia think maybe Kavita could do something as heinous as kill Dale. What if he'd wanted to expose her possible pregnancy? Amelia slapped herself lightly for thinking those damning thoughts.

She felt somewhat sorry for Dale. Mother had mentioned that he hadn't always been so cutthroat. Before writing for the column, he had tried to publish a book that ended up failing miserably. He then went on to make Metropolitan Musings into what it was today.

Not that that should matter, but it was peculiar that he made his living off people like them, the wealthy, the people who threw these extravagant parties for him to report on. Amelia thought to herself that maybe she would have been like him if success hadn't come to her so easily as a Ridley. Amelia slipped on a blue chiffon dress that was vastly different from her riding breeches.

Amelia arrived at dinner and saw roast and potatoes. Something her father loved. It was a simple meal, but she'd had no interest in meat since she was a little girl. Amelia excused herself after prodding her fork into the potatoes and having a slice of lemon-blueberry cheesecake for dessert. After Father and Mother left, she wanted so badly to get under her sheets after this drawn-out day. The winding steps to Father's office seemed longer tonight, the clicks of her heels getting louder and louder until she made it to the landing.

Father had many private offices in the home, but this one was the most special to him. It was invisible to most. A small door led to stairs that led to a long walkway that led to a room with a grand oak desk in the center. She felt almost as if she were about to be interrogated, but by her father.

"I have spoken with the press, and all is settled for now," he said.

Well, I'll be damned. She thought instantly of how Kavita had truly been ahead of this all along.

Father sipped his old-fashioned, then continued. "Those mobsters did it, of course. Retaliating against us for not cooperating with their bootlegging. Especially against Dale, for not keeping his mouth shut."

Amelia's toes felt like they were digging deeper against the soles of her shoes. She could feel the blood draining from her face. Mobsters in their home sounded outrageous. Even she didn't believe this lie. Amelia would have had more peace of mind if one of her siblings had done it rather than some random men who wanted to seek vengeance on her family.

"So what does this mean, Father? Are we still in danger? What about Kavita? Will this ruin her engagement?"

The questions seemed to riddle through her head but not come out her mouth fast enough.

Father stood up, placing his drink down on his desk.

"Settle your spirits, Mellie. There isn't anything to worry about for now. There have been some staff running rumors with other reporters about you and your siblings being there and near him at his death. So people may have . . . suspicions."

Suspicions? The Ridleys were already the family everyone in America wanted to be or wanted to get rid of. In the public eye, a poor boy like Dale, who'd made his come-up, even if it was by bringing others down, was still somewhat more noble than their family. She knew the world saw the Ridleys as *untouchable*. Dale was a light in darkness for them, showing how perfectly imperfect they all really were. If one of them had done it, New York would make sure to have their head on the table by dinner tomorrow.

Chapter 9

Kavita Ridley

The Manhattan Herald
July 11, 1927
FAREWELL TO DALE CAIMEN

It is with our saddest regrets that we announce our beloved Dale Caimen passed away suddenly Saturday night. Dale has worked for *The Manhattan Herald* since he was in high school. He started as an intern, assisting anyone in need of help. It wasn't until he began his column, Metropolitan Musings, that he surprised New York City. People finally learned about social events and got a glimpse of life through the eyes of New York's elite. He had the wit to boot, along with charm and class, as he reported on goings-on from the city we all clambered to read first thing in the morning, before our first cup of coffee. Dale Caimen was adopted by the late Donald and Phoebe Caimen, leaving behind his legacy in his voice at the column.

His passing has shaken the Ridley family, as his unexpected death happened at Saturday's gala. They ask for privacy at this time. We may not have the same voice as Dale, but we plan to continue his legacy with Metropolitan Musings being written anonymously. His funeral will be held at St. Patrick's Cathedral this coming Saturday for all who wish to pay their respects. As Dale once said, "New York is a place where everyone wants their story to be heard, but who shall write them all?"

Until next time, New York's Musers.

Kavita swiped the trickling bead of sweat near her right eyebrow. She fetched the ice-filled lemonade pitcher to cool herself down. The *Harper's Bazaar* magazine was keeping her slightly entertained. She indulged in Parisian fashion, as she thought the style was far better. The French Riviera intrigued her too. She hadn't traveled with her family to France for almost three summers. Her father hadn't cared for France ever since he adopted Amelia.

Kavita knew the only reason their mother made them all go in the summers was so Amelia could be around people who spoke her language. Which eventually made her and her siblings learn each other's native languages. It was like a fun game to her. Within a few years, Kavita could have secret conversations with her siblings, but the one she connected with the most was French and speaking it with Amelia. She'd never understood why her father didn't see the beauty in Europe like she did. Kavita's favorite cousin on their mother's side, Jacqueline, and her parents would frequently visit France and sometimes stay the whole year.

Kavita flipped through the pages of the magazine, seeing that she already owned everything in it, from Cartier jewelry to a Rolls-Royce to the glittering world of New York City that F. Scott Fitzgerald wrote about in his short stories. Nothing stuck out to her. Her imagination clung to her feet in the Mediterranean's bluest waters, then sipping her morning coffee on the hotel terrace while the sun drenched her skin and the breeze cooled her off.

That was what she wanted, but for now, she would have to make do at her family's estate pool to mimic the things she loved. It felt as if she were enclosed in a slightly opaque bubble, where she could see everything going on in the world but they couldn't see what was inside her *spirit.*

She craved the feeling of being hidden, but the sight of her siblings wasn't too bad. They were all in their own little worlds. Henrik tapped his feet along with the gramophone while Louis Armstrong's sound filled the pool area. Adesua was painting something new for an art competition in Harlem that she'd been ranting and raving about. Wei was smoking a cigarette and reading. Diego was looking at cookbooks. Amelia was doing her usual morning dive in the deep end, constantly challenging herself to stay under for as long as possible. She always tried to beat Omar, but he won every time.

Kavita reached for her large sun hat and robe to prevent the rays from hitting her skin. As she flipped the hat over, something red fell from it and down the side of the table. She reached for it as far as she could, too lazy to stand up and get it. The edge was hard and pricked her finger.

It was a peculiar red envelope, addressed to her. Definitely not one of their invitations. She looked on the other side of the pool to see if any of her siblings had seen it as well. Her gut dropped a little, and not from the French 75 she was drinking. The red made her think of the blood dripping down Dale's head. It was a sight she couldn't forget. She got a nearby knife and slit the envelope open.

The white slip of paper had few words on it, but they were enough to get Kavita out of her chair.

> *Don't you and your handsome fiancé have enough dead bodies under you, or better yet, inside you? We know everything, Kavita.*

Only her siblings and the more-than-likely-paid-off police officers knew about her supposed pregnancy. Who would say something like this? She was sure an officer or investigator wouldn't prod into women's issues such as this. If anything, a woman's body and how it worked was the last of their worries. What did they know about her and Franklin? The file. It all led back to the file. At this point, any of them could have it, or maybe they were lying when they said they didn't have it in the hope that one of them would tell the truth. If there was any truth to be told. Dale was dead, and how it had happened wasn't Kavita's concern. Still, it nagged at her, the thought that one of her siblings may have the files and was trying to conceal their dirty secrets.

Kavita didn't feel scared of the letter, but rather the fact that someone, or one of her very own siblings, was attempting to taunt her. Was it because she'd kept the engagement a secret from them? Perhaps Adesua would do this, but they were all shocked, from Amelia to Wei to Omar. None of them really liked Franklin anyway. But whom she married shouldn't matter; she wasn't the one trying to take over the company. At this point, she felt like she could trust no one, but her siblings didn't have to know that, of course. Maybe it was a warning for her to go no further with Franklin. Whoever had written the letter hadn't asked for money. So it had to be one of her siblings.

Kavita crossed her legs and stuffed the letter in her bag. She quickly grabbed her things, leaving abruptly, to her siblings' confusion.

"I got the cold towel you asked for, Miss Kavita," one of the maids said as she walked in her direction.

She waved her off, heading straight for the drawing room. There were too many people in this house. Rotating staff, different friends of her siblings. Anyone could have placed it there. One thing she wasn't going to do was keep any evidence of anything. Kavita looked around, ensuring no one else was near. She threw the envelope into the fire as quickly as she'd read it. She knew what she had done, and someone else did too.

Even after the interrogation, no one had a clue where the file on their family was. This bothered Kavita the most. She wanted to be ahead of whatever narrative Dale had coming for her. She was used to putting a spin on every story that was published, from her so-called scandalous dates to the parties she would attend. It truly tickled her pink, but this time, she felt the darkness of what Dale had been going for. He had been even more conniving than usual that night. She wondered whether the file had miraculously flown into the pond on a strong gust of wind. Kavita hoped for that, but in the ticking bomb of her thoughts, she knew it hadn't. Why should she trust any of her family members? Especially Amelia, who had kept from the rest of them that she was going to be the next owner of the Ridley Line. Kavita had protected her siblings from scandals, but what if hers were far greater than any of their previous ones combined? Her eyes reflected the orange and red embers as she watched the envelope crumple and turn black. Kavita felt pleasure in seeing it disappear. Little did she know that Henrik was peeking through the window behind her, watching her.

She fell to the floor, holding her chest, hit by the same feeling she'd had on the night of Dale's murder. It was all coming back to her. She was fine. That was what she kept repeating to herself over and over. But her body said otherwise. Tears fell down her face. She knew her past wasn't good, and neither was Franklin's. Kavita believed in redemption. Dale hadn't had time to redeem himself because he'd kept bothering her and her family. So she felt in her heart that redemption didn't apply to him.

As she freshened up her face in front of a mirror, faint footsteps approached her hurriedly. They then stopped before anyone came around the corner. She grabbed a mail opener from the mantel to arm herself. Maybe it was the person who'd left her that letter. She wasn't going to wait like an innocent lamb ready to be slaughtered. Kavita quickly approached the corner with the pointy gold opener in her hand.

"Oh heavens!" Mrs. Darla yelped, terrified at the sight of Kavita.

"I am sorry, Mrs. Darla. I thought . . . Never mind," she said, guilt on her face.

"Child, I just came to tell you that Mr. Franklin has called you once again. He wouldn't take no for an answer."

She went to the kitchen. Kavita's avoidance of her fiancé would have to end sooner or later. After that letter, she had no other option. She picked up the phone, only breathing. He knew she was there on the other end.

"We need to talk about last summer, Kavita."

Kavita smiled as a few of the maids walked past her.

"Good."

She hung up the phone and walked out the French doors.

Chapter 10

Amelia Ridley

Amelia was over the fuss of being at the Plaza on a Monday morning. She thought it was ludicrous, as they could have the same meals and better scenery at home. But she knew the lives of society's elites revolved around brunches, business meetings, and family brawls after long, exhausting weekends of parties and charity events.

Kavita usually found a way to escape Monday meetings, but not today, so soon after the fiasco of the party. As Amelia gazed out the window, the working class passed by with their newspapers, glancing at the restaurant with a bit of envy. But she didn't feel anyone would truly want their lives now. Especially with the Ridley file gone and with what Dale may have said to his peers.

"Father, did you know the Grants have moved into the property next door? You know, the grandparents' old estate?" Amelia asked inquisitively.

He nearly choked on his grape. "What on earth are you saying, Mellie?"

"I am being serious. I saw Jamison out on the grounds with his horse. He accidentally crossed onto our riding trails," Amelia said softly.

"Nothing the Grants do is by accident, you hear me, Amelia? Their family, especially his father, despised us when our family's business started thriving. He would scream 'nouveau riche' to anyone who would listen, saying our family couldn't be trusted, as we haven't proven ourselves to them. Be careful with Jamison . . . I know you are smart, Mellie."

Mother could tell Father was frustrated, so she gently rubbed his shoulder.

"Our family may not have as many generations of wealth as the Grants, but we have something they lack, and that is the humility that graces each of you due to your humble beginnings, which is lacking in their children."

This pleased Father, but it upset Amelia even more. No matter what her family did, they would never be good enough for some people in society, who spoke kind words to their faces but spewed wicked hate behind their backs. Amelia played with her food, twirling it on her fork, annoyed at the impending meeting that they could easily have at home. She knew her family wasn't like the Grants, but Jamison was different. He never looked at her with superiority.

Her cousin Sebastien, butting in from the end of the table, spoke loudly. "I, for one, think Jamison truly fancies Mellie. Everyone can see it. That broody steel gaze doesn't fool me for one second."

"Sebastien, you were mighty quiet at the party. I barely saw you . . . You must have found a great dance partner," Amelia said, trying to change the topic.

She blushed slightly when she looked up and saw a waiter escorting in none other than the Grant family.

Jamison walked a few steps behind his father and mother, almost as if trying to conceal himself, even knowing his height revealed him. He held on to the hand of one of his little sisters, who clearly wanted to dip it in the chocolate fountain.

Mr. Grant stopped by the table. "Well, if it isn't the Ridleys," he said merrily as if they were old friends.

Father stood up, grabbing his hand firmly. "A pleasant surprise to see you here this morning, Garrison."

Mr. Grant gestured his hand toward his wife. "The lovely Mrs. Grant wanted to change up from the Waldorf this morning. Hope you don't mind."

Mother interjected before Father could say something nasty. "Ella, please, we are delighted to see you, especially those dashing girls of yours."

Mrs. Grant darted a look at Amelia and then her mother.

"We are delighted to see your eldest here in attendance. I think she and Jamison would make a fine match. Don't you, darling?"

Amelia nearly scoffed so loudly she had to conceal it with a cough. Everything in these spontaneous meetings was so calculated. How would their parents know what a fine match they were when they had spent no time with them, only ever saying vile things about the other family? Now that she'd been announced as the future owner of the Ridley Line, had that changed things for the Grants? Did they think she was too naive a woman to control the company, and they could sweep in with their eldest son and take over? She seethed at the thought of them even considering undermining her. She found it funny, but it also wasn't wrong to entertain the idea. Amelia had always wanted Jamison and her family to join together, but not on terms like this. She was the type who never did anything if it felt forced.

Mr. Grant nodded like this was a perfectly orchestrated performance.

"I wanted to meet with you in a more serious manner, but as both of our families are here, I think it's time we aligned not only on a potential marriage between those two but also on the oil business. I overheard Wei and Omar at the party, and our family would love to bring the two greatest families in the city together."

Father did not hold back his tears of laughter this time.

"You expect me to believe you want—what was it you called me? 'That ole farm boy'?—to partner with your family? I am sure your father would turn in his grave, Garrison. Cut this shit with me," Father said in a loud voice, making the other patrons whisper, ready to tell the rest of the city.

Mother once again tried to save the conversation before it could become an all-out brawl.

"I think we could do this in a less public . . . arena. How about you all come for dinner? We can potentially discuss these rather sensitive topics further."

Jamison said abruptly, "Excuse me, but I have to go, Father and Mother." He nodded goodbye while shooting a glare at Amelia as he walked past her.

This sent tiny shivers down her spine. Why was he looking at her like that? As if she were telling her mother to say those things. If Amelia knew anything about Jamison, it was that he ran from anything and everything when it began to feel *real.* Anytime he would close in on a new stage of love or something in his career, he would leave the country to escape that responsibility. She was sure this time would be no different. She silently laughed at herself, shaking her head, because she knew she ran from him as well. Mirroring each other without even realizing it. Amelia knew she had little patience, but she didn't want that to be the case with him too.

"May I be excused?" Amelia left before even getting an answer from her father.

She grabbed her purse and looked for the nearest taxi, avoiding Mr. Pierre, who was waiting for her in the family car. Amelia was unlike Kavita; she never wanted to drive, as she'd always found cars intimidating. Mr. Pierre was her saving grace. Anytime she wanted to get away, he would drive her to her favorite part of Central Park or to any bookstores or cafés she pleased. He was always there, ready. But today she didn't need him knowing her whereabouts. She nodded her head gently so he would know she would find her way home. Just as the taxi was about to pull out into the street, Adesua and Kavita ran up to the car, tapping on the window.

"Care if we join you, sister?"

Amelia swung the door open. "Of course, my silly Dusie and Kavi," she said in a luxurious high-pitched voice. "Shall we shop to our heart's desire before some daunting news of arranged marriages and potential murder terrorizes our family?"

Thinking of morbid times, Amelia remembered when their father had taken them to his parents' grave in Pennsylvania, showing them where he'd grown up on a farm in a tiny home that looked dilapidated.

Then only a child, Amelia cocked her head and said, "I wonder if your father and mother knew how rich you are now, would they wake up?"

Amelia had had a weird way of describing grief and bringing some light to it while growing up. She hated to see her father sad, so saying something outlandish was her way of coping. Today, they would let all the guilt from the party melt away by indulging in all the beautiful things life had to offer. What were they thankful for? The shops on Fifth Avenue. So that was precisely where they went. Monday morning was always busy in Manhattan. You would see all the lovely flappers with their signature cloche hats and bob haircuts from any way you turned. Amelia couldn't bear cutting her hair, so she always pinned her curls to make her hair appear shorter, just like Kavita did.

Amelia turned to her sisters in excitement as if this were their first time visiting Fifth Avenue. The taxi driver parked right in front of Lord & Taylor on Fifth Avenue. It was the girls' signature starting point. They would work their way up the street to visit each store until their hands gave out, which was their motto. They saw the window display filled with evening gowns, flapper dresses, and various long pearl necklaces as they approached the entrance. A pair of wine-red gloves with black crystals stood out to Amelia. Gloves were something that made her feel even more alluring. The sisters pulled open the brass doors to their ideal escape.

In the midst of the hustle and bustle of the city, this was their oasis, even during the bad moments. They'd first come here when Adesua was eleven and Amelia was twelve. They always had a grand family dinner anytime a new sibling was adopted. This time, it was Kavita's special day. Mrs. Ridley usually had designers come to the home to dress all the children, but she'd wanted to show off her children in the city. She had a desire to get them whatever their hearts desired.

This was hard for Adesua initially, as she saw the prices and would put something back. Mother would look down at her and grab her by the cheeks, assuring her that she could get anything, as the price was just a silly little number. This caused Adesua to laugh and warm up to the thought. Mother found herself distracted, looking at the perfumes and smelling each scent. That was when Adesua's hand was grabbed by a sales associate who had just returned from the dressing room.

"I found this little thief trying to steal a dress. Oh, you wait until I get authorities on you, little girl."

Adesua wept so loudly that Mother bolted and grabbed her hand back from the lady.

"How dare you touch my child!" The lady was puzzled. "How could you assume she was stealing when she was just looking?"

At this point, Mrs. Ridley was fuming, and the heat was evident all over her face. The perfume saleswoman ran in front of her coworker.

"Mrs. Ridley! Mrs. Ridley! I am so sorry. She is new here. We have run into thieves lately, and she may have been too passionate about implementing her training."

The saleswoman ushered the lady back to tending the dressing room. Mrs. Ridley thought for a moment that she was foolish for adopting her children. She knew the world hadn't progressed to where it should be, and it was a moment of failure she would never forget.

They had quietly walked out without getting a thing.

A lady almost the same hue as Adesua had walked out after them, yelling, "Mrs. Ridley!"

Caroline turned to face her, expecting to be scolded for bringing her daughter there.

"I have seen the papers about you adopting these fine children, and I think it's lovely. If you want to shop at a place where you won't feel unwanted, head over to Harlem or the Blackwoods' clothing store. It's my family's store."

This made Caroline burst into tears. She rarely heard anything positive about her and the children, which filled her heart with joy. Without thinking, Caroline hugged her, and the lady smiled.

"My name is Adaline. If we ever run into each other again."

From that day, Adesua said if she ever had a child, she would name her Adaline, or Addie for short. She thought the woman was a guardian angel that had been sent by God. Because that day turned out to be one of their best days together. Now, as they roamed the rows of Lord & Taylor, employees threw themselves at the sisters, giving them refreshments and snacks as they shopped to their hearts' desire.

Their shopper, Martin, ushered the salesgirls over to block off a private fitting room for the girls. There were red velvet chaises and seats in every corner of the room. The phonograph set the mood, playing all the right jazz music to prepare them for a vivacious shopping day. Martin escorted them around the store and set up the room with racks of flapper dresses, silk gowns, and the best fur-trimmed coats.

Adesua went to the perfume counter and stocked up on her favorite perfumes, Guerlain Shalimar and Chanel No. 5. She was also fond of having an eclectic collection of heels. She saw one pair that stood out from the usual neutral colors: strappy dark-purple heels nearly covered with sequins. At the same time, Amelia grabbed the wine-red gloves and a matching dress. She didn't know where she would wear the outfit, but it had her name written all over it. Amelia and Kavita looked at each other, as they knew Martin would have them leaving with more than they had originally intended to get.

Adesua's and Kavita's eyes were like daggers as they homed in on the snack table. Martin had laid out an assortment of finger sandwiches, pink and green macarons, and chocolates filled with liquor. He brought out a nice champagne bottle, holding it behind his back, as the store secretly held it for their top customers. He poured it into champagne flutes. The girls clinked their glasses, as they knew Martin had them now.

Amelia heard giggles and loud voices in the next private suite drowning out the music. Martin excused himself, assuring them that all their needs would be taken care of and giving a curt smile. Amelia stepped out into the hallway after he exited. Something was itching at her as she wondered what the women in the next room could be laughing at.

"Excuse me, ladies, for being so brash, but my heavens, I can't believe they let those Ridley girls waltz in here," one girl nearly yelled to her friends.

Another laughed even harder at the statement. "Martin, don't you think it would be bad press for them to be in here? I mean, ladies, Dale's body is not even cold yet, and they are out shopping like royalty!"

Amelia looked at Adesua, who stopped chewing on her half bite of macaron. Kavita was staring at herself in the mirror, her rage building. Amelia knew that at any minute, Kavita would take off and go into those girls' room to give them a piece of her mind, and she was ready to hold her back if it came to that. Amelia knew this was quite the load to carry. She wasn't one to let sly remarks go by, especially when they were about her family.

Now things were very different. The tables had turned, and the watchful eyes of New York were in charge. If even one of those missing files came out, Amelia saw their future vanishing as quickly as it had arrived, and Kavita wasn't going to help their case. Especially not now.

"I wouldn't be surprised if they all ended up like Marie Antoinette, especially that hussy Kavita. And no one cares about that charity case—what was her name, Anora or something? Whatever it is, they all should burn just like Dale," another woman added.

Kavita turned around and bolted for the door, but just as Amelia had promised herself, she and Adesua stopped her.

"No, we are leaving. Get out of this dress and let's go check out now," Amelia insisted.

Amelia noticed that Kavita's chest was rising and lowering rapidly. She was clearly ready to defend her family, but the last thing they needed was another scandal so soon after Dale's death. She could see Kavita thinking, which she rarely did. Not that she wasn't smart. Kavita was highly intelligent, but she insisted on acting first and thinking of the repercussions later, like how the public could easily twist her actions to claim that she was unsuitable to be a wife. Amelia paid for everything in the hope that it would be an olive branch for not telling her sisters about the plans Father had for her.

Amelia waved another taxi down, exhausted from their escape from reality.

The young driver smiled as he adjusted his round glasses. "I see you ladies had a grand time. Where are you gals headed now?"

"The Ridley Estate," Amelia said with no hesitation.

He whipped his head around. "I knew you ladies look familiar. One day I'll get one of them fancy gold invitations!"

Amelia and Kavita smiled at the man, then looked at Adesua, who had her head resting against the door. She was already nodding off, as she usually stayed home and only went out for events.

"Well, I was thinking of going to Tiffany's, but Adesua looks worn out," said Amelia, slightly disappointed.

Adesua sprang up from where she'd been nearly falling asleep. "No, please, just go without me. I'll be resting up in the taxi."

Amelia and Kavita felt terrible—they didn't want to go without her.

"No, I insist you two go find something that's the cat's meow for me too."

Amelia blew her an air-kiss. "I'll be right back."

Adesua rolled her eyes, knowing how long they would be. Amelia and Kavita dashed through the door at Tiffany's, almost slipping on the marble floors. Now, this was their ideal shopping heaven. Each piece of jewelry was delicately laid out on lush velvet within a clear glass case. But this didn't impress Amelia. She went to the back, seeing the variety of items fit for her desk. Her eye caught a gleaming crystal inkwell and pen stand. She figured she could get both, along with the paperweight she saw.

Kavita was ushered to another room by a new sales associate who was trying to make a good impression.

The young man smiled nervously. "I didn't realize you were going to come in today. My boss said the *Ridley* girls always have appointments."

Kavita was flattered by his shyness. "Well, we decided to do a little spontaneous drop-in. I need something dazzling."

He went to the safe, which was a very large vault.

"Well, I am not supposed to show this without my boss, but you deserve the best. He said you're one of our regular customers."

The young man carelessly put in the combination code within Kavita's eyesight. She thought to herself, *No wonder his boss didn't let him do it by himself.* He carefully put on his gloves, then pulled out the most stunning choker she had ever seen. The deep-ocean-blue sapphire was cut in geometric shapes and set next to eye-catching diamonds. Kavita almost forgot to exhale after placing her hand over her mouth.

"Oh my stars, she is—"

"Gorgeous, isn't she? She should be, for the price. They got her running at around thirty thousand dollars."

"Oh, my father would have a heart attack if I came back home with that!"

The boy smiled and placed it around her neck.

"Well, not too many people could even have the opportunity to say that." He paused, embarrassed at his bluntness. "Forgive me—I wasn't—"

"Don't worry about it. You're right. Maybe one day it will get into the hands of someone who really deserves it."

He smiled and nodded as he carefully placed it back with the other jewels.

In the front of the store, Amelia held up a charm bracelet she thought all the sisters should have. The sales associate perked up when he saw her looking at it.

"We can also provide any gemstone you'd like. I think it would add some character."

She nodded to the man. "That sounds quite incredible. I shall take your advice. What gem should I use?"

A voice came from behind Amelia. "I think something red . . . A ruby would be enchanting for a special trio like you girls."

Amelia cocked her head to the side as her mouth flung open. Mother had come into the store.

"Mother, how did you find us?" Amelia questioned her.

Caroline clicked her tongue in amusement. "Because I raised you girls! I remember our cute little shopping days. Now you have forgotten about little ole me." Mother paused before looking at the gems. She passed them all, pointing directly to the rubies. "Did you know that rubies have so many beautiful meanings, such as nurturing and the spirit of knowledge?"

She paused for a brief moment before continuing.

"I think the most important meaning is love. I think that's something my beautiful three daughters share."

Amelia nodded in agreement, almost taken aback by how blunt Mother was with her thoughts. Over the years, her bright light had dimmed. Between Father's own scandalous doings and her word not being taken into consideration, she had slowly stopped speaking to the girls. She would only offer curt nods or replies that added no value to the conversation. The mother Amelia knew was gone, and that was why they no longer invited her to outings like this. She'd once been a fierce woman who had some control over the family company, until Father pushed her out, saying she should stick to philanthropy work. It was the beginning of her being in her shell at the estate.

Mother's brothers and sisters would tell Amelia how she'd had a plethora of men running after her, but she'd chosen the boy who had no family or money. She'd taken a risk because she thought Father would always protect her, unlike the rest of the men, who just wanted their own empire to become grander with her on board. She'd seen their father as a humble man, but Amelia knew how quickly money changed everything.

"I didn't know that, Mother. You know, I have missed having you around for outings like this. I figured we were bothering you, so we just didn't say anything," Amelia mumbled.

Mother chuckled as she walked, glancing at the cases. She ushered the salesman over to box up a beautiful choker necklace and anything Amelia and Kavita wanted.

"It was only a matter of time, my sweet girl. I want to say how proud I am of you. I know I didn't get a chance to tell you, but you are truly what I wanted to be growing up. I see so much of myself in you, Mellie. I just don't want that sweet girl from Paris with the brightest smile to disappear from dealing with your father, okay?" She said this as if it were a warning.

Amelia went silent. Maybe Mother no longer came out due to her shame over Father and how often they found themselves in the gossip columns. She was never fond of people knowing what she did and where she went. Before her children, she said she could go places and people wouldn't have any idea of who she was. Since they'd come along, she hadn't had a moment of peace. She was amused by it and didn't think it outlandish to have seven children. To Mother, it was completely normal. Amelia started to feel insecure and rubbed the side of her arm self-consciously. She knew that she had grown colder over the years, becoming more like her father. Being the eldest daughter and looking after her siblings for what felt like every second of the day would make anyone feel like their youth and innocence and enjoyment were gone. It was expectation after expectation with Father. Even though he would wave Mother off, insisting she was crazy for telling him that he was being too hard on them, Amelia saw, clear as day, that Mother was always right.

"I am trying my best, Mother, to do what Father expects of me, but me doing small stuff like this for Dusie and Kavi is my only way of being that young girl again. I just find that whenever we are happy, misery slowly finds its way to us," Amelia whispered as she walked around the store.

"Doesn't it always, my darling," Mother responded, almost as if her heart was heavy with regret.

Something in Amelia's spirit felt that Mother also knew all too well how hard it was to try to do what Father expected of them. Amelia watched Mother turn to the salesperson as she paid for everything, then walked out of the store without saying another word, because silence was the only answer at that moment. Something about her was so timid and beautiful. It was as if she wanted to be a fly on the wall, to be there but not be seen. Those few moments meant more to Amelia than Mother could know. Amelia wanted to be more like that. To somehow be able to do her duties at the Ridley Line and also honor her passion for becoming a writer. She would read and occasionally discuss her thoughts on books with Wei and Adesua. She knew she needed to get out of her comfort zone. Amelia looked at the salesman.

"I'll take three charm bracelets with a ruby attached. It reminds me of roses."

Kavita came up from the back, smiling, with a dainty pair of diamond-drop earrings. Amelia smiled at her, waving for her to rush while looking at the clock. It had been more than an hour since they'd arrived, which was far longer than expected. As the sisters walked out, they ran into an elated Adesua, who was walking out of their usual deli with a glass of egg cream.

Kavita shook her head, laughing. "Dusie, did they give you the whole glass?"

Adesua chuckled back. "Well, I wanted to enjoy the last bit of sunshine! I knew you would be in there until sunset!"

Amelia shook her head. She knew she was right. "All right, well, let us go home before Father sends out our brothers to retrieve us like little puppies."

In the taxi, Amelia, Adesua, and Kavita laughed almost nonstop until Kavita slowly drooled herself into a deep sleep. As they drove out of the city, Amelia looked back; deep down, she wanted to live in the city one day. They passed the orchards, spotting two girls close to their age heading inside after a long day, just like them. Adesua gazed out the window, deep in thought.

"Amelia, you remember that hidden closet we found under the stairs when we were younger?" she asked.

Amelia smiled while putting a finger on her lip. "I do, Dusie. That was our little secret place to hide from the boys. They never could find us no matter how hard they tried."

Adesua covered her eyes, thinking about all the times they had played.

"And when Wei started crying, telling Father he lost us, but we'd truly fallen asleep in there from hiding too long?"

Amelia slapped Adesua's leg.

"That was the first and only time I heard Wei cry."

They both gazed out the window, feeling little specks of happiness in the chaos. They approached their estate, the winding road lined by grand trees. Amelia walked happily to her room, which was her peace and solitude. She lay on the bed, noticing a red envelope. She picked it up quickly and opened it.

Dearest Amelia Ridley,
We know what your family did, even if you fail to believe it was one of you who killed Dale. You knew deep down in your soulless heart it was your family. If the Ridleys don't admit their transgressions soon, I assure you your family will reap sorrow and be haunted like no other.

Chapter 11

Adesua Ridley

Harlem on a Wednesday, especially on a beautiful sunny morning, should be its own state with how booming it was, Adesua thought as she set foot out of the car onto 125th Street. Mr. Pierre nodded, reassuring her, as always, that he would be there waiting. Her plan was to meet with Joseph later on that afternoon, but she wanted to cherish some moments by herself. This was her way of getting out of her comfort zone. The tantalizing scents drew her in even more. She silently imagined what her life would be like if she'd grown up here.

In another life, she thought, the sweet caramels, the roasted peanuts, the fresh batch of biscuits, and the sea of friendly faces would have been her home. Her mission was to discover Harlem more and maybe, in return, more of herself.

An elderly man tipped his hat at her as she walked by. "You make sure you come back here, honey, and get you some of my new candles."

He smiled and waved as he placed some final touches on his stall. She was definitely tempted as the aroma of vanilla filled the air. Adesua knew she had a weakness for shopping at the small vendors. If she stopped now, she would return with baskets filled with jewelry, hair products, makeup, and any type of art that caught her eye. A group of young boys started to strum up their instruments, playing smooth jazz, much to Adesua's delight.

Adesua looked through the windows at Blumstein's. It made her smile to see the beauty of all the Black women looking through clothes without the underlying fear of being watched she'd had as a child. At this point, she felt the rumble of hunger in her belly. She stopped by a quaint café called Tilly Mae Table. Adesua ordered a piping-hot coffee, along with pancakes, sausage, and cheese grits. She never would have thought she would like sitting alone by herself. But she enjoyed people-watching as she scarfed down the hotcakes with syrup dripping from her mouth. The waitress looked at her with a smile.

"You're eating like you haven't eaten in days, sugar."

Adesua covered her mouth, her smile widening.

"Every time I come to Harlem, I make it my goal to leave here full and happy," she said shyly while she put her napkin on her lap.

The waitress waved in a playful manner. "Well, you full. Now we just gotta make sure ya happy, don't we?"

Adesua paid the waitress and added a hefty tip that left the woman's mouth agape.

Before she knew it, she had made it to 135th Street and was walking into the Harlem library. She was elated at seeing the never-ending rows of books on history of Black Americans, with African culture alongside. Adesua heard a group of young people, maybe a few years younger than herself, talking about different literary works from people such as Langston Hughes. One boy talked about how much "The Weary Blues" resonated with him because of music being mentioned in the poem. It made her happy to hear how deep the conversations had gotten.

She wondered about her future artworks. Would young kids discuss her art like this one day? Maybe they would wonder what the meaning behind it was. She stepped out of the library, heading back toward 125th Street, and passed an art exhibition. She was surprised she hadn't seen it before. A small crowd of people was staring intently at each piece. Adesua felt she shouldn't walk in, but her feet led her through the doors before she knew it. She found herself looking at one painting that caught her eye. It was Harlem at night, painted in hues of purple and vibrant yellow, with people dancing happily on the street.

There was something beautiful about the simplicity of the colors. The people were highlighted—not the buildings, not the lit-up signs from the clubs. It was the people of Harlem who made it so special and beautiful. She looked down, seeing the signature of Aaron Douglas. She was euphoric at the thought that her art would one day be in rooms like this, just like his. Adesua headed back out to the street, as she found herself too easily distracted.

As she walked by the vendors once again, she saw kids playing in the water by the fire hydrants, all screaming loudly with laughter and tears as they tussled with each other. Little girls jumped Double Dutch as the boys next to them played stickball. Everything was in perfect cohesion in this little paradise. She went back to the man selling candles and got three to give to the host where Joseph had told her to meet at twelve p.m. sharp. The writing on the wrinkled paper in her pocketbook was blurry, but she was able to make out the address: *108 West 136th Street. The Dark Tower.*

The Dark Tower sounded rather daunting to her. She waved off the thought. Joseph hadn't led her astray so far. As she walked up 136th Street near Lenox, Adesua spotted a luxurious town house and felt pleasantly surprised. The entrance had tall, grand windows that reminded her of their estate.

A slender woman with her hair perfectly pinned back arrived at the door.

"Sorry, do I know you?"

Adesua knew exactly who she was. She greeted her warmly, even though the woman was confused.

"Pleasure to meet you. I am Adesua Ridley."

A'Lelia, a woman of age and wisdom, was adorned in long, elegant beads that shimmered in the light. She nodded without much confidence. "Very well, then."

Adesua made her way up the steps, following the woman inside. A'Lelia stopped abruptly when she finally caught a recollection of who Adesua was. She'd heard Joseph mention her, but something now clicked.

"Oh my stars, Joseph done brought a Ridley here!" She paused a moment and smirked. "I was beginning to wonder if your kind was too good for people like us. Adesua, I am A'Lelia. A'Lelia Walker."

Adesua embraced A'Lelia as if they were long-lost sisters, feeling a deep connection to this woman of such significance.

"Such a great pleasure to meet you, ma'am," Adesua said, feeling instant regret. Her time in the South had her calling everyone "ma'am" and "sir." She knew some didn't like that.

"You don't have to call me that, love, making me feel like an old hag! As you know, no matter our age, they are so mad at our fine looks and wealth that these people can barely breathe when they walk past us." She laughed heartily, and it echoed throughout the home.

Adesua gave a nod toward Duke Ellington when he saw her walk in. His music filled the air, enveloping Adesua in a warm embrace. The velvet draperies concealed almost every bit of outside light. The chandeliers glowed softly, adding to the home's welcoming atmosphere. The walls were adorned with eclectic art pieces from local Harlem artists and vibrant African textiles. A sea of honey and warm mahogany faces clinked their wineglasses, their joy and laughter drowning out the notes of Duke playing on the lovely grand piano.

Adesua's heart raced as she found herself among Harlem's finest. Her eyes immediately caught Zora Hurston passionately sharing her latest works with a small crowd. Langston Hughes nodded, his attention thoroughly captivated. Adesua couldn't help but think of her brother Diego, and she wished he could experience this with her. She made a mental note to invite him next time, knowing he and Zora both attended the same college.

"Well, enjoy yourself, and I am pleased to meet you. I have to get you an invite to the Harlem Debutante Ball. Now that you have found your way into *our* world."

Adesua knew exactly what she meant by that. She'd been in everyone else's world except her own, even as a child. Her siblings all got to experience a bit of their culture. She'd lost her way between eating sea cucumber stew and tea eggs with Wei and dancing to old Lavani tunes with Kavita; there was nothing she could claim.

Lost in her thoughts, she saw Joseph mingling with some of their friends. They had gotten close to her over the last few months. Adesua still felt like she wasn't fully a part of their crew, no matter how hard she tried. Although she was slightly full from breakfast, eating felt better than talking to people.

She snagged some deviled eggs and sweet potato biscuits that melted in her mouth. Her throat tightened as she coughed from scarfing the food down too quickly. Adesua ran to the mysteriously colored, strong-smelling punch, which she figured would be better than nothing. It didn't help. Her cough became so loud that people started noticing the disturbance in the ambience.

"Adesua, what do you think about that?" her friend Mabel asked.

Adesua almost choked on air this time for not realizing they'd added her in. Joseph gave her a shuttered look.

"I didn't catch what you said, Mabel," Adesua replied.

Mabel gave a curt smile before speaking.

"About the Savoy—how they are letting everyone enjoy themselves no matter their race, and how more Black-owned businesses are coming."

She moved her head up and down aggressively, trying to catch up and add something of value.

"Oh yes, I think it's beautiful for Harlem. I also love how the *Amsterdam News* is reporting things here in Harlem that are relevant."

One of the girls scoffed at her statement.

"You would know about the paper, wouldn't you?"

Adesua had been keeping quiet since she and Joseph had gotten together, stepping on eggshells around his friends. But not today.

"And what exactly is that supposed to mean?"

The girl put her glass on the counter. *She has enough liquor in her belly,* Adesua thought.

"Look, we don't have to ignore your family has been in some . . . how can I say this nicely . . . heat lately. We don't want any corrupt business goings-on here in Harlem. That may be okay for your type of folks, but we don't need any bad press."

Adesua's nose flared so much that the anger rising from her was palpable. She didn't care whether they noticed her eyes slowly starting to twitch. Adesua wondered what heat, in particular, the girl was talking about, but Dale's murder surely shouldn't have caused her to make such a bold statement. This drastic reaction coming from the same girl who gossiped over any lick of news about white society. She deemed it rather irrelevant, if she remembered correctly. Unless she was referring to something in her file. Dale couldn't have known what she'd done. Or could he? "How dare you!"

Adesua shoved the girl out of the way. She tuned out the noise of Joseph and Mabel calling her back, waving them off as she ran out the door. Adesua was on a mission. She wasn't trying to be in the spotlight; she wanted to make a difference in the community, and that was exactly what she was going to do.

Joseph grabbed her hand, stopping her in the middle of the road. "Where are you going?"

She didn't respond to him. The words that were unspoken were quite intentional for her. He hadn't stood up for her in front of his posse. That was a form of betrayal to her. All she knew was that she was heading for the Harlem School of Music and Arts. Her donations helped keep them afloat and let the kids get new supplies. That was something she was proud of, although it had been a couple of months since she had been there. Something good was being done with her wealth.

Happy to be far away from the Dark Tower, Adesua got to the worn steps of the school. It was quaint, like a redbrick schoolhouse. The elderly headmistress of the school, Mrs. Sampson, stepped out of the large black door. She loved Adesua so much, and Adesua needed that warmth. Instead, she was met with a stone-cold face and a cigarette in one hand.

"Little girl, if you don't get up off these steps . . ."

Adesua was still choked up from the incident earlier.

"Mrs. . . . Mrs. . . ."

"Save it. We trusted you, but you are just like these other folks and their empty promises, having all these parties with donations, and we get nothing! We are going to have to close our doors soon because of you, and this means you are not invited to the recital."

Mrs. Sampson stomped up the stairs, slamming the door behind her.

Adesua looked back at Joseph.

"I trusted you to handle this," she said with disgust.

"Look, the people I gave the money to at the Harlem Outreach Community Center always handle where donations go. I promise you, Adesua, I never had problems with them. One of the politicians has nothing but love for the people of Harlem. I will get it under control."

Joseph grabbed her wrist, kissing it in adoration. He loved her. She knew he would never betray her like that. She let it go, leaving Harlem. Mr. Pierre was back at their meeting spot at 125th Street. Days like this, she was grateful to have a driver. With everything that had happened today, she would have no way to focus.

The moment they made it back to the estate, Adesua made a beeline for her father. He was in the parlor, reading the paper per usual.

"Father, I need your guidance."

Father looked up at her with curiosity. Adesua rarely ever approached him with serious matters.

"What is it, darling?"

Adesua gulped, because of course when she needed him, it was because of a bad business move.

"I think I have got caught up in some business with the wrong people in Harlem. I am not sure how to go about fixing it."

She kept her face confident, ready to own up to her mistakes.

"Why don't you go talk to your mother about this? She's the one good with all that philanthropy stuff," he said in a nonchalant tone.

"But, Father, I know you handle business. I just want to make sure I am donating my funds to the right people and the right places to make a change."

He adjusted his tie. Adesua noticed how uncomfortable he was.

"Honey, Harlem is going to always just be Harlem. I wouldn't lose much sleep over it. You're more than welcome to be a part of the Ridley Line, as I have told you before. We will make a position for you. I'll make sure Mellie sees to it."

Adesua knew exactly what her father was getting at. He didn't see Harlem as a business opportunity. Adesua saw it as another home, and she wanted it to continue to flourish. She wanted to support the up-and-coming talent from there. No, it wasn't the quick money that her father wanted, but Harlem had something other places didn't have, and that was life and *soul.* With that, she collected her bag and left to go to her room.

Adesua went to the top deck of the estate, staring at the moonlight. She wanted to paint the night, filling a blank canvas with her emotions. She went back to her room to get the perfect shade of blue she was missing in her painting bag. Instead, the color red fell out in the form of a letter.

Do you paint with the blood on your hands?

Adesua looked up at the full moon while crumpling the letter in her fist and then throwing it under her bed. A slanted smile went across her face as she shook her head silently. The devil had surely made its way to the Ridley estate, but she knew she wasn't the only one getting these letters.

Chapter 12

Amelia Ridley

The flashing camera lights were something Amelia Ridley would never get over. Not in a good way either. The sound of waves on the dock at Pier 9 almost drowned out the noise of reporters, eager fans, and loud New Yorkers at their press day. It had been two weeks since Dale's death, and the public wasn't having it, from the suspect not being found to rumors that Dale had a tell-all on high society that was going to be released as a book. Some people were whispering that the files he had on the Ridleys had mysteriously disappeared during his murder. Him dying on their estate made them look more guilty than they already appeared to be.

Father insisted they do something before the rumors got out of hand, especially after news of Adesua's run-in in Harlem had begun to get some traction. Surprisingly, for once, Kavita had been left unscathed by the public. Her poor bride-to-be engagement party ruined by a sudden death. This was a turning point for her. Kavita was now the good egg. Amelia was caught in the cross fire because of her pure disdain for Metropolitan Musings. She wasn't too fond of the narrative twist on Adesua. This made the public look at them sideways even more.

Kavita, on the other hand, fed the press what they wanted. Any of her faults, she owned, from dating a married politician to wearing outrageous outfits to making a scene at events. She was the black sheep, and everyone loved that the odd one out was finally emerging from the ashes. Father suggested they put the light back on Kavita since the public now had sympathy for her. Amelia, for the first time, wasn't the sister who had the spotlight for her quiet confidence. If anything, now she felt like a nuisance to her father instead of the shining star of the Ridley Line. Bitterness rose at seeing how Kavita had it so easy. She was getting to marry an ole bloke from New York, whereas Amelia had strict guidelines as to whom she could be with. Amelia didn't have any other choice, as the annual World Alliance Shipping Convention was later that day and the last thing they needed was discussions of Dale's death as a distraction.

"Our family has been distraught over the recent passing of Dale Caimen," Amelia said, taking a brief pause before continuing. "As some of you didn't know, he was very close to our family at one point. He even went to school with Wei and Omar. He would come over with his journal in his hand, always writing. That was the Dale we knew. So when he took over Metropolitan Musings, we were proud of him for always sharing the truth, even if we sometimes looked bad. Because we have all made mistakes. This is why we formally invited him to publish Kavita's good news of being engaged to someone who was never in our circle. An honest man." Amelia gestured toward Kavita and Franklin. They looked nervous but steadfast.

"Which is why, for the first time in the history of the Ridley gala, we are inviting everyone to another party after Kavita's wedding reception. On New Year's Eve, anyone and everyone is invited to the Ridley estate to ring in the new year right. This will be a time for fellowship and love."

The crowd screamed with joy and anticipation for the barriers of high society to fall down right before them. Amelia had winged that last part and hadn't thought through the logistics, but she thought, *May the last be first.*

Omar pulled Amelia to the side at the docks as everyone dispersed. "Mellie, what's really going on? Wei may be too cocky to ask, but as your brother, I want to know: Why are you keeping us in the dark?"

Amelia was taken aback by Omar approaching her in this way. She furrowed her eyebrows in disappointment. She knew that Father had been planning for her to do this, so she didn't feel the need to listen to Wei and Omar. If she was going to be the one to take over the Ridley Line, she didn't need their opinion anymore. Father wouldn't ask other people for advice on small decisions like this.

"It's not my choice how Father wants to handle business. You all act like I asked for this. Father has his own motives, and what say do we have?"

She'd always thought they were on the same team. Now Amelia felt like she was being ostracized for standing up for her siblings. If it wasn't for them and all these never-ending scandals, she wouldn't have to do any of it. As always, she was the one cleaning up their messes. Amelia would rather Wei or Omar do it, but it wasn't like anyone in this family believed or told the truth. Why did they feel like she wasn't worthy of becoming the owner or making wise decisions?

Mother got between them. "Enough. We just got out of hot water with the press, and now you want to dive back in!"

Amelia walked away, heading toward Father and Mr. Pierre. They rushed Amelia into the car to head to the convention, much to Wei and Omar's displeasure. They were upset that she was invited to go instead of them. However, Father had his ways of convincing them that she was the best choice, though Amelia would rather have stayed home, under her covers with a book. When Mr. Pierre gracefully opened the door for them, Amelia stepped out onto West Forty-Fourth Street, taking in the entrance of the New York Yacht Club.

The doorman straightened as they approached. Amelia hurried past her father before he could parade her in front of every eligible man's face. She knew this place too well by now, and headed straight into the banquet hall, pausing briefly to accept a schedule from a white-gloved attendant. It listed nothing out of the ordinary—only talks about shipping innovations, White Star's upcoming passenger lines, and expansions of Holland America. She could already see her father's mind reeling and churning with new ideas for the Ridley Line.

The convention brought in people from nearly every state and worldwide to bring the shipping industry to the next level. Amelia stood out for two reasons: She was a Ridley, and she was one of the few women present who wasn't a wife. She oversaw the safety and well-being of the Ridley Line workers, a responsibility she took to heart.

She remembered her first day working alongside her father at the docks as he showed her the ropes. This was when the men had scoffed at her with every step. Then, over the years, the workers thought it was adorable that she was with Father. But as a teen, when she would accompany her father more seriously, they noticed she would sometimes eavesdrop on the workers' conversations. Although Amelia truly did it in the hope of helping them. She kept notes in a notepad, recording the complaints and occasional cries that brought her to tears.

"How am I supposed to be the man of the house," she'd once heard an aggravated man say to another, "when I can't even bring enough money home to support my family?"

At sixteen, Amelia had marched into her father's office with precise calculations indicating where money could be redirected from showy donations to real-life worker support. He was impressed. In that moment, he'd assured her that she would someday oversee the company. Even then, Amelia hadn't felt that was enough. Wei and Omar had shown loyalty and consistent efforts working at the Ridley Line. As she grew older, Amelia saw the clear differences in how Father treated her versus the rest of her siblings.

To the public eye, she knew the Ridleys looked like they were doing something innovative by adopting children from around the world. But was her father any different from the rest? Amelia shook her head because she knew, deep down, that Father had always planned for her, his blood child, to be the owner. Though Mother could not give him children of her own, he had found a way and would use religious texts to back his decision. He was predictable, and that was one thing Amelia was glad she didn't get from him. Amelia brushed it off, thinking her wits and long-term strategy were best for the Ridley Line—but were they?

Now she sat beside her father in the banquet hall, missing Zelda's book club but knowing this was important. Her father was proud of the work she had done, and he relished showing her off. At the podium, Commodore Harold S. Vanderbilt welcomed everyone seated at their tables for the banquet. Vice Commodore Vincent Astor and Rear Commodore Winthrop W. Aldrich took the podium, mentioning new transatlantic routes, acknowledging Edward Ridley and the Ridley Line, and praising his philanthropy and decades of holding the America's Cup.

Sitting next to her father was Henry Ford, the two of them having their own conversation. Two seats to Amelia's right were Daniel Ludwig, who looked close to Amelia's age, and Stanley Baldwin. Amelia overheard the tail end of their conversation and wanted to offer her input, but she hesitated. She listened further.

"One thing troubling me is how we can prevent future labor strikes with our workers," Daniel said. "As I build my company's foundation, there must be warning signs before these things happen, right?"

Amelia could hold her tongue no longer. "There are plenty of warnings, but most of the time, those in charge choose to ignore them to focus on 'greater' problems. They assume, Who wouldn't want to keep a job in times like these?"

The men, stunned to hear a woman speaking so clearly and confidently, all turned toward her, intrigued.

"Well, aren't you a peach?" Stanley signaled for the others to listen. "Tell me what you and your father have done, 'cause I see it's working in your favor."

"I have been a part of the business since I was young, so I never really saw the workers as workers, but family members of this one big moving machine. I first had my father sponsor housing for workers who traveled from out of state for a chance to work here in the city. I sent five children of our employees to the top schools here, and some even chose boarding schools in my father's home state of Pennsylvania. We ensure proper safety protocols and give bonus incentives for maintaining an accident-free zone. We give the workers something to look forward to."

The men sat, spellbound, seeing their workers as people for perhaps the first time. But Amelia knew, deep within her, that if they didn't have heart or genuinely want better for themselves, their company wouldn't outlast the Ridley Line, no matter how much wealth they had gained. She didn't want the title of the Ridley Line, but no one else noticed the things that she saw them constantly overlook. Maybe it was time she fully stepped into the role.

Daniel was elated at her answer. "Mr. Ridley, you got something grand on your hands, sir. Somethin' grand."

After the banquet ended, Father beamed with joy at Amelia. "Oh, my darling, you shone so brightly tonight!"

Amelia looked up at him. "Thanks, Father. I know I don't have the same bluntness or forwardness as Wei or Omar, but I am happy to make you proud. Which makes me bring this up: Why must we keep who I really am a secret?"

Father sat on the bench before the grand hall, looking down at his hands. Amelia noticed his mood fall as she sat next to him.

"Father, what's wrong? Did I say something?"

His eyes reddened as he looked away.

"I was ashamed of embarrassing your mother even further. Amelia, you are Haitian. People would have treated you differently. I made the decision to hide your Black side in fear of what would happen. Adesua has it easier than you." His voice croaked as he struggled to get each word out.

Amelia's chest felt heavy as if someone had squeezed her heart and wouldn't let go. First, she had forgotten what her birth mother looked like and that she was Black all along. Second, Father thought Adesua had it *easier.* What in the hell was that supposed to mean? Her mind couldn't keep up with what was going on around her. She thought she had experienced heartache before, but this was a feeling like no other. Amelia pressed a hand to her chest, gasping for air through her sobs.

"Sweetheart, please calm down. I worded that wrong. I meant Adesua doesn't have to choose a side. She is seen as a Black woman in her community. With you being mixed race, you're too damn bright for them, and they see you as a white woman. You can be angry at me, but you're my daughter and I am going to make sure you are taken care of," he said, gripping her hands.

Taken care of? she scoffed in her mind. The only one who took care of her was Mrs. Darla. She had been taking care of her siblings for as long as she could remember, while Father was building the company and Mother was going through her moments of insanity. Which now made sense: It was her father who'd driven her mad.

"I want you to carry the mantle, Mellie. You were always destined to make history. Please take my position, sweetheart. I have been getting sick more so recently. I feel that I am confusing myself more and more lately. I don't want to make any wrong decisions. Wei and Omar have both agreed although they were reluctant, but you must make them feel like they have a little control—all right, dear?" He chuckled at the thought.

Amelia's vision blurred. She didn't know exactly what or *who* she wanted to be, especially after the letter saying that one of *them* would be known as a murderer. She looked at her father with concern as she scrunched her eyebrows together. Did he know? Was this his way of doing damage control? It would make perfect sense for Father to have done it. He was always irritated to see a damning headline about their family tarnish their reputation. Father seemingly kept calm in front of Mother, but what if it ate at him?

"Are you going to be okay? What's wrong with your health, Father?"

Father looked down. "I don't want you to worry about that. I have the best doctors in town aiding me. You just may not see me at home as much. I just want you to promise you will do anything to protect our family. If I come to a point where I can't."

"Father, certainly, I will do anything to protect our family," she said while hugging him.

She stepped back into the yacht club's coatroom to retrieve her coat. As she put her hand in the pocket, her finger was poked by a tiny red card.

We know who you Ridleys really are. The world will find out soon.

Chapter 13

Adesua Ridley

If there was one thing the upper echelon of New York City loved, it was the ballet, especially the grand opening of *Swan Lake*. The happiest New Yorker was none other than Mother. The housemaids gleamed as they gave the pristine black-and-gold envelope to Mrs. Darla. She clipped down the hallway so quickly that she nearly bumped into her husband, Mr. Jenkins. Mother sipped her tea as Mrs. Darla walked in with a wide smile.

"It's addressed to Miss Adesua, but I was sure you'd want to give it to her yourself, as I saw who it was from," Mrs. Darla said in a high-pitched voice.

Mother flipped the card and held it to her heart in joy. Moments later, Adesua trailed in and heard the young maids whispering about the invite.

"Mother, what's this fuss about the ballet?" Adesua said, irritated. "You know I told you I will never perform again after—"

"Dusie, darling, I think it may be an invitation. Oh, won't you please open it! I can't bear to wait another moment," Mother said excitedly.

The Manhattan Ballet

September 5, 1927

Dear Miss Adesua Louise Ridley,
The Manhattan Ballet Society is delighted to hear about your return from college in Atlanta. Everyone here at Manhattan Ballet misses your radiant smile. We would love to showcase your art and everything you are doing for the city. We cordially invite you and your family to the opening night of *Swan Lake* on the evening of September 23, 1927, at our prime location, the Metropolitan Opera House.

We will host you all in our prized box seats. There will be a lounge for you and our distinguished guests to enjoy delectable hors d'oeuvres. Please be sure to RSVP as soon as possible so we can ensure you all have a pleasant evening.

Warmest regards,
Elena Fontaine
Director, the Manhattan Ballet

Adesua smiled *and* drooped a little while reading the letter. The slightly empty feeling she'd had when she left her last ballet class had returned. After dozens of performances, she knew she was constantly the only one to stick out in a row of swans. She was always the black sheep—or, in this case, the *black* swan. Elena had tried her best by putting her in the ensemble instead of casting her as the lead, even though she was great. The donors and members of the ballet society suggested blending her in. Still, society was dismayed at the sight of her. She was a blister in the donors' eyes. Who cared if she was the wealthiest heiress of all the dancers? She was never going to be one of *them*.

She'd felt a slight ache when she realized there was no need to waste her time in the world of ballet, which wasn't ready for change. She was staring at her flesh-pink tights, which were not the color of her flesh but of others'. Her face peeked out in the pale swarm that rushed to take the stage. No amount of powder helped, as it made her look like a clown, and the other young children at the ballet would taunt her. Although this was many years ago, no one had known who Adesua Ridley was then. She was no one except a lucky colored girl from a new-money family. The donors all secretly prayed for the Ridleys' downfall. Now she felt a sense of power. Here, they were flocking to her, wanting her to appear at their ballet for good publicity. Why would she say yes to a society that once clamored against the thought of her? To return that feeling and make them feel the same uncomfortable ache she had experienced in their own playground.

"I will attend, Mother and Mrs. Darla. Can you get that designer you found again? Her name was Ann Lowe. I would like her to make my dress for the ballet opening," Adesua said with a slight smile.

Mrs. Darla rushed out of the room, looking back with amusement. "Oh yes, certainly!"

Within hours, Mrs. Darla returned with Ann, hand in hand. Adesua and Mother sat in the main dressing room, where the girls frequently congregated. A room filled with chaise longues, clothes for different seasons, light-up vanity mirrors with an excess of makeup, jewelry, and perfumes. Father wanted the girls to acclimate to each other, as he'd noticed them secluding themselves in their own rooms, especially Adesua.

Mrs. Darla motioned toward her and Mother.

"Miss Ann, this is Adesua, whom I was telling you about, as well as her mother," Mrs. Darla said as if she were a proud mother herself.

Ann, very timid, nodded and smiled as she looked back and forth between Adesua and Mother.

"Forgive me if I may seem forward, but I am most pleased to meet someone like you, as some believed your story to be a tale," Ann said with a slight bow of her head, trying to conceal her smile.

"I must say, Ann, when I saw your work on my sister Mellie's dress, I had a tinge of jealousy at how marvelous it looked. My apologies for the short notice. This is an event that's very personal for me. I know you will make me look my best."

Ann, as if reading her mind, pulled out a brown bonded leather book filled with sketches of her art and fashion.

"Oh, Adesua! I may have felt too much excitement when Mrs. Darla came and said that I had to make some sketches of your dress before she brought me here. Whatever you want changed or added, I will do it. I work very well under pressure and with tight deadlines. In fact, I find pleasure in it."

Ann flipped through the pages and landed on one sketch. In her excitement, it slipped out of her hands to the marble floor. As it fell, Adesua knew immediately that this was the sketch that Ann had made for her. It was *the* dress.

"When Mrs. Darla told me it was for the ballet's *Swan Lake*, I immediately went to work. I really wanted to envision every little piece of your dress. *What does a swan capture in my eye?* I see beauty. I think grace. A swan has a certain regalness that you already possess even at your young age," Ann said with enthusiasm.

She continued, "I wanted something classy but intricate: a white satin dress with an exposed, daring back. The front shall have intricate beading reminiscent of the feathers on a swan's wings. You gonna glide through that place like you're on water, you hear me?" Ann was clearly delighted. Her Southern twang reverberated through the room.

Adesua and her mother smiled, holding up the sketches.

"That will do, and you shall be paid graciously for your immaculate work," Mother assured her.

Ann nodded and grabbed her hand with happiness. Most of the work she had done before ended up free after the toil and labor she put in, but seeing Adesua in that dress in front of all those people would be the prize for her.

> *The Manhattan Herald*
> September 12, 1927
> Metropolitan Musings
> RIDLEY HEIRESS DIZZIES BACK TO HER FIRST LOVE
>
> Oh, I know we wish this was an announcement of a grand wedding of our favorite heiresses, but for now, we see the lovely Adesua preparing for a night at *Swan Lake* with a new designer, Ann Lowe. We hope to see her gliding through the stage. One can wish!

The two weeks flew as fast as Ann Lowe's hands meticulously threaded every bead on the bodice of Adesua's dress. And, oh, was it lovely. Adesua stepped out of the grand dressing room with her sisters. Mother, Mrs. Darla, and Ann stood before her in complete awe.

"My heavens, I thought it was a vision on the hanger, but on you, my dear girl . . . Those bastard donors will regret not letting you be the prima ballerina," Mother insisted as she paced in glee at the sight.

Mother loved to stand out in a crowd, but she loved seeing her children in the spotlight even more.

Adesua sauntered over to Ann and hugged her ever so tightly.

"As an aspiring artist myself, you have inspired such a profound multitude that brings such peace to my heart tonight. I thought I'd never step foot in a ballet production again due to the shame, but you have made me a beautiful swan. And I thank you . . . my friend."

Ann placed a kiss on both of Adesua's cheeks.

"It's time for you glamorous ladies to depart. I don't want you all to be too fashionably late. I'm sure I will see you in the near future," Ann said while heading out the door.

The flashing lights from the camera bulbs made the dark night sky bright as photographers rushed to get the perfect shot of all the New York elite, from the Astors and Grants to the Ridleys, the most awaited guests of the night. The crowd all leaned in toward Adesua as Mr. Pierre opened the door. It was as if the whole world went silent as the lights bounced off every crystal on her dress.

The opera house's grand foyer was the perfect backdrop as Adesua was placed in the center of her sisters. The slim figure of the director extended her hand as she greeted Adesua.

"Adesua, we are all delighted that you accepted this invitation tonight. I hope we will be turning over a new leaf in the near future. I never doubted you, as your beauty and talent always shone through a mist of coals, if I may be so frank. The donors and council, of course, would be elated to have you return if you so choose. Enjoy the show." She hesitated before flashing her bright smile.

"Thank you, for now. I shall enjoy seeing the prima ballerina who succeeded me," Adesua said with a newfound confidence.

Elena nodded and rushed back to the entrance as she waved goodbye. A tall man with gaudy glasses approached Adesua. He was a journalist at one of the magazines downtown.

"Miss Adesua, we all must know who the mastermind behind this dress was, and are they here tonight?"

Adesua laughed through her smile, happy that her dress was mentioned.

"It was none other than my dear friend and designer Ann Lowe; she has done mesmerizing work for my family and me."

The journalist, intrigued, scratched at his paper fast with notes.

"Oh, Ann . . . Ann Lowe, yes, I heard of her recently in Metropolitan Musings. Very interesting. We shall keep her name in mind for future reference."

Women like Adesua and Ann only knew of a world where they were known as mere shadows in the background. She knew that the shadows deserved a moment of light like this.

Questions were being thrown left and right, all very pleasant. This was her time to leave gracefully as the rest of her siblings walked inside the theater to give her a solo moment. That was, until a pesky voice came through the crowd.

"What's going on in Harlem, Mrs. Adesua? I heard of trouble with the School of Music and Arts?"

Her face went as pale as the moonlight in her painting. It couldn't be him. She couldn't make out the face through the crowd. Adesua felt her heart thump so loudly she feared everyone could see through the facade she was putting up. She feared that it was Dale—alive again.

"We at *The Manhattan Herald* have heard about the money issues the Ridleys may be facing after making hefty donations. Is this true, Mrs. Adesua?"

This made her thoughts unsettled. She sighed in relief as she came to her senses that maybe this was a cruel joke from Dale's daunting spirit, revealing someone who mimicked him to spark fear. Surely it was a ridiculous thought, but she knew if anyone would torment them in the afterlife it would be him. Adesua looked at him and smiled before walking into the opera house. There was no answer that would satisfy them. So why waste her breath? Adesua had come to the conclusion they had made up their minds about her a long time ago. She might as well look good.

She sat in her plush red velvet box seat and finally exhaled. Although Adesua missed the attention for doing something worthwhile, it drained her like no other. The Grant family, on the opposite end, gave curt waves as the lights dimmed and the curtains drew open. Joseph gripped her hand when she got comfortable. Adesua wanted nothing more than to be away from him. He hadn't handled anything like he'd promised. There would be consequences for that. Rather than getting herself riled up, she focused on the dancers prancing in formation for the opening sequence.

During intermission, Adesua barely nibbled the hors d'oeuvres, completely losing her appetite once again.

Joseph pulled her aside, noticing how bothered she was.

"Honey, I didn't want to ruin your night at the ballet, and honestly it's just never a good time to say anything to you."

She rolled her eyes out of instinct but then caught herself. Him making it about himself on her night was so predictable. This time was especially off-limits.

"Look, Dale was onto you, not just about the music school but also other things with the mayor, politicians. He was in the middle of a story that went through everything the rich do at these outlandish fundraising parties, and you were a part of it, Adesua."

Adesua stood her ground. "I expect the reporters to tell lies and laugh in my face, but you . . . you have clearly fooled me."

She rushed over to her sisters, who were standing near the entry, clearly ready to go back in. Then suddenly, two elderly couples side-eyed them, and it certainly wasn't a pleasant look.

One lady prodded her husband. "I swear, they just let anyone in the ballet these days. It's a shame, really."

Her husband looked back at Kavita and Adesua. "Indeed, dear."

Kavita was up in arms at hearing the disgusting insult.

"What's a shame is that they let a haggard witch and her pompous troll in here."

Adesua stepped in between them, trying to calm Kavita, but Amelia wanted to join in on the fun.

"Kavi, the only person here tonight who was cordially invited is our sister Adesua. So, of course, they have their breeches twisted because they don't have one ounce of her grace," she said with a smug look toward the couples.

The couples rushed out quickly. This caused the girls to burst out in a roar of laughter.

Adesua looked at her sisters. "You know, I must be doing something really right if they have to spew hate like that."

Kavita grabbed Adesua's hand, then got Amelia's, and they walked back into the ballet with Joseph nowhere to be seen. The rest of the show was nothing short of stunning. Wei glanced at Adesua to see if she was okay after noticing that Joseph's chair was still empty. Before she could nod, the ballet was over.

When the doors opened, a series of sighs and gasps could be heard around the front entrance. Adesua was happy that her artwork was finally getting recognition. She didn't realize it would make people so vocal. She was excited to see her nuanced portraits of a dance trio in different shades of black and white doing jetés and arabesques and looking as if they were dancing through gold and crimson paint. Adesua's smiled dropped when she saw the painting she had worked so hard on.

Red lipstick had been drawn over her painting, spelling out one word and one word only:

Killers.

Chapter 14

Amelia Ridley

Amelia and the rest of the Ridley family were invited to the Hamptons to attend the Grants' impromptu fall gathering at their summer home to celebrate their young daughters' birthdays. Mother was elated to go shopping for the girls the night before, as she hadn't been able to pick out clothes for young girls in years. She chose two lily-white-and-pink dresses with matching bonnets filled with flowers. Mother figured the outfits would be stylish and still comfy in the lingering heat. Amelia waited until the last departing car, hoping they would leave without her, but Mother and now Father insisted she come.

"What happened to make us wary of the Grant family, Father?"

Father grabbed her shoulder. "Sometimes business brings clarity to people's minds after they make rash choices and decisions based upon what I assumed to be their character."

Amelia brushed him off. "Oh, *assume*, is that it? When he consistently brought up where you are from and that our family would never be on their level of class?"

He scoffed. "Amelia, that's enough. You will be going."

She picked up the trail of her floral dress, which was sheer at the hem, and shifted it into the car. Surprisingly, to Amelia, the small moments of closing her eyes peacefully turned into hours by the time they reached the Hamptons. The thought of seeing Jamison again made her heart flutter, even with everything that was going on. Maybe this would give her the peace and clarity she had been searching for. Anything to not be in the city surrounded by mobs of people ready to send her moves to Metropolitan Musings.

The Grants surely had to have raided every flower shop in New York, Amelia thought as they pulled up the winding driveway with probably every Rolls-Royce and Duesenberg parked outside coming straight from Long Island and the city. She saw the large veranda filled to the brim with people with drinks in hand. This was no wake-of-the-morning idea for them. The girls' party had to have been planned months in advance. It seemed every person of importance, and people they went to school with, were in attendance at this supposedly spur-of-the-moment occasion. The Ridleys had been invited last. This was proof that what she'd said to Jamison was true.

Amelia gracefully stepped out of the car, and Mr. Pierre held her steady until her feet reached the pavement. The boys, who had already been there for hours, were spread out in the back of the garden. Henrik, Diego, and especially Wei were being rough while playing a game of lawn bowling with Jamison's younger brother, Elion. She looked over to her left and saw Adesua settling beside Omar with some canvas paper and paint, which was fitting, as they never cared for the uproar of parties in the summer or, furthermore, any time of the year.

Amelia nibbled on a yellow macaron to satisfy the empty craving she'd had all morning. Truly, she didn't want to run into Jamison again. What would she say? She wouldn't apologize for telling him about her fears. Could she possibly even want to marry someone who could get offended over a simple question? Yes, it may have been a loaded question with a variety of possible answers, but if she was to marry him, she needed to confront the harrowing pain that he would leave her. She felt it even more so now, after the second anonymous letter. The Grant family's reputation would be destroyed just by association. But Jamison had never cared for all that—or had he?

Margarete Magdalene—well, now Margarete Thistle—swished her merry way into Amelia's face as she sat on the bench looking out onto the water.

"Is that Mellie Mel!" She covered the sides of her face in an overbearing, dramatic way.

Margarete was already on her third and fourth children at the age of twenty-one. Her toddler twins pulled at her dress, screaming while she urged the first and second to go play.

"I would have never imagined you here at a children's party! Don't tell me you have a secret child we don't know about." Margarete winked as she kissed one of her bald twins on the head.

Amelia knew she had always been sarcastic, ever since their young school days. Margarete would taunt her and her sisters for their skin tones, but it had never fazed them, as they had one another to rely on. Amelia silently thanked her parents for that. Without her siblings, she could have easily turned out like Margarete, having children she secretly despised.

"Yes, Jamison's family has become quite acquainted with mine here recently," Amelia said in a confident tone.

Every girl was in love with Jamison Grant, especially Margarete. She begged her brothers to let her attend the Long Island Country Club to watch him play tennis or croquet. Amelia knew that the implication of her, Amelia Ridley, being potentially paired with Jamison Grant would make a seemingly happily married woman jealous to no end.

Margarete laughed. "Oh, Jamison is over there with our old friend Laurina Key." She waved and winked over at her as she caught her friend's eye. "I think I love the sound of *Laurina Grant*, don't you, Mellie?"

Amelia stood up from the bench.

"Here, Margarete, please have my seat. I can't imagine how exhausting four kids must be. I have to go entertain myself with the lovely band." Amelia briskly left, pretending not to hear another word from Margarete.

She rushed inside, making her way upstairs to get away from the noise. Amelia stepped into what looked like the family library and wandered around. Amelia wanted to stay in the Hamptons more. She skimmed through the books, seeing classics such as *Pride and Prejudice*, *Jane Eyre*, and *Wuthering Heights*. She hoped that Jamison had read a few of them. A creak from the wood floor caused Amelia to turn around and see Elion.

"Sorry, Mells, I was just getting my secret jar of whiskey." He tilted his head behind a stack of books that sat a little forward on their shelf.

"No, I am sorry for puttering around in areas that are clearly not mine," she said shamefully.

Elion scrambled around, grabbing the jar of Canadian Club.

"Amelia, my family loves you. Believe it or not, our fathers may have not always gotten along, but Mother . . . Mother has spoken nothing but kind things about you since we were all children running around Central Park. She saw you as set apart from every girl here in the city, since you were able to speak multiple languages, and by far the most beautiful . . . You have nothing to worry about, I assure you." He smiled as he left the library, waving the whiskey. "Duty calls. Enjoy yourself, Amelia."

Amelia felt a little more at ease. Her worries over her father, her siblings, and now her ever-changing life shifted slightly as she realized she wouldn't mind having in-laws like the Grants. The Ridley children were just like the Grants in many ways. They tried to make sense of the world they were born and brought into, keeping their elders happy, but in reality, a piece of them died with every choice they made.

Jamison nearly collided with Amelia as he rushed into the library.

"Oh, I'm sorry—" Jamison said as he prevented her from falling back.

He walked to the edge of the room and looked back at Amelia. She didn't dare look away, but instead marched toward him as the climax of the jazz band's song soared through her veins. And, oh, she soared as she crashed into him with every intention. He held on to her strongly as he pressed his perfectly curved lips to hers. This felt right. This was right. Whatever had happened before this moment didn't matter, and everything after this moment seemingly didn't exist. He pulled away from her as they exchanged slow gasps.

"I would like to go to the US National Championship with your family, if you don't mind," Jamison said nervously.

Amelia looked into his eyes. "Why do you sound like it hurts you to say this? If your parents are making you do . . . this . . ."

Jamison held on to Amelia, cupping her face in his palms. "Honey, my parents can make me do many things, but choosing a woman I want to spend time with is where they falter. I was running away from that nasally Laurina. It was apparent that my father had sent her after having dinner with her family. She's probably crying to my mother, who I'm sure would be elated to know that we are together."

"Please come, Jamison," Amelia pleaded.

"And that I will," he said confidently.

Jamison walked Amelia down the stairs with the crowd watching. Mother and Father nodded as Amelia walked behind Jamison, his hand entwined with hers.

Surely it was a celebration for his young sisters, but the night ended with a celebration of love that had every single eligible girl filled with envy.

The Manhattan Herald
September 16, 1927
Metropolitan Musings
OUR TWO ROYAL FAMILIES COLLIDE

Amelia Ridley and Jamison Grant: We can't imagine a more beautiful couple than this. Whispers all the way from the Hamptons report to have seen the couple hand in hand. Can't you see the grand wedding rivaling every royal wedding there ever was? It would have been the bee's knees to see young Elion and Kavita paired as well. Talk about a match made in heaven.

Chapter 15

Kavita Ridley

It had been weeks since Kavita had received her red letter. Franklin didn't dare say another word about Dale because Kavita loved to live in her own reality. If it didn't matter to her anymore, the subject no longer existed. Dale was gone, and that was the only thing that mattered. Because the dead couldn't speak. The heat was now back on Adesua. Father quickly paid every paper, once again, to report that Dale's death was an attack by mobsters, trying to deflect the blame from his innocent children.

Franklin had invited Kavita to come to a day party in a secret location to get her mind off things. He wanted to get back to the old "them." The ones who were the life of the party. Kavita was excited for an outing. She'd been cooped up in the house for months under Father's strict orders after Dale's death. The idea of this outing gave her a different feeling than the late-night speakeasies they would go to. Kavita twirled in her sparkling white dress. She slinked down the stairs, waving quickly to her family as everyone ate a late lunch. Her flamboyant cousin Sebastien, who'd just gotten back from France, chased her down the hallway.

"Not so fast, cousin! You think you'll leave me hanging with these boring people?"

Kavita knew he wouldn't take no for an answer. "It's a love . . . emergency. Very private matter. I am sure you understand."

He was about to give a quick response but instead let it go.

"Fine, I will let ya slide this time. Have fun with Franklin. He has to be the perfect kind of crazy to be with you!" He kissed her on both cheeks as if he were still on vacation in France.

Kavita hopped into the private car Franklin had sent before anyone else could run after her. As the car wound over the roads, a peace came over her. The fall leaves were starting to glow in that perfect shade of orange she loved. Quickly, she realized they were not heading into the city, and this made her even happier. The car approached a beautiful conservatory. The tall windows reflected the greenery in the greenhouse, which had perfectly placed overgrown ivy that crept out onto the cobblestone path. It made her feel like she was in a distant land filled with magic.

Kavita was becoming smitten with Franklin all over again without even seeing him. The grounds and gardens were filled with people laughing and chasing each other, enjoying the sun with cocktails in their hands. She even saw that the women were barefoot, throwing their shoes near the fountain. This was her style of party, with people from different boroughs, different working-class people all having picnics together on scattered blankets. The platters of food, with fruit, cheese, and savory sandwiches, kept coming and being passed around. Seeing people relaxing on hammocks or dancing to the live band, Kavita was sure she was in an oasis.

"Welcome to the Garden of Eden," said a sultry Franklin, looking dashing in a cream suit.

She turned toward him, giving him a tight hug, to his surprise.

"Thank you for inviting me; this is absolutely beautiful," she said softly.

He smiled hard at her elation.

"We like to call her the Eden Gala. At the very end of the summer heat, right when fall is starting to come, we host this get-together for any and everyone at this abandoned greenhouse. It started off small, but word of mouth is how it has become so successful," he said quietly.

He passed her a cocktail from a tray. "The heat makes people restless. Best to stay cool."

He grabbed her hand, and they walked the grounds together, Frankling leading her into a different section of the greenhouse. They approached a row of gambling tables all set up perfectly with a great view of the festivities beyond. The thick smoke and smell of cigars permeated the air as a dealer shuffled a deck of cards.

"It's been a while since we've done this," Franklin remarked.

Kavita was more than ready for the high of gambling. The last time she'd played was unlike anything she'd done before. She walked over to the roulette dealer, and he slid over the crimson chips. Being a Ridley came with favors, which led the dealer to put her on credit almost instantly. Kavita placed her first stack of chips on number three. She always loved that number, for whatever reason. A man with a raspy voice spoke from behind.

"Back for more fun, little miss?" he said, with a woman vastly younger than his last ex-wife on his arm.

"Can't let Franklin here get all the good stuff." Kavita looked at the woman, who gazed back at her.

It was gangster Lucky Moretti and some of Franklin's old friends. She knew Franklin had to keep a poker face, not only at the table but also with Lucky. Especially after what had happened last summer. The red letter had only caused her even more stress as she wondered who Franklin really was. Before he'd met Kavita, he worked with Lucky to make a living. She didn't judge him for that because he changed and left Lucky before they met. Now she spoke briefly to keep the peace so he wouldn't retaliate. Surprisingly, even after all her father's doings these last few months, indirectly blaming Dale's death on mobsters like him, Lucky had a peaceful nature to him.

Lucky spotted her look. "Oh, forgive me, my beautiful. Kavita, this is my wife, Francine. She decided to come out and play with me tonight."

Francine nodded in approval. "It's a pleasure to meet you, sweets. Franklin here hasn't stopped talking about you."

Franklin started to blush. "No need for all that, Francine. You know I hear the refreshments are quite great," he said, trying to change the subject.

Lucky focused on the table. "Hey, you two, hush so the miss can focus."

The roulette ball started to bounce in what seemed like slow motion before it finally landed on her number. She felt exhilarated as everyone cheered, hearing her win. Her winning streak continued. Kavita decided to change to number twelve. Until that third round, which became a loss.

Lucky, being the older man, leaned over toward Kavita with optimism. "Look, kid, you know what you're doing. You've won many times before. This is the moment that separates winners from losers. Which will you be?" he said confidently.

This was going to be her last spin no matter what. Her chest tightened as she placed her final bet. The roulette ball seemed to move slowly along the rim until it clicked past her number. The dealer swept away the last of her chips with practiced efficiency. Reality crashed in as Kavita calculated her losses.

The dealer looked up at her with stoic eyes. "Quite a sum you lost, miss. Time to settle up."

The amount would make her father's head spin. Franklin noticed her panic.

"Go get the money. I'll wait," the dealer grunted calmly, but his eyes urged her to hurry.

She looked at Franklin with worried eyes. Kavita was annoyed that Franklin wouldn't pay up for her. That was one of the sacrifices she'd made in the name of love; paying for everything was normal for her. Everyone knew she came from money, but she expected to be taken care of, especially since this was his idea. Nevertheless, Kavita assured Franklin she was fine and left him to catch up with his old friends. She picked up her empty champagne glass and walked to fill it with more champagne. As she was about to pour, she noticed a crumpled piece of paper at the bottom. Kavita assume it was confetti from earlier. Instead, it was a note.

One more glass . . .

Kavita couldn't maintain a poker face this time. Chills ran over her body. She immediately thought the worst, believing she had been poisoned by a disgruntled fan. Kavita grabbed the money out of her wallet, which was in Franklin's coat pocket, to give to the dealer. The hairs on her arms stuck up sharply; she decided to put on her gloves. One finger wouldn't go in, no matter how hard she pushed it in. *The threading must have gotten out of whack,* she thought. As she turned the gloves inside out, another slip of paper fell out.

One more dead body . . .

This wasn't something she could ignore anymore. The greenhouse, which had seemed magical just a moment ago, now felt like a trap, like sulfur and smoke were choking her. Everything around her began to feel small. She walked back to the table and paid the dealer, signaling to Franklin she wanted to leave. He ignored her cues.

Lucky switched places with Franklin, getting closer to Kavita.

"Speaking of owing, I just spoke to Franklin about you and your father. I think it's time for Lucky Moretti to turn over a new leaf. I do a lot for the city of New York that goes unrecognized," he said, then swigged down some alcohol.

Kavita thought about what he did. It was a far cry from helping. If anything, he stole from people who were barely making it. She let him continue so his ego wouldn't be bruised.

"I need to clean up my image a bit. I feel it's the *least* Franklin can do after all I have helped him with. Isn't that right, Franklin?"

The idea of Lucky coming back into their lives hit Kavita with a nagging feeling that something was amiss. Lucky had let Franklin go after he'd done his duty and paid off his debt. There were people envious of him because he'd seemingly gotten off so easily with Lucky. Because everyone knew Lucky was someone you could never escape, no matter how far you got. She waved off her never-ending thoughts. But what if someone wanted vengeance, and a way to pull Franklin back in? Something in Dale's file could have given someone a clear way to force Franklin back under Lucky's wing.

Franklin looked defeated. Oh, how Kavita was tired of weak men flocking to her family, from her father letting Amelia be the person in control instead of Wei and Omar, Joseph abandoning Adesua on her special night, and Jamison keeping Amelia on a string. When she thought about Amelia, she wondered whether she got the short end of the stick from everyone. At first, Kavita hadn't felt bad for her when Omar and Wei called her out at the pier, but truly, no matter what the sisters did, they were in a man's world.

"Sweetheart, are you okay?" Franklin placed his hand on her head. "You looked like you were about to faint for a moment."

Kavita waved her hand, brushing off Franklin's question, trying to focus on what Lucky really wanted.

"My father is so busy. Anytime I talk business, he brushes me away, unfortunately."

Lucky went to her ear, whispering, "For your and Franklin's sake, I think you will have to try a little harder, darling. You know, for old times' sake," he said, winking his right eye and putting a toothpick in his mouth.

"Very well, then. If you both can excuse me," Kavita said curtly.

She ran to the tiny house on the property and called Mr. Pierre to come pick her up. Kavita felt grimier than the mud outside. She sat outside as far away from the greenhouse as she could, waiting near the driveway. Mr. Pierre came within minutes. She was grateful they were still in Long Island. The last thing she needed was for her thoughts to run rampant. Mr. Pierre opened the back door to the only thing that was in her way.

Father.

"Why are you at a place such as this, Kavita? You keep on at it, and I will call this wedding off myself, so help me God." Father slammed his fist on the seat, insisting she get in.

The words continued. A series of insults about her failures. "You lie constantly, Kavita, and I let you get away with it. Not anymore."

She sat, taking in every word. Kavita wanted to let him ramble, but she couldn't bite her tongue.

"He was just like you, Father," she said coldly.

Father turned in his seat as they made it up their driveway. "Excuse me?"

"Franklin didn't have a silver spoon in his mouth when he was born, but he worked damn hard for every cent he has. You know this and I know this. So the least you could do is give him a chance. Why does everyone in our family get chance after chance but people like Franklin don't?"

He cleared his throat, keeping silent. One thing Father would never do was say he was wrong. Kavita was in a never-ending battle of proving not only herself but also someone she loved and cared for. Father being this close to a mobster like Lucky made her feel paralyzed. She took his silence as the closest thing to agreeing with her, for now—or was that what he wanted her to think?

The Manhattan Herald
September 21, 1927
Metropolitan Musings
POLITICS AND PROHIBITION COLLIDE

Politician George Tanner has gotten caught up in an underworld racket scheme with mobster Lucky Moretti. Some say he even tried to get the Ridley Line involved. Dale Caimen had a file showing how Tanner tried to woo his way in with Kavita to get access to the Ridleys and use of their ships for Lucky's not-so-lucky business.

This comes weeks after the Ridleys spoke at the World Shipping Alliance Convention on safety and protecting the piers. Ledgers and telegrams put them in hot water. The office of George Tanner has denied the claims.

Chapter 16

Adesua Ridley

Adesua wanted nothing more than to escape. After what had happened at the ballet, she was hiding from the world. She was convinced that her every move was being intently followed, even more so now that the depiction that she was a murderer, of all things, was painted on her beloved art. In the garden that used to be her safe haven, it had started to feel like there was a public execution waiting to happen.

Omar was insistent that all the siblings gather there this morning. She had tried her best to avoid the garden and maze altogether since Dale's death. Adesua was the first there. It was far too early, and she knew Kavita would be slinking in last. She reached her hand out to the roses filled with morning dew.

"Hard to believe this is where it all happened," a deep voice said from behind her, startling her.

Adesua whipped her head around so quickly that it caused a kink in her shoulder. Wei stood with both hands in his pockets, giving off the ever-so-cool demeanor that he was the one who'd come up with the idea of meeting here.

"Why are you here and not Omar?" she asked.

Wei shrugged before sitting on the bench and lighting up a cigarette.

"Omar, the genius that he is, suggested we should stagger our arrivals instead of us all coming at once. You know how nosy the maids and especially Mrs. Darla are. She would report back to Mother and Father as quickly as we could speak to one another."

Amelia and Omar arrived at the same time, which wasn't unusual, to say the least, as they always either went on a morning walk with their horses or took a quick swim in the pool. Adesua's lips curved downward with a slight thoughtful pout as she put it all together. She quickly understood how they were showing up. Something ate at her, though, and she wondered why she had to show up alone, and how Wei always knew they'd come together. The two rascals of her younger siblings, Henrik and Kavita, showed up, with Diego trailing behind them, stuffing his face with a cherry–cream cheese croissant.

Adesua let out a small laugh at the ridiculousness of them all being there at this godforsaken hour. Her smile disappeared as Omar threw a stack of newspapers to the ground. This startled her, as Omar was the calm diplomat of the seven. His fists tightened as he put his arms across his chest. Wei rolled his eyes while taking a long drag from his cigarette. Adesua could tell by the movement in Omar's mouth that he wasn't ready to say whatever uncomfortable truth he was about to speak. Omar mustered up the courage to suggest an idea.

"We can pretend like nothing is going on, but someone knows something—or better yet, everything," he said, his calm voice ever-so-slightly raised.

Adesua kept finding all this rather comical. Omar was the last to have the file. It was the old elephant in the room. He could cause a fit throwing papers, but she knew the truth and so did everyone else.

"Adesua, you were supposed to get it from me when I was supposed to leave. What happened?"

Adesua knew it was coming, but still it shocked her that he was accusing her of being the one responsible.

"First of all, Omar, it is not my fault that you didn't properly hand me the file in the first place. I have no idea where it went," she snapped back.

Omar furrowed his eyebrows, bringing his head back as if someone had punched him in the face. "'Properly'? What, are you pretending to talk British like Henrik now? No, I placed it in a safe place on the bench so it wouldn't get wet."

"Exactly!" she exclaimed. "That's why I went to go get a towel for Amelia and Henrik, who were dripping wet, hoping it wouldn't mess up any papers. You are all very welcome!"

Wei flicked his cigarette and stubbed it out. "You all need to calm down. A lot happened in a short period of time. Pointing fingers isn't going to do anything."

Diego whipped his head toward Wei, whispering, "You're a fine one to be talking about being calm."

Wei, now breaking his cool, glared at Diego. "What the hell was that, you little—"

Kavita was the queen of discourse, and Adesua adamantly shook her head no, telling her sister not to instigate any further.

"The real question is, what haven't we done? Which I know we have all done something crazy for Dale to act the way he did. Why is it not in the papers right now?"

Adesua was shocked that Kavita, for once, had something of use to say instead of antagonizing the situation. She was right. Why hadn't anything been revealed? It was all still speculation at this point. Henrik had told Adesua he saw that Kavita had burned a red letter, and she wondered whether its contents had something to do with Dale's murder. Was she hiding something that would cause her downfall? Seeing Kavita this calm made her second-guess herself, as the younger sister she once knew was now intrigued by what was happening.

Henrik stepped into the center of the garden and sat on the edge of the fountain.

"I, for one, think one of us has the file. Because why wouldn't someone else take the chance of revealing all of our secrets if they had the opportunity?"

While the youngest, Henrik was as bright as Omar and Wei combined. Adesua looked at each of her siblings, noticing most had their heads down, some exchanging eye contact and knowing glances. It was a silent revelation, they all seemed to think. No one was brave enough to say the words. Except her little baby brother Henrik. Adesua felt heat rise in her body. If one of them had the file, then one of them was the murderer. "My word, Henrik, we just went through a whole interrogation. Do not add to this," she said sternly.

Amelia stood up, shaking her head and throwing her hands in the air. "Everyone, enough! You all have my head spinning," she yelled. "We all need a break from the estate. Let's take a moment to clear our heads so we can properly think of what and where the file might possibly be."

The idea itself wasn't bad, Adesua thought. She did have a fear of the public placing a target on their heads. She had her siblings by her side to protect her, even if one of them was secretly Judas.

Chapter 17

Amelia Ridley

Amelia had a talent for breaking up chaos, unlike Kavita, who thrived in it. Amelia had a way with not only words but also certain acts of service that she knew all her siblings would love. That was simply getting away from everyone and anything. Adesua found her pleasure in painting, while Diego played a game of chess with Henrik, and Amelia and her older brothers bonded over something they couldn't resist: flying.

"Let's go out on the planes with Uncle Fred. It has been some time," she said eagerly.

The boys pepped up as if that were the best thing they had heard all week.

"You know, for a moment, sister, I thought we had lost you to the gazillion balls you girls attend," Wei said mockingly. "I shall ring Uncle Fred this instant."

"Well, I will go for moral support. You know I am not too fond of heights, Mellie." Adesua chuckled, lightening up the tense air.

Amelia entered the car with her siblings and adjusted her leather jacket as they drove down the road. When they arrived, Uncle Fred slapped the front of Wei's car.

"Oh, am I happy to see you all," he chirped.

"Uncle Fred, where have you been?" Amelia exclaimed eagerly.

He wasn't their real uncle from either Mother's or Father's side, but was instead Father's old friend who'd helped him start the Ridley Line. He had since left the company and was now primarily focusing on his nefarious hobbies, staying far away from the Ridleys.

"You know I don't care about all these damn events your father and mother are throwing. I want to see the sunrise and sunset over the water every day, that's all. You kids be careful now. They are all set and ready for ya. Mellie, you should take the hot seat today." He winked at her.

Omar laughed. "Well, maybe Mellie can be like Amelia Earhart. They already have the same name!"

Diego chimed in, "You know what, Omar? You may have a point there."

Amelia waved them off as she and Wei got in the back seat and Omar took the front as the pilot. She adjusted her goggles, feeling the nervousness in her chest. Omar, Diego, or Wei would almost always be the pilot. She occasionally did it, but enjoyed taking in the clouds. The feeling was so far away from it all, from everything she *detested*. That felt like power to her. Solitude was what she wished to have most. She thought deeply of those things; after all, weren't they all born alone in this world? She and her brothers didn't have to put on a show anymore. She hoped that those feelings would stay as Omar descended, getting closer to the ground . . . closer to the *truth*.

"Oh, what a ride, sister. It was beautiful up there. What a great idea today, Mellie. We needed that," Omar said.

She was certain they *needed* a lot of things; surely Father would cover anything up, but Henrik's thoughts did nag her. Why did he feel like one of them would be so reckless as to kill Dale and take the file?

Amelia's face melted into straight lines, her expression as serious as ever. The heat swelled up her back and her cheeks, making them rosy. She was ready to get off the plane as it made a smooth landing, a soft jolt for the most part. Amelia paced around the plane while the boys joined Adesua and Kavita to eat a small snack. She marched over to the wooden picnic table where they scarfed down their apples and sunflower seeds.

"Now that these issues have been brought to our attention, it's time for us to get serious about what really happened that night," Amelia said.

She shot piercing looks at her siblings, noticing that Henrik and Diego had instantly dropped their food. Why were they so quick to react? God, they all had such guilty looks. Amelia was surprised the police had even let them alone. The thoughts that buzzed around in her head were that her brothers must have conversed among themselves to keep things from her and their sisters so they wouldn't leak their precious secrets to the public. Surely nothing that she, Kavita, and Adesua had done was as bad as what the boys had done.

Omar, peacemaker that he was, stood up next to Amelia, grabbing the sides of her shoulders.

"Amelia, I may have been too brash in scolding everyone—"

The tears had already started to fall as her heart raced, and she yelled into the abyss of the field.

"One of us had to kill Dale! Are you happy now? That's what I am thinking!"

Amelia didn't know what was taking her over. Maybe the fear that they could all soon be in jail as accessories to murder, or simply the fact they had some secrets so sinister that even the people of New York would turn their backs on them. Father had worked hard for them to live a life like this. It would be his downfall if one of them had murdered Dale and it was leaked to the world. Adesua and Kavita turned their backs to Amelia, rolling their eyes, brushing off the accusations. Amelia seethed as she watched Adesua continue to paint like this was a calm afternoon, without a care in the world. This one time, they couldn't ignore what was coming for them.

Wei stood up, now taking control of the conversation.

"I have been sure of a lot of things in my life, but I would never kill. I know you and Henrik live in the fantasy worlds of books, Mellie, but this is the real world. There is no damn murder mystery here. Dale died on our property, with no evidence of who or what murdered him.

And if this person wants to put our family in harm's way, so help me, God, I will get rid of them myself by any means necessary."

Maybe her siblings had nothing to do with it, but one of them knew more than they were saying. She knew Wei and Omar would do anything to protect their family, but imagining them killing someone was out of line for her. She had to stop feeding into the frenzy of panic. Amelia knew precisely how she and her family were depicted in the gossip columns. Everything was fabricated to a certain degree so they would appear better to the masses. One white lie turned into three, three lies turned into ten, and they were ignored—well, she thought, until now. Petty dating and opinions were mere folly, but murder was, and would always be, *murder*.

At this point, everyone had started to pack up their belongings. What she originally thought was going to be a peaceful conversation had turned into caged emotions being set free. She was tired of perfectly controlling her reactions. This was *real*.

After they got home, she didn't feel better about the situation, so she went to the garden where Dale's body had been found and sat there. Her eyes felt hot as they turned a sharp red with tears from the emotions she harbored in her chest as she put her hand on her neck, trying to feel the pain Dale had felt in his last moments. Amelia felt empty as she squeezed the thorn on a rose she didn't even realize she had grabbed. The small trickling of blood from her palm didn't faze her in the slightest. Blood had fallen, and so had her family.

Amelia paced back and forth; her silk, feather-trimmed robe followed her. Father was hiding something. If he had been able to conceal that he was her biological father this whole time, he was capable of hiding more. A pain hit her as she thought about her *maman*. Amelia looked at her reflection in her silver oval mirror. She stared at the small brown beauty mark on the side of her face. She couldn't remember much about her *maman*, but she knew she had the same mark. Oh, how she wished she were here.

Amelia was resolute. She decided to wait until the late hours of the night, nearing morning, when everyone was asleep, to go to her father's office. They were forbidden to enter his office without him there. All her siblings had a silent fear of their father, so they never even attempted to go into his office. But all that was going to change today. She peered down the hallway both ways, listening and looking for any movement or signs of lights in the other rooms. It was as quiet as the breath she was waiting to exhale the moment she got into his office.

She hesitated for a moment, considering taking the elevator, but decided on the stairs, hoping it would make less noise. Amelia crept down, almost losing her footing. She knew she should have left her slippers in her room. She knelt, taking them off. As she pressed her feet down on the final step, she gasped as the pressure made a noisy creak that traveled down the hallway. Amelia slapped her forehead. How could she have forgotten about that step? She paused for a moment, waiting for Mrs. Darla or Mr. Jenkins to approach, but to her amazement, she heard nothing except her heart beating through her chest.

Father had no locks on the downstairs office door, which had always surprised her, but he would often tell her there was really nothing of importance in there except lousy business paperwork. She assumed the workers thought this as well, because no man with secrets would leave their office unlocked to the world. *Or would he?* As she stepped in, she left her slippers on the chair. She needed every finger she had to go through the world of papers and boxes her father had accumulated over the years. She didn't even go near the desk, because she knew her father would never keep anything of importance there.

She opened up the wooden cabinets, finding paperwork all neatly organized by year from his different organizations, partnerships, and lastly, the Ridley Line. Amelia didn't know what she was looking for, exactly. She sifted through papers, finding nothing of value other than the knowledge that if her father was ever audited, he would be prepared.

She stood up to take a look around, admiring the details of an oil painting. The painting featured what seemed to be a parallel of night and day, which she found rather odd. She approached the painting, tracing the details of the sun rising over an ocean, with the bottom half of the sun being the moon shining over what looked like buildings. She leaned forward, pushing the painting accidentally while trying to see if the artist's name was on it like the others, but as soon as she did so, the painting clicked as if it was connected to a magnet of sorts. Amelia tried to move the painting up and down, but it didn't budge. She thought for a moment. Father always said nothing of value would be somewhere that could be seen by the naked eye. He would chuckle when he said this, assuring no maids—better yet, no one, period—would find anything in this office. He was always *right*, in his eyes.

She turned the painting to the right, and as if by magic, the wall immediately opened, leading to a narrow hallway. Amelia hesitated for a moment before entering, wondering if she'd lock herself in here, but she knew that this was where her answers lay. Sconces dimly lit the area, but she couldn't see how far down the hallway went. Air enveloped her, making her shiver. As she made it to the end of the hallway, she saw a very large black wooden box on a high shelf.

Amelia stood on her tippy-toes, hoping to reach it without having to move anything, as she knew how meticulous her father was. She was not tall like her sister Adesua. She glanced up two shelves above the one she was near and saw something that seemed misplaced. A very raggedy wooden box with a red leather-bound folder peeping out.

She began to tremble, shaking the wooden box of papers so violently that a black velvet bag surfaced in the middle of the mass of sheets and folders. In the sea of white and black ink, all stacked accordingly, this bag did not belong. She skimmed through the papers, which looked to be contracts. This didn't shock her until she saw notes with her siblings' names on them.

AGREEMENT BETWEEN MR. EDWARD RIDLEY AND METROPOLITAN MUSINGS FOR PRESS COVERAGE

This Agreement shall be enforced starting on 15th of May, 1915.

Mr. Edward Ridley and Mrs. Caroline Ridley

of 17 South Hampton Lane East Meadow, Huntington, NY

AND

Metropolitan Musings

Located at 113 Lexington Avenue, New York, NY 10016

Amelia skimmed through all the formalities and continued to read until she saw . . .

> Metropolitan Musings has been guaranteed the first exclusive arrangement of being able to document any and all significant milestones that center the Ridley family. We shall be the only press to have exclusive access.

Amelia's skin felt like it was on fire. She rummaged through more papers, finding letters in French.

> May 4, 1912
> These dark nights have enveloped my soul. The only light in this world comes from my dearest Amelia. You will find that her spirit is as calm as the moon in a beautiful night sky and as fiery and filled with wit as the sun. I hope you will now cherish this light, as my light has flickered away. Every night you look at

the sky, just know I will now be with the moon as a star shining so bright away from this pain and misery.

Cécile

November 4, 1905

Paris, France

My Love Edward,

I never knew my love could grow for you more. As I sit here by the window, the snow is frosting the windows. Thinking of the last time you were here and how filled with love you made me. I write this with a sense of hope for our future, as I am with child. Not only just a child but a seed of our enduring love. I hope this letter finds you well and is found with joy. I would do everything to be yours. Although it was never intended to happen this way, I am ready to be yours forever, Edward.

All my love,

Cécile Moulin

Amelia placed the letter on her chest. *Cécile*, her loving *maman*. Oh, if she could only turn the hands of time and tell her *maman* to forget the perfect image of her father and to raise her on her own.

Paris, France; 1912

Although Amelia was already roaming the streets of Paris at the age of seven, she would go for her morning walks in her neighborhood, getting chocolate croissants for herself and her mother. Afterward, she would play with the neighborhood cats, Todi and Bing. She wasn't sure whether they belonged to anyone, but she would make them hers by giving them special treats, no matter how much it dismayed her mother. This morning was no different from any other as she tiptoed up the many stairs.

Maman—oh, how she missed saying that name—would be sprawled out on her chair with her head down after her long night shifts at the burlesque show. Amelia was used to waking up at night all alone and fending for herself with what little food she had. But the beginning of the month was her favorite, as a mysterious white envelope filled with a wad of money would be ready for her to spend on some of her favorite treats. She lightly tapped on her mother's shoulder, but she just slumped over more.

"*Maman! Maman*, wake up. I got some breakfast for us," a young Amelia happily said.

She moved her hand, but it slumped to the ground.

"Ma . . . Maman?"

She gently pushed with more force to wake her, only for her dear mother to fall with no sense of her usual jitteriness. Amelia silently sat beside her mother. She must have been tired after a long night's work. She sat for six hours caressing her mother's fiery-red hair, only for her mother, her *maman*, to never wake up again. There was no scolding for buying extra pieces of chocolate from the bakery. There was nothing. She lay on her mother's chest until a barrage of knocks hit the door. Her mother's friend Delilah scolded Cécile from the other side of the door for being late for work. Young Amelia yelled out that her *maman* was sleeping and was in a deep sleep that she hadn't seen before. Frantic, Delilah opened the door with a spare key and rushed to her mother's side, pleading with her to wake up. The only thing that was near her body was a letter addressed to her from the Ridleys. Delilah embraced Amelia so tightly that she couldn't even breathe.

Amelia wept as she held the small piece of paper. She kept rereading it, over and over. If only she could tell her *maman* how much light she'd given her. She was her saving grace as a young girl. All the memories they had together meant so much more to her now that she was an adult, while her father had only been there for her in the form of an envelope filled with money. She now realized it had been from him all along.

As she continued to look, a shadow was cast on the wall. She had been caught. Something told her she should have closed the door behind her. Amelia wiped the tears off her face. She whipped her head back quickly, ready to lie if necessary.

Amelia, exasperated, said, "Jesus, Kavita. You can't just go lurking behind people so quietly."

"Well, at least I still have it in me to scare my big sister," she said with a devilish grin.

Kavita noticed her face was puffy and red.

"Wait, what's wrong . . . What happened?" Kavita grabbed her in a tight hug.

Amelia knew her father kept secrets from them, and she promised herself she'd try to not do the same with her siblings.

"Father has been lying to us all. You know this, and someone is onto us. All of us," Amelia began, ready to start her tirade, but Kavita swiftly interrupted her without a change of expression.

"I know, Amelia. I know everything."

"You know what, Kavi?"

Kavita looked at Amelia.

"I have been getting letters from an anonymous person—and I am sure we all have—regarding Dale's death. Someone knows something, and we need to find out what. We need to go back to the maze."

"Yes, I have, and if I am being honest with you, Kavi, it does make sense if one of us did do something to Dale. Someone got that file that night and is more than likely using it against us, but I'm not sure how. I am nervous that it's one of us sending the letters," she said with despair.

To Amelia, saying this out loud for the first time made the possibility that one of them had done something even more real.

"Well, who do you think did it?" Kavita asked.

"Kavita, it's our family we are talking about. It would be reckless for me to throw out names right now," Amelia snapped.

Amelia took the lead leaving Father's office. She didn't want anyone else to catch them in there. She headed to the garden, with Kavita trailing slowly behind her. Her head was down, staying silent as they walked. They roamed the gardens, making their way to the maze. Daylight had just broken, and the maids were shuffling around the estate. Amelia felt better knowing Kavita was with her. It had been clear from the beginning that they all had something to hide, but to what extent?

While she was deep in thought, Amelia noticed Kavita trail off by herself, holding something she hadn't seen before. It was a brown leather journal, and her sister was furiously flipping through the pages. "I am keeping this. It is about me and Franklin. Something we did last summer. Dale had it written in here and had my interview as the next thing, but he didn't get the chance to run it. I remember him having it in his hand when I saw him. I don't know how it ended up here, but I am keeping it."

Amelia could see that the journal had been hidden in the mud. If you weren't looking for it, you never would have noticed it. She was going to object, but she and Kavita had been through enough. Whatever she had done last summer was surely just as bad as what the rest of them had done. This was a never-ending cycle that she wanted to stop.

"We have to find out who is leaving these letters, Kavi."

Kavita's eyes widened with apparent fear. A heavy hand grabbed Amelia's shoulder and swung her around.

"What are you two sneaky gals doing up this early?" Jamison said with a grin, before he kissed Amelia.

"Just having some sister time. Needed some quiet." She lied so easily it scared her.

Kavita put the journal behind her back.

"Since when did you start writing, Kavita? Never thought I would see the day," Jamison said peculiarly.

"Oh, you know, older sister rubbing off on me. I'll let you two lovebirds talk."

Amelia's heart nearly sank when their eyes met.

"Amelia."

"Jamison."

He reached out his hand to hers as she approached him.

"I assumed you ran away to another country after I hadn't heard from you," Amelia said, annoyed.

Jamison looked down, disappointed. Maybe she'd spoken too soon and he was about to inform her of the sudden departure he was bound to make. After all, Amelia had always said he was a runner. Why would he treat her any differently?

"We can't be together," he said coldly.

She laughed as he harped on and on. Could he be any more predictable? She wanted to say more, but all that she had left was the croak of her laughter turning into tears.

"Look, Amelia, you don't know how bad I want us. I really want us more than anything in the world," Jamison said desperately.

He could have fooled her. He almost looked like he loved her. But for him to leave when she and her family were going through this turmoil was just like him.

"Okay," Amelia said, with nothing left to give.

Problems with men were something she didn't need right now. So she would gladly cut the reins that kept him there if he wanted to go.

"You can leave," she said as she turned away.

He grabbed her hand, bringing her back to him.

"Amelia, the reason I can't let myself have you is because of my family. I would never forgive myself if I bound you to their fate," Jamison said, his hands trembling.

She knew it—she could never be enough, only useful in business, just as her father had molded her to be. Always the one leading people out of their misery but not her own. Jamison was supposed to be her safe place.

"If you only knew half of what my family is going through, nothing your family has done would sway me from being with you. Nothing. So let me make that choice and deal with my fate as long as I can be with you. Jamison, I never cared about any man before or after you. I remember seeing you yell at those boys in school who would taunt me for looking after helpless animals. I remember how you helped me and gave me those wildflowers anytime I was sad. Let me remember more with you," Amelia pleaded.

She hated how pathetic she looked, but as much as she tried to ignore it, she did want to be loved. Finally, he broke. He broke down crying to an extent Amelia had never seen before. His tears brought him to the ground.

"My family has lost it all, Amelia. I have nothing to give you. Don't you see?"

Amelia was bewildered at this statement, as she didn't want to assume what he meant.

"Amelia, I have always wanted you. Even when my father spoke ill about your family, I wanted you no matter what. I remember seeing you, Mellie, that day we raced on the field, and I couldn't imagine myself with another woman from that moment. But once we moved, things went further downhill for my family. This estate was once our grandfather's, but Mother always wanted to live in the city. So we did. I didn't think much of it when we moved back here. Until we saw fewer and fewer maids and groundspeople."

He was out of breath, but he continued. "Father has gambled everything away and put money into things he shouldn't have. That's why he was trying to get in with your father, especially through our relationship. Everything felt tainted as he begged me to marry you once he found out you'd run the company.

"Everything was genuine until it wasn't. Father kept ringing in my ear to escalate our relationship, which truly I wanted to, but I wanted to do so in my own time. I have always lived by my father's rules, so I always left the country when I could to escape his pestering needs when they grew far too great for me. This is why I can't continue this relationship, at least not now. Because Father would do anything to keep money in our family; I can't be with you in good conscience knowing this."

Amelia's mind was melting down as each second went by. Why did he have to tell her this? Why now? But no, this was her life. Her gut feeling, that it had always been calculated, had been right, but she didn't realize it was to this extent. The Grant family wasn't vying for her hand in marriage with their son because she was a perfect match for him, but because their ego had been hit by their crumbling empire. She had saved her own family empire too many times before. Amelia wasn't going to do it for his. She swallowed hard, and a lump stuck in her throat.

"Jamison, I can't—I can't do this. I need to go."

Jamison looked at her with so much guilt. She would have rather he stuck with her than abandon her these last few months. Amelia realized people were only there for her when they needed something or were begging for forgiveness. Now she had nothing to give either. Jamison held his hands over his face. He turned and walked toward home, kicking a pile of leaves hard in anger.

Their families had their own issues, and bringing them together now would only add more to her plate. Amelia saddled her horse, Mya, needing to get away from home after this morning. As she rode to the edge of the estate, she saw Adesua in the back seat of Mr. Pierre's car, looking hopeless. She waved goodbye to her, but it seemed Adesua had her own share of worries.

Chapter 18

Adesua Ridley

Adesua hadn't expected to see a block party when she pulled up to Joseph's family's barbecue in Sugar Hill. The entire street pulsed with life, families spilling from one brownstone to the next. She had never seen anything like it. Her smile gleamed bright as Mr. Pierre opened the car door, revealing a group of young girls in their Sunday best playing hopscotch. Adesua walked up to the tall double doors, knocking gently.

A girl younger than herself peered out. "Whatcha knocking for? Just come on in."

Adesua smiled as she waved off Mr. Pierre.

"Forgive me, I wasn't sure if I had the right house; I was looking for Joseph," Adesua said politely.

"Oh, you must be that girl my brother was talking about. I am his younger sister, Sara."

"Pleasure to meet you, honey. I'm Adesua. Now, where can I put this? I brought some mac and cheese."

Sara shot her look. "Oh, Adesua, that's the name? Hmm, well, that was a bold choice for you to make. Don't you know the aunties always have control over the mac and cheese?"

Adesua did not, in fact, know of this unspoken rule, but they were going to have to let her slide this one time. She set the glass tray in the kitchen next to three trays that already had spoons dug into them. Sara chittered and chattered away, walking her outside, where Joseph's extended family had gathered, though it looked more like a reunion of old friends of all ages.

Joseph's face lit up when he spotted her. "My beautiful woman made it all the way out to Harlem for little ole me? I am flattered." He chuckled and kissed her on the cheek.

"Well, I wouldn't say 'little,'" Adesua teased.

"Come here. I want to show you around."

The dancing area thrummed with couples and children jumping and swinging in every direction. The string lights above them twinkled overhead like stars. He brought her to the closed porch, where a few older women sat.

"And this right here is my beautiful momma and my auntie Adaline." He motioned to two ladies with their legs crossed, sipping on what seemed to be tea, but Adesua knew better at a party such as this.

"Momma, this is Adesua, the one I told you about," he said, his confidence suddenly wavering.

She sat up, recrossing her legs and pouring more cloudy drink into her glass.

"Adesua, hmm? Tell me about yourself, gal." His mother twisted her lips.

The lady beside her smiled brightly, quite in contrast to his mother.

"Well, I just graduated from college in Atlanta a few months ago. I came back home to see where I want to—"

"Oh, Atlanta, you say? I got some kinfolk down there. Is that where you originally came from, girl?" his mother asked, slightly more intrigued.

"No, ma'am, I'm originally from Illinois. I did have some family from the South, my adoptive parents told me," Adesua said, smiling at the small similarity they shared.

"'Adoptive'?" His mother's voice sharpened. "Joseph, don't tell me she's one of them Ridley girls."

Adesua was used to the crazed looks of others who didn't look like her. But this was new. She thought they'd understand—they'd experienced the same racism and injustices, after all. Who cared if she was adopted? And who cared if she was a Ridley?

They did, apparently.

"Momma, listen—"

"Now, Irene," the woman next to Joseph's mother cut in. "Settle yourself. I know the Ridleys. Met her mother years back, when Adesua was just a little thing."

Irene rolled her eyes at her sister and then looked back to Adesua. "I just didn't realize Joseph was bringing you here. I'd have kept on my good clothes." She chuckled.

"That Mrs. Ridley is a kind woman, so you need to stop being ugly." She looked at her sister, then continued. "I am Adaline, again, by the way. I know Joseph has introduced you to probably every person at this party. Take a seat, darling."

Adesua sat with her legs crossed, trying to keep the nervousness and disappointment off her face. Then she remembered who Adaline was. The lady who'd helped them when she and Amelia were young. The connection stunned her.

"I mean no offense to the girl, Addie, but, honey, you aren't one of us, no matter how dark your skin may shine," Irene said. "Raised by them white folks, probably don't know the first thing about her own people. I won't have my only son giving me grandchildren who—"

"With all due respect, Mrs. Blackwood," Adesua cut in, digging her nails into her own palms, "you have no right to speak to me and my family in this way. You think I chose to watch my family burn alive? You think I chose the Ridleys? I have done everything possible to get closer to my people, but I am only pushed away by the likes of folks like you. I went to a Black college, date Black men, support Black communities. But it's never enough for some people."

Everyone looked at her silently, shooting cutting glances at Joseph's mother.

"Well." Irene smoothed her skirt. "She sure has a mouth on her, doesn't she. Joseph, she's got spirit, I'll give her that. You can bring her back." Mrs. Blackwood paused, easing the tense lines on her face.

She and her posse went back inside the house while Adesua slowly exhaled. She looked away to stop herself from crying, staring at a man's mouth with a cigar that hung limply from it. It made her think of a memory she thought she had long forgotten.

Illinois, 1913

The world closed in on Adesua when she awoke one Sunday morning to a dark fog spiraling down her chest. She figured she was trapped in a nightmare that would never end as she gasped for air . . . good, clean air. The night before, her mama and daddy had yelled in fury and rage as Mama prepared the family dinner. The thunder had seemed to bang on their doorstep. She liked it when the weather was like this because the thunder would drown out every poisonous word her mama spat at her daddy. A young Adesua had left the table without even being noticed. Now she was being shuffled out the door and thrown onto a mysterious bed that was not hers.

A voice echoed through her ears as her eyes stayed shut.

"Young Black gal, probably no older than six or seven. Her parents both died in the fire, and it seems a cigarette from the father could have caused it. We asked neighbors if the girl had no family there. Her mother and father both originally came from the South alone. So she's on her own here now, Ida," a man said with a hint of sorrow.

Adesua lay in that orphanage bed every night, hoping her mama and daddy would miraculously walk through that door. Hadn't Jesus returned from the dead, and so many others in the Bible, just like Mama had taught her?

The day Adesua was adopted was a blur to her. She remembered how alone she was for weeks, then months, then two years. Every child Adesua would meet who had the bluest eyes or even an unruly face filled with freckles—they were all adopted before she could even introduce herself. All because of the shade of her skin, which glowed as bright as the sun, making the tears in her eyes gleam. Every potential parent immediately looked over her, going to the next child to ask their name. She knew they looked different from her, but what made them so much better? She saw one boy throw a toy in a lady's face, and he was still adopted! She knew from that moment that there was nothing she could say or do until Mother—her new mother, Caroline—came directly to her.

"You are the one we have been looking for, honey."

She smiled as she remembered walking up those grand steps, looking at this enormous white house that felt larger than life.

Every night, her new bed would be drenched with tears. She'd been brought into a new family and world that didn't seem possible without her mama and daddy. She knew, as loving as Mrs. Ridley and Mr. Ridley were, they were not Mama and Daddy. Adesua dreaded the thought that she would never again find herself in their arms. And, oh, their love. She wished she could go back to the day before the fire and that last fatal fight. Her mama would wake her up with the smell of golden, buttery biscuits, sausage, and eggs, and Daddy would kiss her on the cheek with a murmur of "I love you" through his slender cigarette that blew wispy clouds from the side of his mouth.

She snapped out of her deep trance.

"I am sorry, Joseph. I wasn't expecting—"

Joseph pressed a finger to her lips. "No, it was my fault. I hoped seeing you here would change her mind. But mothers can be a little . . .

complicated, no matter what color," he said. "Let me make it up to you on the dance floor."

She knew he respected her but wished he had spoken up more. Maybe this was another unspoken rule of Black families she didn't know about? Adesua made a silent promise to herself that she would no longer let people make her feel like her existence was a burden. Their discomfort was their problem, not hers. Joseph took her hand and swung Adesua around until she was dizzy and smiling. She could tell he was distracting her from this and something else.

"What else is going on, Joseph?"

He grabbed her hand, taking her away from the crowd and walking her toward the street.

"Adesua, I love you, and I am really trying to make this grow, but is there anything else you need to tell me?"

She hesitated because she could barely trust her siblings anymore. Why would a man that she had just brought into her life give her any loyalty?

"That's the answer I needed. Adesua, I am trying to protect you, but it's getting out of hand. I paid the school. When I gave it to the committee, I was informed that you owed money to another organization, and it went there. They refused to give me any more details," Joseph said with sadness tinging his voice.

"I will get it under control, Joseph. I thank you for your kindness and generosity for the school. I know who I need to talk to."

She gave Joseph a kiss on the lips, reassuring him that he wasn't the crazy one or at fault. Adesua was, and she knew it. She thought everything she had done was careful, but it wasn't. She sent her goodbyes and thank-you's to the family for letting her enjoy the day with them. Long Island was the only place to hide. Harlem was slowly moving her out day by day.

Mr. Pierre was waiting for her with open arms. "What's wrong, kiddo?"

His strong British accent startled Adesua. Mr. Pierre was a silent man. A keen observer but always watchful and protective over each of them since they were children. None of them knew much about Mr. Pierre's life before the Ridleys, but he was their family.

"Nothing, I just needed a hug without words." Adesua hugged him tightly.

He gave her exactly that. No other words were spoken on the drive all the way back to the estate. He stopped looking at her in the rear-view mirror.

"Dusie, don't forget how bright your light is. Even now, you've always been a star in my eyes. Don't let this world stop you from what you need to do. No matter what they say."

He turned off the ignition and opened the door once more. As she headed upstairs, she heard arguing in the foyer.

"Father is in the Hamptons, doing nothing because he is losing his mind!" Wei exclaimed with his arms in the air.

"There's a right way to do this. We go behind Father's back, and he finds out. Me and you are done. He will take away everything we worked for," Omar said calmly.

Wei shook his head, walking back and forth.

"No, we need to do it soon. The board has already talked about his loud outburst. Him being senile. He will ruin the Ridley Line."

Adesua walked away, but her heel got caught on the floor, causing her to trip and break a vase of roses. *Another thing broken,* she thought.

Wei swiftly came and picked her up. He checked her arm, which was now bleeding from the broken shards of glass. He set her on the foyer couch. This made Adesua laugh because her legs were functioning just fine. Wei ran upstairs to his room and came speeding down with a small paper packet.

"Here, I am going to put this on you. It's called Yunnan Baiyao," he said comfortingly.

This was a drastic difference from his earlier tense attitude about Father.

"We just need a little. This little packet can heal almost anyone," he said as he rubbed her arm gently.

Omar had left by this time. Adesua knew he didn't want to be confronted about the conversation he and Wei had just had.

"Wei, about the night Dale died. I just want to apolo—"

He stopped her before she could finish.

"Dusie, not now. Let me just do this, okay? We don't have to mention that ever again. He is gone for a *reason*." He was getting riled up again just thinking about it.

Adesua let him leave without pestering him further. No one wanted to face the truth. It was easier to instead pretend it had never happened. But someone knew, and they were waiting to be slaughtered next, just like Dale. This time, it would not be by the press, but by the people who had prayed for the Ridleys' downfall.

Chapter 19

Kavita Ridley

Streams of loud noises were nothing out of the ordinary for the Ridleys. Kavita started every morning after a long night out on the town just the same. The maids came to her room at the same time, like clockwork—no earlier than nine and no later than ten. Kavita could roll into her room right when the sun rose and be up first thing in the morning. She claimed it was a gift because God knew how reckless she could be. On this morning, Kavita would sink into a tub filled with oils and flowers. Her hair was matted due to the amount of pins she'd put in it to make it appear short.

Kavita was tempted to cut it off into a short bob like her friend Lila or her sisters, but she always hesitated when she brought the scissors to her locks. She felt like her hair was the only thing that connected her to where she came from in India. Her raven-black locks fell all the way down her back.

She parted her lips and sang a note so high that it stirred Henrik. He could hear everything in Kavita's bathroom because his room was beside hers. Kavita sang a song that he hadn't heard in a long time. She and Henrik would sing songs together when they were younger.

Kavita threw on her custom orange kimono-inspired robe. She walked hard, almost like a toddler, to Henrik's room. She opened the door to see the back of his ashy-blond hair. His ear was pressed to the wall before he whipped around.

"Haven't you ever heard of this little thing called . . . um, knocking?" he asked.

Kavita rolled her eyes, grabbing his arm. "Haven't you ever heard that it's bad to eavesdrop?"

Henrik shook his head while batting his long eyelashes with a simple, closed smile. "Okay, you've made your point. What do you want?"

Kavita gave him her devious, wide smile. Henrik knew she was about to ask him to do her bidding anytime she gave him a crazed smile like that.

"Oh no, whatever it is, I am not covering for you, pretending to be you in your bed with a wig—"

Kavita put her finger over his mouth to stop him from rambling.

"No, I want us to be a team."

Henrik furrowed his eyebrows in utter confusion. He was sure she had gone mad now.

"Look, I know all those pins in your head may have made you lose a few brain cells, but what 'team' could I possibly be on with you?"

Kavita rubbed Henrik's full head of hair like he was a golden retriever. "Oh, my little brother, you have so much to learn. I know you want to play music outside of your room."

Henrik's cheeks flushed pink in embarrassment. No one mentioned his love of music due to their overbearing Father and the Ridley Line. So he'd hidden it from his family.

He stuttered, trying to outwit his sister. "First off, Kavi, we are the same age. You are three months older than me because God had to show his thanks to the world by having you born in November. Secondly, I play music as a hobby. You should think about getting one." He grabbed her arm and walked her out.

"You and me, some of my girlfriends I want you to meet, and Franklin at the Golden Goose tonight in Harlem. Maybe you can show off some of your moves!"

"We leave at eight, Kavita! No later than eight," Henrik exclaimed as he slammed the door.

⌬

Kavita put on her sheer black stockings with the velvet black lines that traced up her legs and crystals sewn in. If she was to accompany her brother and maybe even join the open mic tonight, she refused to blend in with the crowd. She wanted to be a showstopper, just like how she had seen Josephine Baker all over the gossip columns the night before. Kavita slipped on a three-tiered red-and-black fringe dress. Kavita knew the dress code was red, but she was a rebel; she had to add a little bit of herself into it. She never was fond of looking like everyone else. She layered on pearls and diamond necklaces to add sparkle. She started to pin her hair in her usual updo before suddenly remembering what long hair meant to her.

People like her were one in a million. They followed what she did. She could have followed the trends of how they wore their hair, but she was the trendsetter. Kavita slowly took the pins out and let her hair fall down her back. She looked back at herself in the mirror, taking in the length of it. It mesmerized her that she had kept it up for the past few years. Kavita found ruby crystal clips and pinned them in her flowing hair.

A triple knock came at her door. Every sibling had a distinct way of knocking, which Kavita had memorized, but more than one sibling used three knocks. She couldn't quite hear who it might be.

Henrik tapped twice, paused, then tapped once more as if he were unsure whether she had heard him knock the other two times.

"Come on in."

Henrik closed the door gently behind him.

"You see how that works? A little polite knock goes a long way!"

Kavita brushed him off as she pinned more crystals to her hair instead of a bed of flowers. Her hair looked like a constellation of stars.

"Henrik, what are you doing here? I thought you said eight o'clock sharp."

Henrik rubbed the temple of his forehead in laughter.

"Kavita, that was twenty-five minutes ago."

Kavita whipped back toward Henrik, storming over to retrieve her watch from the closet. She laughed as she stepped out, holding it out to him.

"Well, see, it was an emergency."

Henrik sat on the edge of her bed. "Oh, sister, pray tell. Hastily, of course."

Kavita slipped on her strappy black velvet heels that matched the lining of her stockings perfectly.

"I shall be on the way first. I need you to make an excuse to Father and Mother for why I shall not be in my room."

Henrik walked to the door leading to her private stairwell.

"I don't know why they gave the most mischievous child a stairwell. I should have gotten it. Anyways, never mind that I told them I heard you vomiting all morning again. You are covered. You might want to lock your door tonight. Mother seemed frantic. I told her not to worry; I said you were reading a book in bed and I'd check in on you."

Kavita grabbed her beaded clutch and followed him out. He turned and peeked out the window to see that she did nothing to prevent them from coming in.

"You have no fear, do you, Kavi?" Henrik laughed as he walked down the steps.

"Everyone knows you're the favorite child, along with Diego. You two have never got in any trouble. So Mother and Father are always going to take you at your word."

He nodded gleefully as Mr. Pierre opened the doors for them.

"Yeah, you may be right for the first time, sister."

Kavita ignored his comment as she fussed with her dress. She'd always been obsessed with the intricacies of beading. She wondered who had taken the time to make a dress so beautiful. Henrik swore up and down that he and Kavita were nothing alike because of her recklessness, but here he was, sitting in the car with her, going to a speakeasy. She chuckled to herself at seeing him nervous.

"Is this your first time going to a theater or a club?"

Henrik straightened up, trying to look cool.

"Of course not." He put his index finger on his thumb, a tell that he was lying. Kavita knew the little tricks and antics he would do whenever he lied or was nervous.

"You know these clubs mean nothing in the grand scheme of things. It's just a bunch of sweaty bodies too close together."

Henrik looked at her with pleading eyes. "Can we just have a fun night without, ya know . . . you drinking? I know I shouldn't ask, but I get scared and don't want to be the reason something bad happens to ya, especially with us together for the first time on a night out on the town."

Kavita felt a twist in her stomach at the question. She didn't like being called out for how she drank, especially not by her younger brother. It wasn't her fault he'd grown up to be such a prude, locking himself into the music room and teaching himself every instrument.

"You shall have nothing to worry about tonight, brother. I'll be as sober as Amelia when she writes her books in the early morning." She chuckled softly.

"You know I love you, Kavi. I want you to be happy."

Kavita started to hide her smile but let him see it anyway. She grabbed his hand.

"And you know I love you too. Now, let me introduce you to my friends."

Henrik looked petrified; his facial expression said everything as if he were screaming it out loud. Mr. Pierre opened the door, and Kavita and Henrik slid out of the back seat. A group of girls pointed at Kavita the moment she got out.

"That's Kavita Ridley!"

Kavita waved and smiled while holding on to her brother's arm. Henrik had a way of dressing more casually than everyone in the family, with his suspenders and brown woolen pants. Kavita was sure that those girls would be the first to report to Metropolitan Musings that she was out with a poor man.

"Henrik, why must you wear those dowdy clothes?" she groaned. She hadn't even realized in her room what he had on because she was so focused on making sure her hair was flowing just right.

"Well, Kavi, some of us don't crave attention and truly just want people to love us for what we are, not what we have."

Henrik looked back at the girls and flashed a smile. He had a handsome face but looked like an infant beside his brothers. He had a tall stature, but his skin was buttery soft, without one blemish, which made girls question if he was no older than fifteen. Kavita knew Henrik would look better if he let her or Amelia dress him, but he was stuck in his British ways.

Friday nights in Harlem were abuzz with anticipation. It marked the end of the workweek, but more importantly, it heralded the grand opening of the latest speakeasy, discreetly nestled off Fifty-Second and Fifth Avenues. The Golden Goose, a hidden gem, had only opened its doors a fortnight ago, and the news had swiftly reached Kavita and her friends Lila and Ellie, who, as always, managed to stumble their way out of the car.

A flock of men and women stared at Kavita as she passed them in line, as she always did. She figured if they all enjoyed reading about her every morning so much, it was her right to get these special privileges. She hit the goose-shaped brass knocker three times, as instructed. The security guard dressed in an all-black suit popped out and instantly recognized her. Kavita pushed the door open a little more before being stopped by him.

"Well, sweetheart, I let you skip the line, but you gotta say the code to get in."

He chuckled, knowing it was nonsense. She did it anyway, ripping the paper out of her clutch.

"The geese strike at midnight," Kavita told the man.

He pondered for a moment before pushing it open. "I could have sworn it was a goose." The man broke out into mad, roaring laughter. "You have a good time tonight, ladies. Let me know if anyone gives you trouble."

Kavita was no stranger to the dimly lit, gritty atmosphere of speakeasies, but the Golden Goose was in a league of its own. The narrow, creaky stairwell led to a hallway adorned with royal-blue velvet wallpaper and golden sconces. The warm glow of the sconces cast a golden hue on Ellie's fiery-red hair. The distant sound of a jazz band grew clearer with each step, and Kavita pushed open the door to a breathtaking sight that widened her eyes. She could tell Henrik felt nervous.

Kavita was struck by the beauty of the Golden Goose. She was enchanted by the fact that the rooftop was now a garden oasis with twinkling fairy lights and the moon's reflection on the shiny black tiles on the floor. Ellie grabbed Kavita by the hand.

"Kavita, snap out of it. Four chairs have our names written all over them."

Lila and Ellie flopped onto the ruby velvet armchairs, almost blending in with them in their red dresses. Kavita took in everyone wearing different shades of red, and it was pleasing to see the backdrops of the surrounding greenery. Kavita looked to her right to see a small elevated stage and a band that started to play dramatic entrance music.

She looked at Lila and Ellie in happiness, wondering why the music was getting louder, and the crowd clapped.

"Have any idea who might be performing?" Kavita asked her friends, who both shrugged.

An eavesdropping girl—probably a fan of Kavita's—interrupted. "It's not just anyone. It's Josephine Baker. I would think the city's most famous girl would have known."

Lila caught that as a jab and was about to say something to the girl before Kavita cut in for herself.

"Surely I probably should have, but that's usually for the unknown girls of the city to know. So I leave that job to them."

The girl was snatched away as her friends side-eyed her for overspeaking.

Although only two years older, Lila hugged Kavita like a proud mother. "Thatta girl! You show them who Kavita Marie Ridley is!"

As Kavita returned Lila's hug, the crowd hushed as the spotlight illuminated Josephine Baker. Kavita and Henrik gasped at the sight of her. She was like an enigma, an angel descended from heaven. Her two-piece outfit was covered in crystals, diamonds, and feathers. Kavita had never seen anything like it. She imagined that was what space would look like; the singer was like a pattern of stars, and they were the dark sky. Josephine swayed her hips with vigor and elegance.

You couldn't tell whether she was moving fast or slow. The audience roared in applause at the end of her dance. Josephine caught Kavita's eye, in awe. As she stepped through the crowd, she headed straight for Kavita. Josephine cupped Kavita's face in her soft hands, which caused heat to rush to Kavita's cheeks. Her wrists smelled like jasmine and sandalwood. The rumors about how she smelled like a million bucks were true, Kavita thought. She would never tell them her secret scents, though.

"You're truly as beautiful as everyone says, Kavita. I've been fond of you since I first heard about your family."

Kavita's eyes grew big, as she would have thought she was irrelevant to someone like Josephine. She had recently finished her first movie, and Kavita was just a girl who had risen from rags to riches. Nothing was exciting about Kavita when compared to Josephine.

"Fond of me? You're too kind, Josephine. I'm in the graces of one of the most remarkable women of our time. I hope to be half the lady you are someday."

Lila and Ellie shifted their chairs to move closer to be in Josephine's presence.

"Ahh, excuse my manners, ladies. How gorgeous you both look."

Lila, excited to get a word in, grabbed Josephine's hand. "You are a stunning performer, and I hope you plan to stay in the city. It's missing someone like you."

Josephine laughed while rubbing Lila's hand.

"I have to return to France. Although, I wish!" She stood up, bringing Kavita up with her.

"I'd love for us two to meet again. It always brings me joy to see another woman who looks like me. We are truly the diamonds in the rough, and you better never forget it. You hear me, hon?"

Kavita smiled because she knew it was true. There weren't many people in places like this who had the same golden skin tone. Kavita nodded and hugged her. Josephine pushed her back.

"Oh no, honey, we kiss on both cheeks like the French do now," she said kindly.

She took notice of Henrik and gave him a kiss on the cheek too. Josephine mingled with the crowd, her security close behind.

While looking at her brother, Kavita noticed a shadow come into view. It was Franklin. She let go of Henrik in shock. Franklin grabbed her hand, kissing it. "I missed you so much, dollface."

He grabbed hold of her and kissed her passionately. It was almost too passionate, even for Kavita.

"If you'll excuse us, I have something to tell Kavi," Franklin said charmingly.

He pulled her into a corner, looking at the view, then her.

"Kavita, I want you to look at me and keep smiling," Franklin said, beaming, nearly laughing.

"I need you and Henrik to leave immediately. Don't tell Ellie or Lila, as they will make a scene. Lucky has found out your father had a deal with Dale and ratted him out and the politician with the Farely Shipping Co. for bootlegging. That ship was taken over by police. Now he wants your father to pay for his losses."

Kavita wanted to hit him. How had he found out? Father kept his business a secret. What if this was all a joke to get Franklin back in with Lucky?

"You know what I think—"

"Kavita, leave now. I won't promise you make it out of here if you don't do it now, and quickly. Have a smile on your face and tell your friends you are using the restroom and tell Henrik you need help with something. Whatever you do, don't tell him." Franklin leaned in and kissed her on the cheek and walked away with a smile on his face.

Kavita told her friends she had to go meet with someone and for them to not wait on her. The girls were already too tipsy to even care.

Henrik saw men in hats who were very much armed coming up the stairs. He grabbed Kavita because, after seeing Franklin and his sister conversing, he knew they were there for her. He beelined straight for the exit door the performers took, away from the rest of the crowd.

Mr. Pierre stood out by the car, waiting with a gun in his hand. Franklin must have informed him as well.

"Kavita and Henrik, hurry!"

Mr. Pierre waved his gun as men came through the next alley, aiming guns toward them and shooting.

"Damn it, Kavita, what have you done now?" Henrik asked as they piled into the car.

Kavita didn't say a word. Mr. Pierre zoomed through the bustling streets to their estate. Not that it was any safer there.

Chapter 20

Adesua Ridley

The Ridley estate was eerily quiet, the only disturbance being the phone's incessant ringing. Each ring was a piercing reminder of Joseph's persistent calls, a sound that had transformed into the source of Adesua's mounting irritation. She wasn't sure why she didn't want to be bothered by anyone today, especially men. Mrs. Darla picked it up yet again.

"Yes. Yes, Mr. Blackwood. I will tell her you called."

Mrs. Darla hung up and shrugged, as she had no cure for a man in love. The phone rang again, and this time, Adesua answered.

"Look, Joseph. I am dealing with some important matters I have at home, just as you have yourself sometimes. I know it's hard to believe a woman is ignoring your calls."

The voice on the other end laughed before she could finish.

"Would a ticket to the Harmon Foundation Gala change your mind?" he asked, sounding amused.

Adesua pondered for a moment. Because surely it would make her look rather suspicious to change her mind so quickly, but this was more business than her frolicking around with his family and peers, who seemingly despised her.

"Oh, forgive me, Joseph. It's been a whirlwind of . . . Never mind that. I would be delighted to go. If anything, this would get my mind off things."

She could tell Joseph was more than likely shaking his head with a wide smile on his face.

“Well, darling, I thought it would be a great place for you to make new connections, since you say I don’t pay attention to your world,” Joseph affirmed.

“Of course, lovely. I will meet you there. Seven o’clock, okay?”

Adesua hung up and looked at Amelia, who was pacing left and right. This made Adesua’s nerves falter once again, making her second-guess everything.

“I can’t go to this gala Joseph invited me to—there is no way. What if there’s another person who’s out to get me, like at the ballet? This worry is consuming me,” Adesua said, her voice heavy with genuine concern.

Wei strolled over to the cabana chair, his gaze fixed on the tranquil view of the water, its surface mirroring the calmness of his thoughts.

“Adesua, no matter what you do, you will have lovers and inevitably haters as well.”

Adesua wanted to tell Kavita and her brothers what was going on in Harlem, but she could barely hold on to the little sanity she had left.

“I should probably call and cancel. I don’t know what I was thinking—”

“That’s enough,” Wei interrupted. “None of that matters anymore. Dale is dead. Let’s discuss this another time. You know Henrik and Kavita like to eavesdrop. I do want you to be careful. I have been receiving some rather odd things, so just keep an eye on your stuff and don’t let anyone get into your belongings, okay?”

He gave her a hug, and Adesua watched him leave the cabana area, heading to the art room.

“You’ll be fine tonight, Dusie,” Amelia added.

The Harmon Foundation Gala was like something out of her wildest dreams. Seeing people who looked like her, but with their art transcending their names. Her name was something she knew she would never escape, but being here felt like finding the family and community of like-minded individuals she had been searching for. Adesua never liked the galas her family threw because anyone who approached her at those parties was doing so just because she was a Ridley. Here in Harlem, who she was didn't matter. But no one was as impressive as Adesua in her blue satin dress. Joseph tilted his head with a smile, grabbing her hand and ushering her to the ballroom floor and sending her into a twirl.

"Oh, don't you look breathtaking," he said as he kissed her on the cheek. "I am so happy you came, my dear."

Adesua smiled, happy to see his reaction, as this conversation was much more pleasant than the one they'd had before. She wished that life could be simpler, where the only worries she would have were what party she would go to next or where she would donate money. It would be to the arts, or to young women and children, or to both. Now her life was all that, but it came with a price to pay for wealth and fame, as turmoil and pain would surely follow.

"Adesua, it's only the beginning for you. I can see you up there after a long day with the kids, getting awarded for your beautiful artwork," Joseph remarked as they sipped on their drinks.

Adesua nearly choked. She loved the idea of children, but having them now was something she couldn't want less. Adesua thought she was broken in a way. She loved the traditional values of men like Joseph, but she didn't necessarily love when it applied to her and her future. As she cleared her throat, a man who Adesua assumed to be William Harmon announced the winner of the Harmon Foundation Award for Visual Arts. He held a check for $500. Aaron Douglas walked up to the stage, accepting the award with a gentle speech.

"Although I have won this award, I want you to know all our work means something far greater than we can imagine. For centuries, we have communicated through art, whether with fables, religion, or the simplicity of showing love. It all resonates deep within us until we inspire others to create their art. I would like to hope tonight, with all of us surrounded by beautiful minds, that these moments can offer something far greater than this money—how we define the future. Whether it is black, white, or any color in the rainbow, it shows we all have a story to tell. Thank you."

Adesua and Joseph nodded silently to each other, knowing how important it was for people like them to be recognized for the things they'd done. Although the night was coming to an end and she had an even bigger day planned for Wei tomorrow, she was finally present in the moment instead of lost in the hundreds of thoughts that were going through her mind. Moments like this were few and far between, so seeing it together with their very own eyes made them each think of what they could accomplish. Even if their goals were vastly different from each other's.

Adesua loved a good birthday party—and she loved planning them for her siblings even more. Today she was hosting a yacht party for Wei, who was never one for surprises. But Adesua would do whatever she wanted to make it memorable. She felt he was not fond of knowing what happened next because of what happened at the ballet. He didn't like surprises or not having control of every setting they were in.

Wei always made sure to oversee any event they had or attended to, but his birthday wasn't one of them. Adesua had cried for weeks in her room. Every time Wei tried to comfort her, he was met with a door slam. So when she looked at the calendar and saw his birthday was approaching, it was the distraction she needed from the hounding press.

Adesua rushed into the kitchen, where Chef Laurent and Diego carried out trays of food alongside a perfect vanilla-buttercream cake with cherry filling, "Happy Birthday" scripted atop in red icing.

The yacht, waiting patiently off Huntington Bay, was docked and ready, and they all stepped onto the boat with gifts and decor. Adesua invited his college friends from Yale, the Grant brothers, and his new friend whom he had hired as an assistant. His college roommates, Nathaniel and Gregory, were already filled with alcohol, which made them sway in the growing breeze and nearly fall overboard.

"Boys, the party hasn't even begun," Adesua called out.

They ended up swigging more alcohol in cheer.

"Oh, sweet Dusie, every Yale boy knows the party starts before the party," Nathaniel yelled.

Wei was roughhousing with them. "Our Yale days are slipping behind us, brothers!"

Adesua lit the candles, covering them with her hand, and called everyone to crowd around the cake.

"Wei, come on, front and center, so you can remember this moment tomorrow morning before you boys get sloshed."

Kavita chuckled, hitting Diego and Henrik.

"Hey, me too. I can be one of the boys."

Wei came over, rubbing Adesua's shoulder in gratitude while removing the hair covering her face.

"All right, all right. As long as my baby brother and sister will do the honor of starting it off for me!" Wei exclaimed.

Kavita sang slowly as Henrik played his harmonica. Then Adesua chimed in, as did the rest of the crowd. Adesua loved her sister's voice. She felt Kavita could be a star in her own right if she wanted to, instead of feeding the gossip columns petty drama that she knew was beneath her and their family. Adesua looked over to see Amelia and Jamison holding hands. It made her smile, seeing her sister doing the things she said she would never do.

Wei blew the candles out and stared at them longer than usual. Adesua thought that maybe Wei had made a real wish this time, unlike the other times, when he would quickly make his way to the food and celebration. This time, he relished the moment, and she saw Amelia take notice of it too.

"Thank you all for everything. Let's make this a night to remember," Wei said.

Jamison laughed. "Oh, like remembering the book club you started in college? Boys from Dartmouth, Columbia, and every college in between wanted to be a part of it."

Adesua raised her eyebrow. "You're telling me Wei had a serious book club?"

Nathaniel turned around with a chocolate-covered strawberry, barely making coherent sentences. "Some would call it 'a book club.' Some would call it 'a journey of tasting the forbidden nectar we all so love,' all while, of course, learning everything about the fine arts!"

"Now, this has intrigued me. Do tell, boys," Adesua said jokingly, wanting to embarrass Wei even more.

Gregory pitched in, saying, "All I am saying is that the room would be filled with smoke. I couldn't even see the letters on the pages."

Adesua saw two people board the ship who looked strikingly like Wei. He turned around excitedly and ran toward them, speaking in their mother tongue, Cantonese.

"Everyone, this is the Zhang family. My friend Kai came to the Ridley Line for work and greatly assisted us. This is his sister, Shuye. I have been spending time with their family when I've been away lately."

Shuye and Kai bowed their heads with kindness.

"Thank you, Wei, for inviting us," Shuye said, then turned to Adesua. "I saw your art at a festival I went to by myself and recognized your name. Your work is stunning," she said softly.

Adesua hadn't seen a beauty like hers before. Her eyes were as dark as obsidian. They were perfectly set and lined with kohl. Her hair was perfectly put together with an array of pearls and gold pins clipped into her onyx, finger-waved locks. The pale-green satin *qipao* with intricate gold and cream threading hugged her figure very well, almost appearing white or even silver in the sunlight. Adesua thought it was magic. Shuye *was* magic, as she flipped out a fan that matched her dress.

"Shuye, you are a work of art, hon; I am surprised I have never seen your face in town before."

Shuye blushed. "I am just now getting out more, thanks to Wei and my brother. If I'm honest, I couldn't find anyone that wanted to be my friend."

Kavita shot a look at Adesua. They both knew exactly how she felt—an outsider in a world they were brought into.

"Well, you have a friend in me, especially my sisters." Adesua smiled, grabbing her hand.

Just as the group was getting acclimated, the sun began to set. Their cousin Sebastien arrived with twenty more people.

"You all call this a birthday party? See, that's why I brought reinforcements," Sebastien yelled as he popped a bottle of champagne.

Adesua walked up to him, upset.

"Sebastien, this was supposed to be an intimate party for family and friends. You are turning this into a circus."

Sebastien rolled his eyes playfully. "Honey, when has Wei ever been quiet in his life? You and I both know he loves a good time—a rowdy time, at that! Besides, this big ole boat could fit hundreds. I think you are being rather selfish," he said with his right eyebrow raised.

Adesua saw Amelia coming to her defense.

"Sebastien, I think Dusie is trying to say we didn't even prepare enough food for all of these people, and it would be rude for any new and unaccounted-for guests not to be fed, right?"

Sebastien waved to a group of their family servers dressed in all white with silver food trays.

"That's why I called Mrs. Darla days ago to accommodate these lovely folks. You know I'm the favorite cousin. Now, enough yapping and thinking, you two. Let's have a grand time."

Adesua looked at Shuye and Amelia, then sent an icy look to Sebastien.

"You wouldn't dare—"

"I did! Oops, I see him walking up the stairs now. How about I take the lovely—" He looked toward Shuye in confusion.

"Oh, I am Shuye. A friend of Wei's," she said, tilting her head down.

"Shuye, Shuye, Shuye, oh, I am sure you are a friend. You are destined to be my cousin's wife. I see the stars aligning now. You know, I am a matchmaker. It's a God-honest gift, I assure you," Sebastien said gleefully.

Adesua turned to Amelia, exasperated by Sebastien's antics. "Mellie, take care of our new friend Shuye while the boys act silly."

Adesua walked past the crowds of people to get fresh air near the edge. Then she saw him. Not Joseph, but her childhood friend Theo. His cream suit and slightly unbuttoned pastel-blue shirt matched her dress almost perfectly. She thanked Sebastien silently, because after the ordeal with Joseph, she needed a break from reality. Her eyes homed in on him, as did his on hers as she got closer.

"Addie Louise, I never thought I would see you again."

She hugged him, and he held her closer. Theo kissed the top of her hand as if it were routine with him. She looked up and saw the sun hit the streaks of gold in his hair. He smelled ravishing in the woody-amber scent he was wearing.

"How have you been, you big-time tennis player? You got too good for us in New York and left us for France!"

He gave her his slick side smile, which Adesua had always loved.

"Well, I had to, seeing you getting all loved by Joseph Blackwood. You two are a beautiful couple," he said with sharpness.

So much for a break, she thought, chuckling to herself.

"Yes, we are. Well, I hope to see you at the national championships," she said with haste.

Adesua gave him a quick side hug, then departed. The last thing she needed was to get intertwined in a love scandal, but she did miss the time when her life wasn't full of so many tasks. When she and Theo were good friends, they'd spent their time playing hooky and going to Coney

Island. He was one of the few who'd stood out for her, never caring what she looked like. She shook the what-ifs from her head.

As Kavita and Henrik took the stage, Adesua exited her trance. Kavita's partner, Franklin, went up to the stage. Where had he even come from? She was taken aback by all the people who surrounded her. Franklin, exhilarated, took the mic and looked out at the crowd.

"I want to say I have been listening to this fine lady sing up a storm across town with the soon-to-be-famous Henrik as a musician. They will perform a nice original song for you and special guest Duke Ellington!" At this point Sir Duke had become almost a necessity for all their family occasions.

Diego took Adesua's hand, dancing as the music whisked them away. Adesua saw love around her with every turn. Amelia was twirling with Jamison. Wei offered his hand to Shuye on the dance floor. Kavita gave short looks of love to Franklin. And Mother and Father were smiling in the shadows of it all. Adesua knew then that love was all around, and she prayed it would blossom into new flames as red as the roses that fell around on the dance floor, commemorating the celebration of life and love—but hopefully not blood.

Chapter 21

Amelia Ridley

For the first time in years, she had the estate all to herself. The boys were out in Chinatown, Adesua was in Harlem, and Kavita was with Franklin. She would always say how much easier her life would be if she were an only child. Amelia knew in her heart she didn't like being alone. Even if they were a nuisance to her, her siblings were her responsibility in some way, giving her more purpose in life, which she hadn't imagined possible when she lived in France.

Amelia planned on spending the whole day tending to her horses, especially Mya. All she desired was a day of peace and quiet. She was going to get it by being far, far away from the—

The phone rang. She kept putting on her socks, then put her boot on her right foot. It rang and rang. What was the point in having servants if they couldn't do a job as simple as picking up the phone? She guessed they were all taking it easy for once too. Father and Mother were still in the Hamptons while Father recovered from supposedly being overworked.

She answered when the incessant ringing kept going.

"Ed, where have ya been, honey? We miss you over—"

Amelia slammed the phone back on the hook. Everyone knew Father's cheating ways had never stopped. He'd just gotten better at hiding it over the years. The phone rang twice more. She was going to give this lady some choice words. She picked up . . .

"Miss Amelia Ridley and her siblings are expected to show tonight at eleven p.m., or secrets will be spilled." The voice paused.

Amelia dropped her other boot to the ground, scrambling to get paper and a pencil to write down everything she heard.

"Masks are required. Come to Surf Avenue near Coney Island and give the secret code words *Leave your secrets at the door* to the Merriweather Co. antique store."

Amelia sighed. So much for having a day to herself.

Somehow or other, Amelia was able to get in contact with all her siblings for them to be home in time to get ready for the secret masquerade ball. Maybe, just maybe, they would be able to find out who was really behind this, if they all had the same game plan. What secrets had to be left at the door? Why must they all be there? Maybe this had something to do with the file that was missing? If that was the case, she must attend.

Amelia didn't have to convince anyone to join, as they were all currently walking down the path with ridiculous costumes and masks on. The boys all had a laugh about it. Amelia and her sisters were the only ones who considered coming to an unknown location as a potential threat. The "Merriweather Importing" sign looked like it was one nail from falling down. A crate of globes and antiques filled the small shop. An elderly man with a magnifying glass pretending to look at something pepped up when they entered.

They were pointed to a pavilion that was filled with already drunk guests waving money in the air. There was an auction going on. She noticed art pieces that had been in Jamison's home from his travels. She put her head down as she realized he hadn't been lying; his family really did need money. Amelia had forced herself to believe that Jamison's way of going from so loving to quickly isolating her had to be simply because of his recent issues with money. Now she felt remorse for him. It felt like he was a clown putting on a show for the rich. They walked in the direction of the pavilion heading to where the party was.

One thing did bother her, though: the meaning behind all the dress protocols and the secret key words being so *secretive.*

"The princess has escaped her castle, I see." Jamison came up from behind her, wrapping his arms around her waist.

Wei made an expression as if he were going to be sick. "Not too handsy with my little sister."

Amelia walked off with Jamison to get away from the noise.

"Why are you so happy, then sad, acting as if we couldn't really work together knowing both of our families have issues?"

Jamison looked up in the sky, inhaling a deep breath of air.

"I was being weak like my father. I have to pick up his slack and unwillingness to do whatever it takes to get our family back to where they need to be. At least my mother and siblings. I have made some investments that are coming to fruition. But Mellie, I just don't know yet. Having this party was for all of us. Everyone that's been picked apart by the gossip columns just because we were born into this world. I made sure no press had word of it. So you don't have to worry; I am not like your father."

Amelia let go of the breath she had been holding, stifling her hope that she wouldn't hear the wrong answer. Finally, it was the words she wanted to hear. He did this for them, or "for *us*," as he said it. That was more than enough for her. She kissed Jamison because maybe this time he would choose her. She sure as hell didn't want to let anyone into her family's never-ending world of games. At least Jamison knew how it was to be front and center of the gossip columns.

"I am going to go by the water for a moment. I promised myself some time alone today, but I thank you and I love you."

Amelia hadn't said those words to him in a very long time. She meant it. Not because of the distress she and her family had been through, but because he'd kept fighting for her even when she didn't think he was.

"I love you too, Mellie."

He kissed her on the top of her head. She walked over to the pier to sit and stare at the moonlight. A woman approached her, smiling, wearing a red dress and mask. Amelia was really starting to hate the color red, all that it reminded her of.

A red letter.

"Some lady told me to give this to ya; it's for a fun game. Have a nice time, toots!"

The woman handed her the letter and then galivanted back to her posse, laughing. Amelia knew it couldn't be from her, as she seemed just as clueless as she was. Amelia was frantic as she read this letter.

One more chance to come clean with your secrets. Those masks can only hold for so long.

If only life were as easy as sending bribes, but whoever the mystery person was didn't demand money, but instead for them to admit their transgressions. They seemed to want only one thing: the downfall of their family. That was their prize. It wasn't that the letter was any worse than previous ones, but more so that, this time, it felt even more serious. Something so short and confined meant their patience had run thin. She could tell all her siblings had been in an uproar since Dale's death. Perhaps things were all amiss because they were receiving letters just like she was. Amelia ran over to them, lifting up the card. Henrik and Diego put their heads down as soon as she showed it.

One by one, their faces looked away in disbelief over this never-ending secret-letters fiasco. Kavita, in her ever-so-dramatic way, started cursing left and right.

"We should have never come here, Amelia. This was all Jamison's grand idea anyways. He has to know something!"

Jamison eased his way into the group after hearing his name, thinking it was about something pleasant because of how well the party was going, but to his surprise, it was the opposite.

"You all go home. I am going to handle this with Jamison alone," Amelia said sternly.

Wei and Omar almost interjected, but it was no use when it came to Amelia. She was going to get her way just like Father. Kavita and Adesua gave her a kiss on the cheek and made sure once again that Jamison would take Amelia home. As she saw each of them pass the Merriweather shop, she knew she was in the clear to say what she felt to Jamison without one of them sneaking up behind her.

"Jamison, I have been keeping some things from you . . . I want to be honest with you like you were with me. Dale had a lot of secrets about each of us, but for me, it was that I am Edward's biological child. None of my siblings know this." Amelia wiped a tear from her cheek, taking a breath.

"Father kept it from the public because he figured it would ruin his credibility and the family's allure of having seven children adopted instead of owning up to having me with a Black French woman. It would harm my mother and further deepen the problems with my brothers, since I am to be the next head of the company."

This was who she was. Whether he took it well or not wasn't something that concerned her any longer. Jamison was the first to hear the full truth. It felt good taking her bottled-up feelings and expelling them onto him. He took a few moments in silence, taking in every word.

"I hear you, Mellie. I really do, but—"

But. That was the one word in the English dictionary she despised the most. Because anything after the word all but negated every word he'd said before it.

"But all I am hearing is that you all had a secret that Dale was going to tell the world . . . You all didn't kill him, did you?"

Amelia's eyes welled with tears again, and it wasn't because of red letters this time.

Chapter 22

Kavita Ridley

The Manhattan Herald
November 7, 1927
Metropolitan Musings
OUR FAVORITE SOCIALITE WANTS NO SPOTLIGHT FOR TWENTIETH BIRTHDAY!

Our favorite heiress, Kavita Ridley, is twenty years old! It seems like yesterday when she joined our beloved Ridley family. We are a little somber to say that her wild escapade days may have come to an end. As everyone knew, she would soon tire of the wild double life that seemingly every Ridley child has been living except for Mr. Edward Ridley's prized eldest sons, Wei and Omar.

A swarm of satin, silk, and feathers flew over Kavita as Adesua and Amelia threw options for her grand birthday slumber party at her. Kavita enjoyed being at home now. The more mess she found herself in, the more she realized why Adesua enjoyed staying out of the spotlight and at home. She felt a change in herself, as now going out with her friends felt forced, and the fact that her sisters knew how to treat her on her special day showed what she had been missing out on with them. The people who mattered the most were her family.

Sebastien stormed in like he was on a deathly mission. "Kavi, honey, we mustn't lose the day! Which one have you decided to wear?"

Sebastien pestered her, holding different silk pajamas lined with feathers up to her skin. Kavita hated having to choose a color, because she loved so many. One day, she loved lavender and would get everything in that color; then another day, she would want a particular shade of pink that was not too salmon nor too hot.

Sebastien clicked his fingers at a quick pace. "Sweetheart, none of us are getting younger here."

She pointed to the forgotten pajamas thrown to the side under the pinks, baby blues, and purples. "That one. I want the emerald one."

Sebastien looked displeased, as it didn't have the same bells and whistles as the others.

"Oh my, Kavi always wants to be the underestimated one. Never worry, my dear. You shall wear the gold crown. It will match perfectly with the green," he said as he sauntered away.

Kavita tried to interject. "Bu—"

"Bu-bu-but nothing. You are the birthday girl, and you *will* look like it."

Kavita looked to Amelia and Adesua for aid, but they were of little to no help, as Adesua slipped on the orange pajamas and Amelia slipped on the black.

Kavita saw hordes of girls swarming through the front door as Sebastien escorted them in, allowing the maids to attend to the guests and help them choose from the finest pajama sets and nightgowns in the enormous powder room near the ladies' grand hall bathroom. This made her smile, because there were faces she hadn't seen for a while, some for years. Amelia had invited the neighbors' daughters, who lived in the small cottages. She'd always seen Kavita look at them as they passed their quaint homes and knew that she longed to meet them in some way. Adesua invited some artist friends and other ladies Josephine had introduced them to at one of their galas. Sebastien invited all their cousins from Illinois and Pennsylvania.

For once, Kavita forgot her life from before. Today, she was celebrating a new beginning. Even though the ping of sadness occasionally hit her, she was surrounded by people who cared about her, or at least wanted to. She just never let them in. A poke on her shoulder from her sisters, and she knew it was time. A satin blindfold was placed gently over her eyes and she was led through the house. Kavita laughed as she thought to herself, *What haven't I seen in this home?* But she loved not having control for once. Her cheeks started to hurt, as this was the most she had smiled in ages. Her bare feet felt cold as she stepped onto the icy marble. She couldn't tell whether they were in the kitchen or the ballroom. She heard shuffling and giggling and then a loud gasp.

"You have my cousin's delicate feet bare on the floor!" Sebastien scolded the maid—hopefully playfully, Kavita thought. "She is the queen of the night. Go get her slippers immediately, thank you."

Although she was slightly annoyed at Sebastien's overbearing command, she knew how frazzled he got with large events. The fur did feel good on her feet, though, so maybe he was right. As Amelia removed the blindfold, she found herself in the grand ballroom. It was like her own version of heaven on earth. The long tables of food and delicacies caught her eye. It was everything she could imagine. All the food she loved looked absolutely divine, from samosas, Peking duck pancakes, deviled eggs, empanadas, and chicken-tikka skewers. But, for Kavita, the desserts may have been her favorite part. Milk- and white-chocolate fountains flowed next to a bowl of strawberries, and the colorful macarons almost looked like every girl in there with their colorful pajamas.

Kavita was rushed with hugs and a glass of a cloudy drink. She smelled it instantly, and to her delight, the chai calmed her. She didn't know why, but at that moment, she didn't want to drink alcohol again. The room, filled with pillows and vibrant rugs on the floor, reminded her of a dream. The feather-stuffed mattresses were covered in plush blankets and small bedside tables. The jazz band played light music while everyone was eating at the seven rows of tables.

Kavita clocked Amelia, staring at her with happiness.

"I want to make a toast to my dear baby sister," Amelia began as everyone raised their teas and juices.

"As she enters into a new level of womanhood at twenty, we all wanted to show her how much we love her with a party featuring everything she holds dear to her heart, from beautiful saris and champagne towers to a new Cartier vanity case lined with emeralds. She has grown into the fiery, courageous spirit we always knew her to be, and we know she will bloom into the love flower she chooses to be, and we will be there for her when every petal dies and a new one grows. Here's to new beginnings."

The league of girls clapped their hands, hugging each other. This was what Kavita had been missing. She saw she wasn't alone in this story of life. Yes, her story sometimes felt like she could go no further, but she was making that choice at that very moment. Right now, the scandals didn't matter. She never paid too much attention to the chandeliers but wished to hang from them like a flying monkey. She chuckled to herself. If anything made her happy, it was not the trails of gifts lined up in the corner, but instead seeing everyone enjoying themselves at the perfume bar and the spa area, along with the artists drawing their portraits and the fortune teller she'd avoided the whole night.

In the middle of her thoughts, Mrs. Darla came rushing into the room.

"Your doting fiancé is at the door, Kavi," she said giddily.

The girls all followed her to the door. Franklin stood there with a bouquet of yellow tulips. He knew how much she'd started to hate red roses everywhere and that she needed some sunshine in her dark life. In another hand, he held a gold locket necklace. She opened the locket to find dried marigolds pressed onto the glass with a note in his handwriting saying *I love you.*

Kavita hugged him so tightly that she thought maybe this hell was slowly coming to an end. The never-ending threats were tiring.

If she were the person doing it, she would have confessed a long time ago. Kavita felt the person was holding back for whatever reason. They wanted the Ridleys to own up to their mistakes to the world so badly, but that was a thing a Ridley would never do, blood or not. She thanked Joseph before shooing him away and getting back to the festivities.

Her birthday cake was the most perfect ten-layered caramel-honey cake she could dream of. As she blew out the candle, she wished it all would disappear. What exactly did she want to go away? She wasn't entirely sure, but she hoped and prayed that God would figure it out. That was the only fortune she needed to hear tonight.

The morning light seeped through the draperies onto her golden skin. It felt good, like she hadn't been outside and her spirit was begging her to run into the light. Some girls stirred when she stepped beside their beds to reach the garden. For a moment, she didn't feel an ounce of sadness. The sun removed any thoughts she'd had before. Kavita never understood why the darkness made her feel despair even more deeply.

Was this why every time she went out at night, she had to have her friend Lila by her side? In the light, she felt renewed. When she stooped down, she grabbed a lone rose that had fallen from the bush. Kavita thought of Dale as she grabbed the rose and ripped off one of its petals. She looked to the sky.

"I am sorry for what I have done, and if I could trade places, I would . . . Actually, no, I wouldn't, but I promise I will make better choices and live a life to be proud of, not in the shadows."

It was a sorry excuse for a prayer. She knew that. But it was better than nothing, in her eyes. Dale had had his own karma coming for him. It wasn't her job to get in its way. She'd just made it easier. As she stepped through the garden, she peered into the ballroom again. She turned around to find an older woman who favored Kavita in many ways. The elderly women back in her home country had tried their best to provide for Kavita when she lived on the street. Her heart twinged with pain as she thought of it.

❖

India, 1915

The sun was mercilessly beating down on the people of Bombay, especially a very young and spirited eight-year-old Kavita. She now knew only of survival, ever since her parents had died months prior. The light in her bright eyes had dwindled. Kavita ambled through the tiny alleyways, smothered by crowds of people, feeling as if she couldn't breathe. The aroma of spices warmed her empty belly, which growled persistently. Her eyes watered, and she tasted the salt of her tears to calm her hunger. Kavita's small frame allowed her to get pushed against the crowd effortlessly. She went to each vendor selling food, pleading for a bite.

They slapped her hand and shooed her away. She roamed the streets farther, eventually seeing crowds of protestors all chanting in unison. A man held a placard that said "Swaraj for India." Kavita knew terrible things were happening, but she never understood their meaning. The air was thick with emotions due to the political climate. Gandhi was onstage with crowds gathered around. His speech on the power of truth (*Satya*) inspired a young Kavita.

She felt even weaker, so she made her way to the back of the crowd and passed out. Little did she know that this would be her saving grace.

"Neer! Neer!"

Kavita heard the faint voice grow louder. She knew she didn't feel well, but her name was not Neer by any means. She struggled to open her eyes and saw two girls a little older than she was, cradling her in their arms. Kavita's eyebrows raised in amazement when she saw one of the girl's intense eye color, the shade of a sparkling green gemstone.

"I heard you, Sulochana, and I see. She is hungry. We gotta take her to Anath Ashram. The sisters will help her," Neer replied.

"What's your name?" Sulochana asked while tilting her head in curiosity.

"Kavita. My name is Kavita. Malabar," she said, then fell back asleep.

Kavita found herself wrapped in another young woman's arms. She was unlike anyone she had ever seen before. Her fair skin was scattered with dark-brown spots, and her eyes matched. The young missionary, Emily Thames from Lake Forest, Illinois, had traveled back to India, where her family had been living as missionaries for the past decade. She wanted to help unfortunate youth just like her family did. Kavita's almond-brown eyes sparkled in the sunlight when she saw the white walls filled with vibrant paintings. The lace curtains swayed in the slight, gentle breeze.

It had been an eternity since Kavita had slept in a bed. Children's laughter echoed through the hallway, a sound foreign to Kavita's ears. Neer and Sulochana waved at her when passing her by. It startled her but also filled her with a strange warmth. Emily's gentle touch on her head reassured her, dispelling her fears.

"You don't have to be afraid now. You are safe here. Breakfast will be served soon."

This felt like a setup to Kavita. She pulled the bright-colored quilt over her head, half expecting to wake up from this dream. She was waiting for someone to grab her and hurt her with false promises, but something in her heart told her that this might be real. Kavita pulled the quilt down, seeing Emily's inviting face again. The woman smiled at Kavita for reassurance. "I also have some fresh clothes for you here after you wash up."

Kavita was shocked that everything was true. The dining table was set with a variety of metal plates and cups. The children, all similar to her age, sat politely, waiting for their food to be served. Suddenly, she saw poha, *idli*, and fruits brought by another older woman who she thought looked like her but had soft lines on her face and white hair. Kavita sat quietly while her hunger slowly started to fade away.

"For what is done is done. Pain for more pain on others wouldn't be how they wanted it." The lady pointed to the sky. "Live life anew and let go." The fortune teller shuffled her feet, leaving as quickly as she had approached. *Pain for more pain?* Kavita pondered the lady's words. *Who would have more pain?* She'd endured it enough.

Henrik met her outside as she sat by the cold, empty pool taking in the fortune teller's words. He held a small piece of a burned red letter.

"I know you have been getting these letters too, Kavita. We all have; it's not just Amelia and not just me. One of us did something, and it sure as hell wasn't me." He paused, looking at her seriously.

Kavita was uncomfortable seeing him so stern.

"I was there when Dale died, and I saw you. You are the reason for his death, aren't you?"

Well, that was no way to treat the birthday girl on this dreadful morning—or better yet, *mourning*.

Chapter 23

Adesua Ridley

Adesua glared at the cigar hanging from the man's mouth.

"Dusie, you all right? Let's grab some drinks," Amelia said.

Adesua smiled while nodding. They were at the US National Championships, a yearly event that held a special place in their hearts and was their favorite outing as a family. It had been a long time since they'd felt like that. With all the parties and galas, it was easy to forget who they were at the core—people who enjoyed simple things, like a tennis match.

Spectators waved at her and all the Ridleys as they walked by.

Adesua perked up as they headed to the clubhouse. It amused her, as mostly everyone here never watched the tennis players. They were here to make a fashion statement; she and her sisters accommodated the wish of the masses. A group of young girls chattered at the nearby table. She assumed they were laughing at the exuberant hats on all the ladies.

One of the girls approached her with a smile.

"May I have you and your sisters' autographs? We hear about ya in the papers all the time, miss." The young girl retrieved her journal for them to sign.

"Of course, dear," Adesua said happily as she walked over to the table where Kavita and Amelia were sitting to sign it.

Kavita, enthralled not to be seen as something terrible for once, went over to the girls. “Better yet, darlings, I got a journalist who can get a photo of all of us so we can be on the front page. How ’bout that!”

The girls eagerly nodded in bliss. The young man positioned everyone together for a group photo, then the camera flashed brightly.

“Have a pleasant time, you dolls,” Amelia said while Adesua held on to her sister’s arm.

“My stars, can you believe we used to be that young, gushing over God knows who . . . Time goes by so fast.” Adesua chuckled.

Jamison approached Adesua and Amelia, holding a white box. Adesua did a double take, thinking it was an engagement ring, but the box was too flat.

“Mellie, I found this brooch while in town earlier. I think it would look beautiful on you.” He opened the box, which contained a modest but beautiful emerald-colored brooch that matched the color of her eyes.

It was lovely, Adesua thought, how Jamison seemed to fall under Amelia’s spell. Adesua saw Jamison walk past her, and she felt a tap on her shoulder. She couldn’t tell who it was right away.

Jamison pulled his hands out wide, covering whoever was before him. “Theodore Montgomery, as I live and breathe. How are you, brother?”

She turned to the table, pretending to grab something from her clutch as the man made small talk with Amelia and Jamison. They seemed even closer after his family’s masquerade party. Adesua found it odd. She’d been sure Jamison was a runner; anytime there was conflict, he was usually the first one out.

Adesua turned around abruptly after reapplying her red lipstick. She hoped he would stroll away, but he turned to her with a smile.

She saw that Theo was engrossed in her looks.

“It seems God may have answered my prayers after all.” Theo approached, kissing her hand. “You look like a sunflower with that yellow on—better yet, an angel from heaven today, as always, Miss Adesua.”

Adesua dipped her head down, thanking him and avoiding eye contact. He stepped closer to her side as Kavita ran over to the table with their cousins from Mother's side.

"Theo, stop being silly."

He flashed her a smile. "You couldn't just let me have a little fun!"

Adesua rolled her eyes. Jamison was clearly confused by the interaction, but saw the apparent attraction between the two as he held Amelia's hand and sipped his drink.

"Adesua, Theo here is one of the best up-and-coming tennis players in the country. His family comes from Canada. I assure you, he is a mighty fine man."

Adesua smirked. "I never assumed he wasn't until now. Are you sure Mr. Theo didn't pay you to say that?"

Theo brashly looked at her from the corner of his eye, bringing his smile to the side.

"All right, Jamison, you did good work. Not your best, but that will be all for now." Theo slapped Jamison's shoulder jokingly, going along with Adesua's story.

"Jamison, me and Theo went to school together briefly before I went to the all-girls school," Adesua said calmy.

"Oh, you sly foxes, you got me good. I must admit, Dusie thought I had a hand on Cupid's bow." He chuckled.

"Well, you fine folks, I know I will see you again. I have to attend to some business. Enjoy the match," Theo said, flashing a bright smile.

Adesua waved off his advances. The last thing she needed was another man fawning over her. She feared the papers would release the secrets about her. She knew Joseph had good intentions toward her, but she couldn't stop wondering whether he was the person she needed to spend the rest of her life with. Adesua thought of all the married people she knew. None of them ever seemed happy in the balance of things. Some just settled to have the comfort of a person.

New York, 1916

Adesua had never seen such a beautiful but simple view of horses running in the fields. She sat on the fence railing, watching Amelia do her jumps to get ready for a competition. Adesua marveled at how elegant Amelia looked in her perfectly planned choreography with her horse, Mya. She hoped that one day she would look like that in ballet. Mother had made sure each sibling found their special talent, and ballet was something Adesua had vied for from the moment she saw her first performance. Adesua smiled at the figures of ballerinas prancing in her head.

Wei came up from behind, climbing the fence to sit next to her. They were both in awe. No matter how many days it had been, this was their home.

"I wonder if this is a dream we haven't woke up from." Adesua smirked.

"Well, if it is, I hope it lasts forever," Wei added.

He jumped down and went to the nearest wooden post, pulling out his pocketknife. Wei began to carve their initials into the wood.

"Just in case it is one, we will leave our mark here somehow." He chuckled.

Adesua silently prayed, hoping her birth parents were happy wherever they were, but she knew she had finally found a family that was going to love her more than the orphanage ever could.

Amelia got off her horse and ran up to Adesua and Wei. The staff took Mya back to the stables.

"Last one back to the house has to give their dessert tonight to the winner," she said while running.

Adesua took off running, getting way ahead of Wei. She felt fast, but there was no way she was faster than he was. All she knew was that no matter who won, they had all won in this life because they had each other.

Two young women bumped into Adesua so hard it made her fall back. She wanted to slap them all on the face on that balcony. She knew that was what they wanted her to do. To make a scene in front of the "fine" folks, proving she didn't belong there. Years ago, Adesua used to fall for this type of anger provocation and get stirred up. They wanted to say, "See, she is crazy!" With rumors going around about her and the potential false business promises, the perception of her meticulously created persona was slowly changing.

It was inevitable: What went up, must come down. With admirers came imitators who wanted to have and do everything she did, but secretly hated her for it. Now it was time for her to rise again.

"Excuse you, ladies." She smiled, taking a sip of her drink.

They scoffed, rolling their eyes in unison.

Diego tickled the side of her stomach. "Dusie, you haven't tried any of my little desserts at home recently. Miss our late-night kitchen talks," he said with a smile.

"You and Henrik might be the only people in the house who have stayed so pleasant throughout this whole ordeal. I didn't want to dampen your mood with everything I've got going on."

Diego shook his head in disbelief, in an *if you only knew* kind of way. She could tell he had something on his mind as he put both hands in his pockets.

"Adesua, I haven't been honest with all of you. Dale had something on me too. I just didn't want to go into the details. I met someone in Harlem months ago, and I fell in love with . . . *him*."

Adesua held her breath, unsure of what to say. She didn't want to interrupt him, but she also didn't want him thinking that she didn't care. Instead of words, she grabbed his hand, encouraging him to keep going.

"Dale was going to release it, as he was one of his rivals. I don't know, Adesua. I feel sad because I will have nowhere to go if Father finds out. I am sure of it."

"We are going home now." Adesua grabbed his hand, heading to his car.

Adesua loved that Diego didn't even question her. He trusted her more than most and, more importantly, more than he trusted Amelia. She had to have something to do with all this. Adesua had no proof, but she was determined to figure out how . . .

⚜

The drive back from the US National Championships in Queens to Long Island was quick, as all the traffic was going into the city for the games.

She was sure that her siblings would be looking for her, but at a busy game like that, they could be anywhere, and that was what she loved about the city. She hoped in her heart that Wei and Omar would goof around and think she was entertaining a new man like Theo. But the only thing she was entertaining was the truth. Which was getting further from the Ridley family each passing day.

She and Diego went to the stables, where Amelia kept her cherished things in a box buried in front of the apple tree. After digging, Adesua felt not only the sweat beading down into her eyes but also her heart beating out of her chest—which went silent when a navy-colored box appeared. She held her breath as she lifted the cover.

Adesua and Diego gave each other knowing looks as they knelt on the ground all covered in dirt. Diego rummaged through Amelia's journals and treasured relics from Paris. He knew that what they might find could change everything. Amelia kept everything in this graveyard of secrets, under a tree that was supposed to be filled with beautiful memories.

Adesua was baffled that Amelia would keep her life's treasures in a spot underneath a tree. Maybe that was why she did it. She knew in her heart no one would think she was silly enough to do such a thing. Oh, how she was very wrong. As they rummaged through old journals, they saw another small bin that was halfway open. Adesua removed the lid, scanning the first paper she saw: Amelia's birth certificate.

Acte de naissance

Mère: Cécile Moulin

Père: Edward Ridley

Diego's eyes widened as he stared at Adesua.

"Wait . . . this means she wasn't—"

"Adopted," Adesua interjected.

Chapter 24

Amelia Ridley

Amelia wandered up the steps to the Grant family's house, because being at home didn't feel like home for her. The grounds at the estate felt emptier than usual as she knocked on the door persistently. She smoothed out her brown-fur-trimmed yellow coat as she waited impatiently. Seconds turned into minutes. Nothing. Their butler and maid were usually very prompt in answering. She turned away, sighing. Amelia had hoped Jamison could see her in this outfit, inspiring an impromptu date, but maybe she should have rang first.

Just as Amelia was about to leave, she was startled by the sound of a scuffle at the door. Elion, still in his pajamas despite the late hour, appeared. His presence starkly contrasted with the calm afternoon, capturing his unexpected attention.

"I'm sorry, Mellie. Jamison said he'll speak to you another time." Elion's words hung in the air, heavy with disappointment and uncertainty. His voice, usually warm and cheerful, now carried a weight that Amelia could not ignore.

His eyes mirrored her own, and the uncertainty of when "another time" would be only added to the tension in the air.

Amelia's confidence in her relationship with Jamison was shaken at that moment. Ever since she'd confided in him about what had happened that night, he'd never wanted to leave her side. He felt the same remorse she had, but maybe she'd gone too far? They had rarely gone days without seeing each other over the last couple of months, as they often spent their time with their horses, writing poetry, or discussing new ideas for her books. This sudden change left her feeling uneasy.

She tossed around the fall leaves, feeling the same wave of emotions she'd felt the night of Dale's death. Something was off, but her mind was too tired to investigate. The leaves crumbled behind her, and she turned and noticed her father.

"How is my Mellie dear? I feel like I haven't seen you in a long time," he said apprehensively.

Amelia paced, looking down at his boots.

"If you're about to go hunting, then I want to come with you."

Father nodded, smiling. He knew how hard it was to get Amelia to do anything with him lately. She found it rather peculiar how quickly Father had returned to health. One minute, he'd looked confused, sick, and senile. Now he was going hunting like he had when she was a young girl.

"Fine, I will wait for you to get out of that scruffy coat. The animals might mistake you for one of them." He chuckled as he headed to the shed that housed a row of shotguns. Mr. Jenkins and Mr. Pierre were waiting nearby to offer assistance.

Amelia loved the fall. Maybe the brisk, cool air that flowed through her hair brought her a certain level of happiness that she was otherwise missing from her life. She looked at herself in the gold-plated full-length mirror, adjusting her brown cloche hat with a green feather attached to the edge. She put on her brown tweed jacket with hints of blue and green and her brown knee-high leather boots. Amelia knew she had other pressing matters to attend to, but spending time with her father was her priority.

Amelia rushed out the door while looking at her diaries and the scattered pages of her books on her bed. She thought about putting them away on her desk as usual, but she was sure Father was probably tired of waiting. She shut the door quietly, ran out, and gave Adesua a slight nod and a smile as she walked past her room. She rushed down the stairs and ran through the field, past the stables, and to the far point of the estate, to the shed where Father waited.

"Well, 'bout damn time. I was about to leave you," he said with amusement.

They passed the dense oak trees with their hunting dog, a golden Lab named Bowman. His tail wagged as he heard rustling sounds in the trees above.

"Father, I am sorry I haven't been there for you or checking in on you. Since you've been sick, a lot has been on my mind," Amelia said solemnly.

"Mellie, you really don't have to do this alone. You know that, right?" Father said strongly.

Amelia smiled as she put the shotgun down. "Father, I know you could help, but why spread more pain? You need to worry about getting better and making Mother happy."

She definitely said that as a jab. Although she cared for him, she loved her mother too. Amelia saw the pain behind his eyes. Father might have loved her, but she knew he'd used her mother's family to get where they were today. She thought that would mean Caroline had his utmost loyalty, but that wasn't the case.

"I know you did it, Mellie."

Amelia moved to the right, turning her body to square up to her father. She felt her face tense as her jaw locked in anger. Father knew a lot of things, but he didn't know *every*thing. She lifted one of her eyebrows as her anger slowly turned into a soft smile. Amelia had, in fact, done it, and she'd done it so well that Father had had no idea what she was really capable of, and that brought her a small amount of joy.

"How? I have done nothing wrong," she said, each word slowly oozing out of her mouth.

She didn't bother defending herself. Her father knew that any choice she made, whether it was life or death, was for good reason.

So there was no point in fluffing the edges to make it seem better. Amelia felt herself losing the fight she once had in her. From the way she snapped back at him, she noticed that she was turning into him. Amelia had done a lot of wrong, and here she was, justifying her wrongdoing, just as he had. It made her skin crawl to think of how similar she was to him. At the same time, she knew how necessary it had been to get rid of Dale, and it had nothing to do with keeping Father in the public's good graces. But she would let him think that for now.

"I know everything. That's why I have been protecting you and covering up your loose ends. Dale promised me over the years to put you all in the press to make a name for ourselves. Because if we are all being talked about, Mellie, that means we are good to do business with. I controlled each of your images without you knowing until it got out of hand and Dale went rogue." He paused, fetching Mr. Jenkins to get him water.

"I was going to handle Dale myself, but I am proud of you, my flesh and blood, for seeing the issue and handling it with grace. This is why I am preparing the world to see you as the new owner when that time comes. You handled business, even with death on the line. I didn't think you had it in you, Mellie." He laughed, nearly choking on his water.

Amelia bit her bottom lip, upset at how calmly her father was taking this.

"Yes, I wanted Dale dead, but it was an accident, Father. Those files . . . what they said about us . . . They couldn't be released. You don't understand what was said."

Father looked to the side as he rubbed the top of Bowman's head.

"Oh, I know, my sweet daughter. I *know*." He laughed again.

"So why are you just now telling me this?" Amelia asked in confusion.

Father kicked leaves off his boots before replying, "Because I knew you weren't ready. You still held your siblings' opinions too close to your heart. I had to wait to be sure, and you have proven to me you're more than capable of doing what needs to be done." He chuckled. "That's why I am getting Kavita married off as soon as possible, and I will send the boys somewhere so they won't be in your way."

Amelia's heart felt like it was about to come out of her chest. She didn't want her brothers to go away. Yes, they had their moments of ego, but that didn't mean she wanted to do this alone. Father was more demented than Amelia had thought. He truly didn't feel like her siblings were a priority. It was all vanity to showcase that they were somehow better than everyone else. Father wanted to be the innovator, the man to change the game, and he would do it at any cost. She wondered what Father would have been like if he had stayed in Pennsylvania. Would he still have turned into the soulless man he was today?

Movement to the left caught her eye, and she saw a pheasant. Amelia whipped up her shotgun, and a gunshot pierced the air. The bird flopped to the ground, to their excitement. Father walked over to see the bird.

"Dead."

Chapter 25

Kavita Ridley

Central Park was beautiful that morning. Not because of the birds chirping or the kids frolicking in the cool weather, but because of Franklin. He'd been by Kavita's side ever since Lucky's men had targeted her. She only felt at ease going out during the day. The Mob wouldn't be so bold as to come for her in broad daylight, she hoped. Franklin convinced her to leave their little picnic spot for an adventure.

He hailed a cab so Kavita wouldn't get tired. She loved how he knew how she was with her heels. She stubbornly refused to take them off. He then led her down some wobbly path in a busy alley. They continued to walk until they made it all the way to West Forty-Sixth Street. The lively, loud markets and workers started to fade away. Franklin stood in front of an empty redbrick building that looked like it needed some love. He walked to the large oak door and lightly tapped on it with the weathered brass knocker.

"Is anyone home? I must have scared them away." He laughed as he tapped once more.

He motioned her in after he unlocked the door, which led to a staircase. Kavita looked around to see if anyone had noticed her entering. She had feelings of peace when she was with him, but she knew how her sister Amelia would react if she saw her in a predicament like this.

He smiled, noticing her deep in thought.

"You are the first person I have brought here. Ever since I got into real estate and became a broker, this was my first goal. So here is my first property. I hope to have tenants here by the end of the year."

Kavita looked around and saw the charm of the place. Even with the peeling dark-burgundy floral wallpaper, dirty cracked windows, and stale air lingering in every corner, she could see that it had potential.

Franklin watched her taking it all in, feeling slightly embarrassed, as he knew she was used to finer things.

"I know it's not much, but it has character, and this area will be booming in a few years. I mean, look how close it is to everything. Some people laughed at me, but I feel it. I also hope to smooth things out with Lucky, in a way. He's just so hard to speak with."

Kavita looked up at him, saddened that he saw her only as someone who was used to a life of luxury and that she and her family were the cause of the problems with his old boss.

"Franklin, I think it will be lovely, truly. About Lucky . . . I will talk to my dad about it. I didn't tell him what happened that night in fear that he wouldn't let me leave the house or see you again." She cleared her throat to get rid of the settled dust. "But I want to clarify that, when I was young, a place like this would have seemed like a palace to me. I once slept on dirt, only being fed breaths of air. So don't think I feel like this place isn't worthy. Anyone would be lucky to live here one day."

Franklin clasped his hands together, smiling, then looked away in deep thought that made his smile slowly fade away.

"Lucky wasn't just some old boss to me, Kavita. Before we get married, I want to be completely honest with you. Lucky is . . ."

Oh God, she thought. If this man had been lying to her this whole time, her heart wouldn't be able to take it. If he was still doing business with Lucky and was putting her and her family in danger, she had to go no matter how much love there was between them.

"He is my uncle, Kavita. My father was murdered many years ago. As time went by, I was slowly welcomed into his world, and I began to see Lucky for who he really is . . . a murderer. I believe he is the one who killed my father after he felt betrayed. I think that night you were shot at was because he thought I was with you." Franklin was visibly struck by sadness.

"I fear we should leave, Kavita. Your father can handle this, but Lucky is a man of vengeance. We can start somewhere new—in Paris maybe, or wherever you want to go. I can have my brother look after my properties. We can start a new life," he said hopefully.

So much was happening that Kavita couldn't keep up. She sat on the steps of the staircase, looking up at him. She was tired of running and escaping from things that could ruin her happiness. Kavita had thought for once she had it right in agreeing to marry Franklin. She'd had her wild, carefree phase, going to every mansion party in New York, where everyone assumed she was happy. In the quiet moments, she knew she went to parties to cover her deep sorrow. She had been trying to fill a void she didn't know how to fill.

"Why can't I just be happy again?"

Franklin knew she was right. He swooped her up as the bride-to-be she was.

"Let me take my beautiful future wife out for a day on the town. I am sorry. I just don't like hiding anything from you, Kavi," he said, then gently kissed her on the lips.

She kissed him back harder, holding on to him. He moved her dress up ever so slightly as he gripped the long locks that fell down her back. Franklin closed the curtains and threw a blanket over the floor before coming back to her. Her heart started to thump a little louder, and in the early-morning hours, it seemed to echo throughout the house. She slipped off his jacket, which fell to the floor.

Franklin traced the lines of her chin with his large thumb, going down from her neck to her belly button. He gripped the sides of her waist before the room seemed to fade into euphoria for them both.

The front door slammed open. Men armed with guns, knives, and rope. Kavita let out a scream, throwing her bag at them. Franklin yelled and cursed at them, saying they were family. An older man pistol-whipped him in the head, making him black out. As two men grabbed Kavita by the legs and arms, carrying her, she fought back as hard as she could. A wet cloth was placed over her nose, and she soon saw the darkness she'd tried so hard to escape.

Chapter 26

Adesua Ridley

Chinatown had a beauty that Adesua would never get over. Paper lotus lanterns flew above her. Bright neon tubes advertised Cantonese restaurants. Wei snagged a copy of *Shangbao Chinese Journal of Commerce*, while Henrik and Diego took in the smells of the amazing food around them.

Young boys yelled, "Fresh dumplings and hot rice!"

Adesua whispered to Wei in Cantonese, "Delicious."

Wei saw how her eyes got brighter looking at the food and quickly grabbed some bills to give to the boys in exchange for dumplings and rice for Adesua.

"Here, don't say I don't do anything for you," he said with playful annoyance, putting his arms around her and Henrik.

Wei stopped suddenly, making everyone look at him mischievously.

"I, for one, need a little break. Anyone want to go to the massage parlor with me?"

Henrik and Omar had shot their hands up by the end of the word "massage." Adesua looked at Diego, who seemed uncomfortable with the idea. They had a silent agreement that they would stick together.

Wei noticed immediately. "Very well, then, Dusie and Diego. Go have fun galivanting around a tea shop. The real men need some time to relax," he jabbed mockingly.

Adesua shot a look at Diego; she could tell his feelings were hurt, though she knew Wei was coming from a good place.

Diego stood a little taller. "I mean, we can walk by. I'll take a look. I also don't want to leave Adesua alone."

Wei came up to him, roughhousing with him by playing with his hair. "See, my little brother is a gentleman."

As they approached the building, they spotted a sign with large gold brushstrokes that read "Herbal Baths & Massage." As the door opened, they could see the steam from the cedar tubs roaming through the air. The masseuses wore dark silk *chang-san* and were doing *gua sha* and cupping on the clients. Wei immediately went to the back to slip on a robe like the professional he was. Henrik and Omar soon followed.

Adesua looked at Diego and spoke louder than usual. "I thank you for not leaving me alone. I would like to explore a little bit more, if you don't mind."

Diego eagerly nodded his head at the opportunity, waving at the boys. They were already in a deep trance with their massages, to their advantage. She took Diego's hand in encouragement, and they headed to Pell Street. The Dragon Tea store was a stark change of pace from the massage parlor. The circular moon gate doorway perfectly matched the tea shop. She walked up the winding wooden stairs to get a better table and a view of Chinatown.

Adesua paced back and forth with Diego, wondering when they were going to tell their siblings about what they had found. With Kavita's wedding coming up, there was no time that was good. The birth certificate was proof of a circle of lies that had started before they'd even joined the family. She wished that was the worst of it. Adesua pulled out the diary from her bag. She had wrapped it in a piece of floral cloth to conceal it.

After going through pages and pages from Amelia's diary, more heinous details came to light.

Adesua scanned through the diary more while Diego took a bite of his shrimp toast.

Jamison has been avoiding me, and so has my family.

I wish I could go back to the simple life I once had.

I always have to clean up after everyone's messes . . . Now I have to do it for Father?

It all started when the fire breathers ignited more than just fire around me. It was anger. Dale . . . We had a dire problem that needed to be contained.

Dale had to be killed, there was no other way.

Adesua paused before continuing to read. The bottomless pit in her stomach felt like it was growing wider, like a black hole. The emptiness swarmed around her now that she knew what she had been chasing was potentially in the palm of her hand. Tears fell down her face as the life she once knew was long gone, and it was almost as if it had never existed. The Amelia whom she'd thought she knew was keeping foul secrets, acting as if they were all imbeciles.

Adesua saw red as she slid the diary across the table, pointing out a line to Diego. His mouth flung open, the remnants of his food falling out. She looked out to see a crowd of people below on the street rehearsing and dancing together. It was the street-side lion dancers. The papered coils made her think of the night of Dale's murder with the fire-breathing dancers, just as Amelia wrote in her diary.

The Night of Dale's Murder
July 9, 1927

Adesua stood up and headed through the maze she knew all too well. She hated the scene that had been caused by her brothers' making a huge ordeal out of the rowdy guests. The garden maze was the only place she loved besides the art room, but she didn't feel alone, and the rows of roses seemed to reach out to her. She heard footsteps approaching from behind. Adesua, in a panic, took off running, ready to arm herself if needed. She sighed in relief when she saw Wei's familiar face.

"It's me. I come bringing hugs," he said jokingly.

Adesua ran up to him with tears flowing down her face and kissed him. It was as if a flashing light happened the moment their lips touched. She immediately backed away.

"Oh, Wei . . . Oh, Wei. I am so sorry. I don't know what's wrong with me. I wanted to hug you. I—I don't know why I did that," Adesua stammered.

He hugged her, bringing her back in.

"Dusie, it's okay. It's okay. I know you meant nothing by it. You were scared. We were all scared . . ."

Wei pondered for a moment, as he felt different too. He remembered Kavita making a remark, asking if they were finally feeling good, and it all made sense.

"Adesua, I think Kavi and her friends may have done something to the punch." He sighed. The spiked alcohol was why he felt such rage. He'd nearly blacked out while fighting those boys.

"We will handle her tomorrow. She is still being frivolous, trying to make a statement that's not needed. Let's head back and inform the others," Wei said.

Dale Caimen stood there, smiling with a crazed look, as they turned the corner.

"I always thought Kavita would be the family's downfall, but boy, oh boy, was I wrong. So don't worry about trying to lie your way out of it. I saw everything. You got one messed-up family."

"Dale, please. It wasn't like that. He is my brother. Please don't do this."

He laughed, mocking her. "'Oh please, don't show how sick my family is. Oh please, don't release the biggest story of your career.' You Ridleys are a hoot, aren't ya. Blame your father for putting ya in this situation. See, that's why I took a picture to memorialize the moment." He turned away.

Dale turned back; his anger wasn't gone yet. Compared to Wei, his short stature was obvious, but that didn't stop him from invading his space, winding his arm back to throw a striking blow at Wei's face. Adesua saw the anger in Wei's face, as if his life had flashed in front of his eyes.

Diego and Adesua pieced together how Amelia could have killed Dale. They recounted the moment after Adesua saw Dale with Wei. They'd left in a panic, not wanting any more trouble. Which made Adesua go near the steps at the back of the house, where she saw Kavita come out of the maze. They debated on telling the rest of their siblings about what they knew about Amelia, but as each day passed, more secrets that they had all been hiding kept returning from the dead.

Kavita had also gotten into an altercation with Dale when Adesua and Wei were seen caught up at the maze.

Chapter 27

Kavita Ridley

The throbbing in her head kept pulsating. Her wrists started to go raw from the tightness of the rope. She began feeling sick, wondering if Franklin had done this to other women. Kavita had a feeling in the depths of her gut that maybe this was his way of truly clearing his name with Lucky. Was this whom she was set to marry? Was Franklin a person who got a thrill from torturing others for fun or survival? The smell of gasoline wafted to her nose, and her head slammed against the floorboards with every turn. Her eyes started to brim with tears.

She had never imagined dying at the hand of the man she loved. Blindfolded, Kavita could only see darkness. Streams of moonlight peeked through, but nothing more. The men were silent in the car, as if they, too, feared the same fate. Kavita refused to feel sorry for herself. She had been playing with fire for so many years. The heat had finally caught up with her, with nowhere to go.

The car halted with a jerk, sending her head to the back of the seat once more. As the door swung open, Kavita didn't put up a fight like she'd been planning to. Instead, when they grabbed the back of her shoulder, she let them. The tears falling down her face were real, but she wasn't going to be a threat to them. A threat meant more men. More men meant more protection for Lucky. If she were easy, the threat for her would be lessened. She hoped this would give her family a chance.

For once, she wished she'd listened to Franklin. Her heels felt too tight around her swollen feet. Each toe throbbed with every clumsy step she took. Kavita limped as one man let go of her, further indicating they didn't see her as a threat. She leaned forward, getting too off-balance and falling to the ground. Although her vision wasn't clear, she could feel the blood trickling down her knee. A man's strong arm wrapped around the backs of her knees, while his other hand held her neck. He carried her the rest of the way.

Kavita moved her head to the side, smelling a familiar scent. Oil and the fishy smell of the water. She was at the shipping docks. Fear appeared in her mind. What if they were shipping her away or making her be a slave? Without her family, she would be nothing. The blindfold was peeled off, and she saw only Lucky. The man who'd carried her was long gone. Her heart held a smile for her because her face surely couldn't.

Lucky stepped closer, looking into her eyes.

"Franklin sure does know how to pick 'em. It's a shame you are such a beautiful lady."

Kavita said nothing. She wasn't going to give him the satisfaction of her pleading for forgiveness. She knew how this worked, but to what end, was her only question. A rat scurried across her feet as the damp, moldy air surrounded them. She wanted nothing more than to see Lucky wrapped like a pig ready for slaughter. He was as vile as one, and should be treated as such.

"I can tell you got a million words a minute in that pretty little head of yours. Don't get any slick ideas just because I am here alone. I will kill you in an instant, you hear me?"

Kavita nodded aggressively, keeping her eyes down. The old Kavita would have spat in his face a long time ago. But her constant poor decisions had gotten her this far. Maybe acting like Amelia was the way to go for now. Her sister never let anyone know what her next move was.

Kavita, on the other hand, wore her emotions on her sleeve, where they were waiting to roll and pop off on anyone and everyone.

"Speak up, girl, just like your father did," Lucky said, slamming the palm of his hand on a table, causing an echo inside the warehouse.

Everything was boarded up and covered in white cloths. The only thing she could see was the stars peeping through the broken ceiling panels.

"I don't let my own son ignore me, and I surely ain't starting now," he spat.

Lucky paced in circles before striking her hard on the face.

"That's the problem with you young women. You forget your place in this world."

Kavita's face started to swell from the hit. She still would not give him the satisfaction he wanted. Although she could feel her eyes turning red, that was all he would get from her. Aside from a cough as rough ropes were tied tightly around her chest.

"If your sister comes in here with any funny business, so help me God, your body will be at the bottom of the Hudson River before day breaks. Do you hear me?"

Kavita looked up. He had threatened her, but mentioning her body as if she were no longer in existence scared her more than she wanted to show.

"Oh, there it is. Fear. I can smell it on you. That's all I need."

Kavita blinked fast at the thought of her body sinking with weights around her. Dying alone was her worst fear. Not a lot of things haunted her, but the thought of water slowly filling her lungs pained her. Lucky was not testing her this time. She prayed to God for the first time in a long time. She whispered to herself, "Amen."

"Honey, you're going to need more than God to help you today." He smirked, reeking of alcohol.

There was something poetic, in a way, for Kavita to arrive here by the same shipping dock, and dying here would be coming full circle. But if she was to die today, she would make sure she wasn't the only one going.

Chapter 28

Amelia Ridley

Mrs. Darla scrambled to Amelia's door and began knocking aggressively. Amelia flipped her covers back, barely getting a chance to put her feet in her slippers. More knocks slammed on her door. Amelia slung the door open in anger over the disruption of her sleep.

Mrs. Darla grabbed hold of her.

"It's about Kavi. Go out to the maze—your brothers and Adesua are out there waiting," she said, out of breath, then plopped onto Amelia's bed.

Amelia threw her robe on over her nightdress and ran outside to see all her siblings except one—and *Franklin*. She walked up to him and slapped him in the face.

"What did you do to her?"

"They took her, the mobsters your father spoke about," Franklin said. Amelia turned, heading straight back to the estate.

Wei grabbed her arm. "Franklin has pleaded with us not to tell Father, or he feels like they will get rid of Kavita."

"He wants only you, Amelia, alone. He knows you're taking over the Ridley Line and wants a deal with all his wishes fulfilled since your father ratted him out," Franklin added.

Amelia looked at her siblings, back in the same position, once again, where she had to make the tough decisions.

"Wei, Henrik, and Adesua, you go in a separate car. Franklin and I will arrive together," she said.

They rushed to put proper clothes on to make it in time. It was still dark outside. Franklin and Amelia drove quickly out of Long Island to make it to the shipping docks. Amelia didn't like the feeling that was enveloping her. Her sister had gotten in the middle of something that wasn't her doing, but her father's. Franklin slowly pulled in and parked the car. The sudden roar of an engine blared. Lucky emerged from the driver's seat, then pulled Kavita out with her arms tied behind her back. Lucky's cigarette dangled from his lips with the embers glowing ominously.

"Well, well. Isn't this sweet? Got the newest leader of the Ridley Line," Lucky drawled, a hint of madness in his voice when he laughed. "Makes my job easier, doesn't it, Franklin, my boy?"

"Your . . . boy?" Amelia whipped her head around to Franklin.

She had no idea about their ties. If Kavita weren't in love with him, she'd be sure to have him killed by tomorrow. Amelia knew Kavita was a fool in love, but not this foolish. She remembered when Kavita swore up and down that Franklin would protect her at all cost. Yet here they were, failed by more men in their lives.

She saw Henrik hiding behind the crates, doing just as she'd told him. They knew this shipyard front, back, and sideways. This was their playground.

Lucky's savage grin widened. "Oh, darling, that ain't the half of it. Tell her about Montana, Franklin. Tell her how you played her like a fiddle at that gambling table. How you were gonna take the money and run," Lucky said mockingly.

"Kavita, I was . . . I would have never done that to you." Franklin was fuming, trying to redeem himself.

"I trusted you, Franklin. Now you have put me and my sister in danger," Kavita said, heartbroken.

"These damn entitled lovers are something, ain't they, Amelia?" Lucky interrupted, slipping his hand into his coat pocket.

"Now for what I really came here for. I want to strike up a plan with you. My name will be cleared because I am going to be putting the blame on one of my disloyal men. From that point, you, Amelia—or ya father, whoever will be in charge—will need to make sure all my lovely cargo gets here untouched and ready to be served to the fine people of New York." He laughed like a maniac before continuing. "Your father has made me lose so much business that this is the only way to redeem even a sliver of it. You hear what I am saying, girl?" He spoke in a low voice, flashing the pistol to make sure she understood.

Amelia felt at a loss with this. Lucky clearly had a gun and was ready to use it at any moment.

"Yes, Lucky, we have an agreement," she said in defeat.

Kavita spoke up weakly. Amelia tried to wave her hand down for her to stay calm, but it was too late. "I don't give a damn what you lose, you bastard. I am going to make sure every press from New York to California knows what you did here today."

Amelia and Franklin took a step closer to brace for what Lucky might do next. She took a look at Henrik, while Lucky homed in on Kavita.

"What did you just say, bitch?"

"No matter what our family does, we get away with it because we are the family everyone craves to be. You will always be known as less than a criminal for stealing from the poor. So no, my sister will not be doing your bidding."

Franklin had taken so many steps, he now held on to Kavita and was backing her slowly away from Lucky.

"Lucky, listen, it doesn't have to be like this. We can find another way," he desperately pleaded.

Lucky scratched his head while waving the gun.

"Don't you get it, Frank? People like them always win. This is why they both gotta go. Let them be a lesson for the rest of those who consider trying me again."

Amelia screamed so loudly that every other noise was drowned out. Kavita closed her eyes. She now felt what Dale had. Even through Amelia's screams, death was silent, the air around her gone.

A gunshot rang out.

But it wasn't just Lucky's. Henrik held a gun up high, frozen there as if he were a statue.

The crack of the shots from both of their guns had split the night. As Franklin lunged into Lucky's sight, he pushed Kavita down as the fatal bullet hit him. He crumpled, crimson blooming across his shirt.

"Franklin!" she screamed in agony.

"Kavi . . . I want you to know—" Franklin's final breath dissolved into silence as he held her hand.

Kavita's anger filled the sky.

"Franklin, please. Please wake up, I love you."

Henrik stood at the edge of the darkness, his father's Smith & Wesson smoking in his hands.

Chapter 29

Adesua Ridley

Adesua gnawed at her hands, nearly causing them to bleed. She thought of Kavita, praying for her safety. Her legs were knocking together, making the car shake.

She turned to Wei in distress.

"Why did Henrik go instead of you? He can barely protect himself."

Wei looked as bothered as she was over the whole situation.

"Amelia was right. Henrik is tiny and can blend in with any workers that might be there. Way more than the rest of us," he said, pain in his voice.

She knew it was Wei's desire to protect them all, and knowing Kavita was sitting there possibly being tortured was enough of a damning thought for them both to be sent over the edge.

A gunshot went off. Adesua didn't even have time to figure out if she was danger before her sisters and her brother Henrik were there. She ran so fast her heel came off, and she didn't even look back. She didn't know if Wei was behind her, but it didn't matter. She was going to help her family.

She saw Kavita on the ground next to Franklin, all tied up. Her worst nightmare had come true.

"Wei, help her!" she screamed, so loudly that even the gulls shrieked with her. As she got closer, she saw Wei had passed her kneeling on the ground next to Kavita. Her heart felt like it came out of her chest. Seeing Kavita and Amelia alive was all that mattered. *But wait, where is Henrik?* She looked up at Amelia in pain. Adesua could see Amelia knew what she needed to say.

"He is behind the crates, Dusie. I think he is in shock over everything."

Adesua ran behind the crates and found Henrik on his knees, crying.

"Oh, come here, baby."

He wailed loudly in her lap. "I thought I killed Kavi. Did I just kill someone? Adesua. Adesua." He struggled to speak through the tears.

She looked into his icy-blue eyes. The innocence and light that was once there was slowly fading away. Her heart was tightening with each and every moment, and she wished she could take this load off his chest.

"What happened? Where are his men?" she asked.

Henrik looked up at her in tearful remorse. "They are gone. I heard him say that he didn't need a scene and can handle one girl by himself with Franklin. He kept remarking that Franklin would never turn against him because it would be a death sentence for him."

Adesua nodded, saying no more. Henrik was frustrated with the blood on his hands. Even if it was to protect his sister. To take a life was to lose some of your life. She knew he felt that way. As her clarity came back, she started placing the blame on Amelia. Had it always been her plan to do this? To have her innocent brother become a murderer like her?

Now Pandora's box was slowly coming open. She and Wei in the same car made sense to her. Maybe she was going to do the deal with Lucky anyway. This concerned her, because whether they brought the cops in or not, things could end very badly, with Kavita dead or, worse, all of them dead but Amelia. If she had any suspicions that they knew it was her . . . they could all easily be a sacrifice to protect her.

Adesua grabbed on to Henrik, going back to a now-untied Kavita and a long-gone Franklin. He looked at peace. But Kavita looked far from it. Her heart began to race again as Amelia then turned to look her in the eye. Her voice hardened.

"Adesua, go retrieve Dale's camera and journals. They are in the trunk," she said sternly. She rushed back with the camera in hand and the black velvet bag filled with evidence against Lucky and Franklin, and Amelia nodded to Wei. "Put them in Lucky's car. Henrik, go fetch the police. This ends today."

Daylight had broken, and workers began to scurry around the scene in shock. Most walked by and headed to their proper work area as if this was just another normal day to them. Police came in a hurried fashion, blocking off the murder scene before civilians and reporters could come rushing through. Any time the words "Ridley" or "murder"—or better yet, both—were used in a sentence, it got around fast in New York.

Flashing lights came shortly after, and they all turned their backs to the cameras. Who were they kidding, trying to hide? Adesua knew better than the next person that everyone knew it was them. The infamous Ridleys had truly been caught committing a murder this time. Nothing anyone could say could change this narrative.

Days passed by, and just like a bad nightmare, it all repeated once again. Each of them was separated to be interrogated for the murder of Lucky Moretti and his nephew Franklin. The investigators and police chief scratched their heads.

"You do see how troubling it is that we are back here, correct?"

Adesua nodded in agreement. She didn't believe it either.

"We have interviewed your other siblings, and they have all said the same thing. I believe, in my heart, that you have something else to say. A truth we haven't heard yet," he said apprehensively. "One where the story isn't just your baby brother, Henrik, randomly having a gun and protecting his sisters. One where Wei wouldn't just sit there and let it happen. We know his track record, and you're telling me he let his baby brother take the fall for that? I don't think so."

There was no lie in his statements. Amelia had made sure they all had the same orchestrated story: a frantic Franklin trying to keep Kavita alive, saying Amelia had to go alone, but she didn't in fear that Lucky would kill her. Same words, same story. All jumbled up just a tad so each version could have their own personal flair. One sibling would be in hysterics, the other would be nearly fainting while talking about them potentially dying at the hands of mobsters, and so on.

Adesua thought about how she knew Amelia was Dale's killer and how she could end the lies for everyone. Who was to say that Amelia wouldn't keep them in danger? Or worse, make sure they all had blood on their hands? Yes, they had lied and had secrets, but death was another matter she wouldn't dare step on. Amelia had motive to keep her title in the company. If the world found out who she was, even Father couldn't save her.

"No, my brothers and sisters were very brave to take a risk that could have ended their lives," she said curtly.

Instantly the police chief and investigators gave up. They all had an alibi and all had perfect reasoning. It was self-defense. The police knew, deep down, that something was off. She could tell in their eyes that keeping their lives was more important than their line of work. Because messing with a Ridley now seemed like a ticket to heaven or hell.

Another detective wandered in.

"One more thing, Adesua," he said, bringing out a red envelope.

Damn it.

"You ever seen a little thing like this in your home?"

Adesua wanted to lie quickly, but they had it in their hands. There was no fire she could throw it in and watch it crumble. It was there, alive, almost as if it had its own beating heart.

"Yes, I have," she said stiffly.

He tossed the letter on the table for her to read.

one signature . . . one shipment . . . should've let your sister do the dirty work, but you Ridleys are all the same, thriving off hurting poor people. Your time to come clean is wearing very thin. But that's what you Ridleys do, take risks until it's your downfall.

"So can you explain what they mean by this?"

Adesua cleared her throat and then her thoughts before speaking. She was now the one in the hot seat. Maybe she should have told on Amelia, and this wouldn't even be relevant.

"People have tried to extort our family for many years. Especially more so now that we are adults. We have been blackmailed and falsely accused of things simply because people we thought we could trust were truly the bad guys. So yes, someone thinks that I have done something with politicians, but they couldn't be further from the truth," she said in one breath.

Amelia tapped on the door, with the police chief now by her side. Adesua hadn't even realized he had left.

"That's enough now, gentlemen. We have gotten confirmation on everything," he said, pleased.

Amelia walked all the way into the room with the herd of men gawking at her dress. Adesua had never seen her wear a dress with a slit so high, or fishnet stockings with intricate details. It was like she wanted to take the attention away from everything else.

"I have agreed with Miss Amelia here to provide more police protection to keep any aggressors and blackmailers away," he said with a smile, rubbing her shoulder.

Adesua felt sick watching this exchange happen. Amelia had morphed into someone she had never seen before, a vixen playing her cards to abolish all the terrible things they had done. She did have a moment when she thought that she should be grateful they weren't all behind bars, but it was indeed unsettling seeing her sister in this way. Adesua and Amelia walked out of the police station together. She silently prayed, hoping this was the last time she had to do this.

Mr. Pierre opened the car door for them to step in. Adesua sat there silently, with thoughts racing in her head.

"You can say it," Amelia said coldly.

Adesua cocked her eyebrows at her. "Say what?"

"That I am a terrible person."

Adesua looked out the window to avoid eye contact with her. She knew Amelia could get her answer by looking at her face.

"Tell me what happened to Dale that night," Adesua said.

Chapter 30

Amelia Ridley

The Night of Dale's Murder
July 9, 1927

Amelia was huddled up in her secret spot in the maze. She loved that she could watch and see everyone from this view. There was a small opening in the shrubbery in front of a concrete slab chair, perfect for sitting and being closed up, with no one to bother her. After her confrontation with Dale, she wanted nothing more than to get away from this party, but Father had forbidden her from going to her room while guests were here. He made sure by having Mrs. Darla do checks just to see if she would disobey.

She couldn't rest like she wanted, but she could write about it in her diary. Amelia felt a twinge of jealousy that Kavita was getting married before she was. It gave Father something more to complain about. She didn't understand why she and she alone must be the face of the Ridley Line. She had to be the perfect woman. She had to dress a certain way. Oh, and she couldn't get angry in the way she really wanted to. As her father would say, people didn't remember kindness, but they did remember when you snapped.

The paper of Amelia's diary began to get wet from the trickling beads of sweat falling down her hand. It was hot—unbearably so. She took another swig of the juice concoction that was being served and a glass of wine. No one knew how much she battled drinking. It was her only escape from the constant pressures put on her by her father.

She heard Kavita's voice, even though she tried her best to conceal her yelling from the crowd.

"How dare you, Dale. How dare you come to our home on my special day and ruin this for me?"

Dale shrugged as he took another sip of his drink.

"Kavita, it's a business. Your father knows this better than me. You chose to get yourself tied up with a mobster family. Wasting your potential. Hell, you would've been better off with me than the scum of Little Italy."

Kavita slapped him hard with all her might.

"You're going to regret doing that, little one."

She heard them walk away. Well, at least Kavita did, as she was cursing up a storm as she walked out of the maze. Amelia stayed still in fear that Dale would see her. She clicked her tongue in disgust over his—

Footsteps got closer and louder. Had someone found her hiding spot? Hysterical crying was all she could hear. Then, suddenly, she saw it was Adesua, with Wei running behind her.

"You can't just keep running away from what you feel, Adesua."

Adesua put her hands in the air, falling to her knees.

"You don't understand, Wei. I can't show these people how it hurts me. I can't. They will use it against me every time. You should know this. This is why you never show emotions. So why can't I?"

Wei stooped down next to her, taking a sip from the champagne bottle before leaving it on the ground.

"Because, Adesua, I don't want you to harden and get cold like me. I want you happy. The past ten years with you have made me a better person in more ways than you think. The way you—" He stopped himself.

Amelia could see through the greenery that the way Wei was looking at Adesua meant he wanted to say more. She covered her mouth, hoping her heavy breathing wouldn't be heard. Wei leaned toward Adesua, kissing her on the lips passionately. Amelia's eyes widened in shock and heartbreak. How long had this been going on? Adesua pulled her head back in confusion. Amelia figured that she was feeling as shocked as she was. Instead, she went back in, kissing him again. He grabbed her back, closing the gap between them. A flash of light hit Amelia's eyes, making her flinch.

Their eyes were still closed, and they remained locked in a passionate embrace, until Adesua pulled away, walking in the other direction.

"Wei, we talked about this last year, and the year before that. I am not doing this. We are siblings, Wei. It isn't right," she pleaded with him.

"It's not our fault we were adopted together. I didn't ask to be brought into a home with someone I'd fall in love with at fourteen, Adesua. You know that's not fair," he said, his voice laced with guilt.

Adesua's face hardened. Amelia could see her demeanor drastically change before her eyes.

"I am with Joseph, and he is the one I will marry. Not you. Not someone I share my last name with," she whispered.

Clapping could be heard coming from the opposite side of the bush Amelia was hiding behind.

Dale.

He put his hands on the sides of his face, smiling.

"My, oh my, what a performance that was."

Adesua's face dropped more than it already had.

"Look, Dale, we can—"

"Oh, cut the shit, Adesua. You can, what? Explain? I saw it all."

Now Adesua looked down in silence as Mr. Pierre came to a stop at the estate.

"I will let you girls finish up."

Amelia knew Adesua had been looking in her room, but she wanted to remind her they were both involved in some way.

"Why didn't you tell me you saw? What else happened? How did Dale die?"

Amelia looked at the stables, then back to Adesua.

⟡

Dale placed his briefcase behind him near the bench. He stood up, taking in the view of the large pond. Amelia saw that she could easily open his briefcase and get what she needed out of it. She grabbed the papers and every journal she could. He was still taking swigs of his cocktail while admiring the moon. She thought, for a moment, that if he picked the briefcase up, he would realize how light it was. Amelia quietly placed rocks in the bottom. Until one fell out of her hand and rolled down the path.

"Who is there?"

Shit. She figured she could make a run for it, but her heels would slow her down. Dale ran behind the shrubbery, spotting Amelia and grabbing her hand. She threw down the papers and journals as he dragged her out of her hidey-hole.

"You thought you were slick, didn't you?"

Amelia tried to pull away. "Unhand me now or I will scream," she said with exhaustion.

"Oh, you don't wanna do that. You know why? Everyone will see what you and your fucked-up little family have done." He gripped her hand tighter, whispering each word in her ear. "Actually, my apologies, Amelia, I was mistaken by saying 'your' when truly it is *our* little family."

Amelia looked straight through him as if he weren't there, stopping dead in her tracks. He let her arm go. She couldn't move, and she didn't know why. The words that flew from her so easily had been taken away, as if by the slight breeze from the Long Island Sound, whispering its way through the garden.

She didn't feel air flowing into her lungs but instead was preoccupied by the endless questions that she was ready to throw at Dale. "What did you just say?"

He widened his mouth, showing his widely spaced teeth, which looked like a row of gravestones.

"My sister. Oh, how I wished to say the words, my little sister. You thought you were special, huh?"

Amelia knew exactly what he meant, but what proof did he have? It was his word versus hers. Of course, anyone would want to be a part of the Ridley Line. Dale Caimen was no different.

"Oh, I can see those gears in that lil' head of yours working, little sis. Father got rid of me as soon as he and Caroline got married. My poor, foolish mother drank herself to death and only left me with a letter and a . . . You know what, how about you open it," he said, his voice laced with intrigue and the slyness of a snake.

Amelia snatched the envelope from him. A thick black-and-white photo of a woman and her father. How many lives had this man who was her blood lived? Did Mother know about this? Surely there was no way. Amelia slowly crumpled up the photo.

"Oh, not so fast, little sister. There is more proof of that coming right to you—or better yet, to Metropolitan Musings." He winked while mocking her. "You know what makes this all better? You sick Seven Wonders really thought you were better than me, when all along I was better than you. I never thought about looking into my mother's belongings, as they were a sacred grave to me. Who would have thought that I would find a photograph of good ole family-loving Mr. Ridley holding my mother. A slew of letters and then nothing." His voice trembled.

Amelia had enough issues on her hands, and having to deal with Dale as not just her brother but . . .

"Then I got to thinking, as I was ready to send in this exposé of what a fraudulent family you all are. I thought, wait a minute, you are just another little Black girl that he has been hiding this whole time.

They could barely tolerate Mr. Ridley with his adopted children, but a Black bastard child couldn't be any better in my case." He smirked.

Amelia rolled her eyes, as his theatrics were starting to irritate her and she felt rage at the idea of this cesspool of a human being related to her in any capacity. She refused to give him the satisfaction of seeing her fear. The only thing she felt was the world closing in around her as he slowly came near her. "And whatever do you mean by that, Dale?"

"I think that Mr. Ridley . . . Excuse me, as this is all new to me." He chuckled before continuing. "That he would be elated to have a fully white child—and a male, at that—to, let me think . . . take over the Ridley Line," he whispered loudly enough for her to hear. Amelia felt everything crumble before her. Everything she had worked so hard for, all the lies and secrets she'd protected. It was all going to be a waste when Dale was done with them. She knew there was some truth to what he was saying. Father truly had no loyalty to anyone but himself. She thought for once Father was going to have her and her siblings' backs if she complied. But with Dale being Father's biological child as well, Dale would make sure they would have nothing if Father let him be in control. Amelia paused momentarily, knowing that Dale Caimen was always doomed to failure. From the corner of her eye, she saw the gleaming champagne bottle. She kicked Dale between the legs, making him scream in agonizing pain.

"Oh, you little bitch, you're gonna regret—"

Cloink. Dale fell to his knees on the ground. He placed his hand on the top of his head, which was bleeding. Amelia held the heavy champagne bottle, which she'd thought would have broken on his head but had instead stayed intact with its heavy, thick glass. He stood up on one knee, bracing himself so he wouldn't fall into the fountain. She hit him again in the same spot.

"It was always you . . ." His voice trailed off.

His eyes rolled into the back of his head as he fell, his head hitting the edge of the marble fountain and his body sinking into the water.

Adesua gripped her dress so hard in fear of the words she'd heard. It had been no accident. Amelia had murdered Dale.

"I love you, Adesua. You have to believe me. It was self-defense. He grabbed me. I feared for my life."

The estate's wide doors opened, and all their siblings poured out of the house, heading to the garden.

"What's going on?" Amelia was confused by the ruckus.

"Father is having another press day for us. Reporters are already in the garden," Omar called out.

Amelia was shocked to be hearing of it last, as Father usually told her everything first. Father had shown his true colors, making it clear that he would turn on all of them if he had to. Yes, she was the favorite by far, but he had a meticulous reason for everything he did. His springing another press day on them without her knowing was sure enough a sign that she could no longer follow in his footsteps. It was hard for her, as she had been under his wing her whole life, to now turn against the man she and her siblings saw as a king who did no wrong. Amelia was ready to play the games her father had made them play their whole lives. She looked at Adesua as they both slid out of the car. Amelia silently gave her a confused glance, as she didn't know what was going on either.

The garden was beautiful, with six fountains going straight down the middle, whereas the mazes both had their own ponds and sitting area. If it wasn't the place of Dale's death, maybe she would have liked it more.

She didn't know if Adesua believed her or not, but she hoped in her heart, after all these years of being a family, that she wouldn't betray her. They all stood front and center in the garden. There were about thirty members of the press all waiting, writing down every breath the siblings took, every glance they gave, and every lie they were about to tell. She was sure of it, but she wondered why Father had not prewarned them. This concerned Amelia because everything her father did was so calculated.

Father took a step up onto the podium. Of course he was raised above them all as they stood next to him on both sides. Mother stood nearby, quietly, but she was there.

"Our family has been under an attack I wouldn't wish on my worst enemy," Father said, forcing a tear. "And this has troubled my mind recently, escalating my illness. My health has declined gravely to where I can't ignore it any longer. I can't seem to remember things that are necessary for me to keep going for . . . I am not sure how much longer."

Amelia hated seeing her father like this. She walked behind her siblings, heading to the podium. He looked confused and shocked as she stepped up onto the podium beside him.

"I will be handling all affairs until Father gets better. I do believe the constant pull and tug with the press revealing things about our family has exasperated him to no end. So please give us grace during this time, as Kavita, my beautiful sister, is in mourning over the tragic death of her fiancé," Amelia closed out, thanking everyone for their time.

The press took pictures in a frenzy. She could feel the envious looks of her brothers Omar and Wei next to her. She didn't dare look at Adesua. Father stormed into the veranda and closed the doors, and Amelia followed her father's lead.

"Amelia Rose Ridley, how dare you embarrass me in front of all those people."

Amelia looked at his empty eyes square on.

"I have *lied* for you. I have *killed* for you. I sure enough can *lead* for you," she said in a single breath. "I will go to the board myself, because clearly you are not in your right mind. To hold a press conference without letting anyone know. Not even me? We can't keep playing these games, Father."

Father wept for the first time in years. The last time was when Mother had threatened to leave, giving herself the upper hand. When she stayed, his tears dried as fast as they'd dropped. Amelia left without acknowledging his sadness. All the years of her father's corrupt actions would catch up with him sooner rather than later. She wasn't going to let this empire—*her* empire—fall because of his incompetence.

Amelia got in her Rolls-Royce, heading for Jamison at his family's Hamptons estate. She was informed by Elion that he had left in a panic in need of an escape. From Kavita being kidnapped and now Father losing his damn mind, Amelia needed her escape, too, and her only form of peace was now Jamison. No matter the issues that he had with his family, Jamison had always found his way back to her side.

Amelia walked up the long winding driveway at the Hamptons summer home, thinking of how different it had been when she was there with Jamison in the summer. No longer were blooming flowers covering the driveway; now it was just fall leaves and brisk air. There was only Jamison's car in the driveway, so he must be home alone. Amelia brought her hand up to the door to knock, but hesitated. She smiled to herself. There was no need for formalities when he was home. If they were married, she would have walked in without warning.

So that's what she did. Amelia wanted to spook him like she had when they were young children playing hide-and-seek. She silently giggled to herself, covering her mouth. It was the first genuine laugh she'd had in months. She walked to his room, seeing it was empty. He was more than likely in the library.

She opened the door to the grand library, seeing Mrs. Darla at the table with papers around her and red letters in the fire. Amelia froze at the sight. She began hyperventilating. Amelia had held her guard up for so long. How had it come to this? Jamison's eyes almost seemed hollow, as she could look right through them. She knew that she had been lied to.

"Mellie, oh no, Mellie, listen, honey," Mrs. Darla said, falling out of her seat while trying to console her.

Mrs. Darla came up to Amelia, trying to brush down her hair with her hands and then cupping the sides of her face. She leaned in, whispering in her ear, "I promise. I promise on my soul I won't tell anyone about Dale. You deserve a chance."

This was a betrayal she hadn't felt in her life.

"Darling, listen. Listen to me. We had no choice, sweetie."

Amelia stopped crying and looked at her. "Everyone has a choice. Jamison, I can understand, but you . . . You, Mrs. Darla, you were my *family*."

"Honey, I know. I am still family. You have no idea what your father has done to me and Mr. Jenkins. He has taken advantage of our kindness for years. My husband doesn't know this, but our children, they lost their jobs. We needed to provide for our grandchildren in some way, Mellie. Your father barely gave us two pennies to rub together," she cried hysterically.

Jamison sat there in silence. Amelia knew he wanted to disappear, but she was going to make him feel her pain.

"You, Jamison . . . I trusted you. You were supposed to be my future, and now it is all gone," she said, frantic.

"No, it's not, Mellie." He stood up and came over to her.

"Mrs. Darla and I were burning everything before you came in here. The press offered us a substantial amount of money to find the exposé Dale had written about you all, but we waited and waited. Neither of us had the heart to do it. Which is why you are seeing all the papers in that fire. Because I love you."

"But why, why would the press offer money? How did they know?"

Jamison looked at Mrs. Darla, seeing if it was okay to speak. "We didn't look deeply into the file before going to the press. They told us if we gave it to them after you all gave your statements about the night of the murder that we would be offered an amount even you would have taken. Mrs. Darla told me how Mr. Jenkins pleaded with Mr. Ridley for a loan, but he laughed in his face in return. She was angry, with every right to be so, Mellie," he said in a somber tone.

Mrs. Darla continued, "The more we found out about the secrets, the more we knew it wasn't no measly scandal that Kavita had gotten herself into but that this was something that would put you all in grave danger. We didn't know if Dale had already said something to the press.

When everyone was in a commotion, I grabbed the file, and Jamison followed me out of the garden, demanding it. Then we spent the time to figure where to go from there, and here we are now, burning it. I did feel for Dale, but you seven are my children."

Amelia couldn't think about love, but she did feel her heart soften for Mrs. Darla. She and her husband had raised her and her siblings. The least Amelia could do was provide for Mrs. Darla and Mr. Jenkins's family, as they had done for her.

"For your loyalty, I will protect you and take care of you, Mrs. Darla. I am going to be leading the Ridley Line, so whatever salary you need to help you and your family, I will make it so. You have my word."

Mrs. Darla got on the floor, nearly kissing the ground Amelia stood on, grabbing her legs and thanking her profusely. She looked down at the maid with pity. Was this the power her father felt looking at others? She knew she was slowly morphing into the leader of the family, and this moment settled it for her.

Chapter 31

Kavita Ridley

Mr. Pierre took an eager Kavita to the Metropolitan Life Tower, as she'd requested. She hopped in the car where she and Franklin used to sit. A flood of memories she suppressed returned to her. Seeing her fiancé lifeless made her think of Dale and the moments before his death. It had all come crashing down on her in an unbearable way, and she hadn't slept for days. She'd had enough.

"I will see you later, Mr. Pierre. I'll find my way home."

He nodded silently, raising his eyebrow in concern. Kavita never liked to be driven by him, so her getting home by herself wasn't out of the ordinary. She went to the top floor, looking at the city that made her who she was today. A cloud of smoke covered her face as she looked over the rooftop of the Metropolitan Life Tower. She tapped her slender cigarette over the edge, and the ashes flew away. She loved the view of the smaller buildings from here. It was as if she could grab each of them and put them in a dollhouse. She sometimes felt like a doll trapped in a home in this so-called city. Everyone was perfectly placed where they should be, and then there was her. Kavita knew that she and her siblings would always be out of place in a world like this.

She inhaled longer, slower drags of the smoke, and it swirled through the thoughts that overtook her mind. New York City wasn't the wrong place for her; the levels of society bothered her the most—the debutante balls, charity events, after-parties, and the endless amount of showboating. Someone was always trying to outdo another here, just as these tall buildings tried to do so tirelessly. Kavita had seen the masks fall off the elites who pretended to be so high and mighty, but honestly, they were as frail as the bones of this city. They fueled the downfall of one another. She wondered what the island felt now that it was being sunk by the countless buildings and never-ending people roaming the streets with their secrets. Kavita chuckled, thinking the island would like to run away too, like her.

She thought about the first time she and Franklin met, bringing tears to her eyes.

New York, 1926

Kavita leaned against the wall, gazing at the sunrise. This was her secret spot, where she didn't have to be bothered. Some mornings, she liked to be up before the city that never sleeps and see people through their windows, scurrying to leave for work, some gazing out the window with their coffee and a book. It was all beautiful chaos in a way that she couldn't put into words. A deep voice broke the silence as she waited for whatever creep that was probably following her to make himself known. She had a pocketknife and cigarette ready to gouge out his eye.

"There's nothing in the world like a New York sunrise."

Kavita turned with her perfectly arched eyebrows raised, the engraved red-and-gold pocketknife Wei had given her the night before in her hand. She slowly took the slender cigarette out of her mouth.

"Listen, if you're here to try any funny business, I'll carve my name into your chest. You hear me?"

The man took a few steps backward with both of his hands up in the air as a way of surrendering, showing that he meant no harm.

"Well, no 'good morning'? 'How are you doing today, sir'?"

Kavita looked him up and down. In her anger, she hadn't realized how dashing he looked. His nice pin-striped pants, pleated straight down the center, were so sharp they would cut her before she did him in. Kavita doubled down on what she'd said, worried he was still some crazy stalker.

"You're going to try to make me, Kavita Ridley, believe you don't know who I am?"

The man stroked his mustache with his thumb and index finger while giving a wide smile. "Am I supposed to know who you are, darling? Because so far, you may be the only beautiful woman in Manhattan—or, as a matter of fact, the state of New York—with a knife ready to maim any man who compliments her."

Kavita turned away, hiding her smile.

"Oh, no need to turn away. I could see that smile from Long Island," he said playfully.

Kavita, now annoyed, stepped closer to him, knife still in hand, twirling it around her fingers.

"I suppose if you were trying to kill me, you would have done so a while ago."

He nodded as one perfect piece of gelled, curly hair fell over his eyebrow.

"Well, I'm glad, out of both of us, you were the one to say it, darling."

Time stood still as moments went by in silence. Kavita loved when people knew how to be comfortable in silence. She would always be met with a "What's wrong? Why are you so quiet?" from the many men she would encounter. This was a first for her, and she secretly enjoyed it. The man cleared his throat as he looked in his pocket, noticing he had smoked his last cigarette the night before.

"Do you mind sharing one, Miss Kavita?"

Kavita stared at him while blowing cigarette smoke in his face.

"A lady like me doesn't smoke, and even if I did, I don't smoke with strangers."

She laughed as she looked back at the skyline, now fully awake with newspapers slinging left and right. Kavita dreaded going down because she knew people would look at her with disgust or pity because they knew, in some way, the Ridleys would always win. She didn't care—or at least, that was what she wanted to trick her brain into thinking. The man took notice of her change of expression.

"Well, Miss Kavita, wielder of intricate pocketknives. I'm Franklin, and normally, I'd say what a pleasure it is to meet you, but I must say I fear for my life."

Kavita slowly put her hands in her gold clutch purse, reaching for her last Chesterfield. She dangled the cigarette in his face like he was a dog waiting for his toy.

"Since we are no longer strangers, I guess I'll let you indulge in my last, dearest cigarette, Mr. Franklin." Kavita smiled quite deviously as she held her lighter to his cigarette.

He had broad shoulders that looked like a perfect headrest when she tilted her head. Kavita pondered on why she hadn't seen someone like him before. He was very well dressed, with his black silk tie and gold cuff links, but she noticed some wear on his hands around his knuckles. That alone told her he wasn't a man from a wealthy family, which brought her comfort for many reasons. He wasn't there to drain her existence by talking about frivolous societal things that she didn't care about. Suddenly, she was hungry to know everything he was thinking behind those earthy-chestnut eyes.

Kavita had been this way ever since she'd moved to the States. Any boy or man she crossed paths with whom she fancied, even just a little, she imagined what her whole life would be like with them if they were together. That was something she and her sisters had in common. They'd visually planned out what their weddings would look like or what shade their children's eye color would be. Kavita would hope that if she had a girl, she would be just as demanding as she was. If she had a boy, she'd pray he wouldn't be a fool like his father for picking Kavita Ridley to be his mother.

Franklin approached her while staring her in the eye.

"I must say, behind your sunset eyes, a million thoughts must run, and I'm quite curious to know what's on your lovely little mind."

Kavita's eyes widened so much that her lashes hit the tips of her brows.

"How bold of you to say. There's nothing little about this mind."

He took a step closer while stubbing his cigarette out. His figure was daunting, standing over Kavita.

"Now, you know I didn't mean it like that, darling. I'm used to being bigger than everyone, and you're so petite."

Kavita half smiled as she looked up at him. He was towering over her, an inch or two taller than her older brother Wei.

"Funny you say that. Most men say I'm quite tall," Kavita said while noticing an angry man yelling at what looked like his wife or daughter in one of the windows.

Franklin straightened his tie while moving a step closer.

"Well, I'm not just any man, sweets."

Kavita smoldered, observing the moment while he took her in.

"Lucky for you, I'm not just any woman."

She took a step down, heading for the door. Franklin ran after her.

"So you're just going to leave without saying goodbye?"

Kavita's eyebrows arched in a cocky manner. Her smile widened while she tilted her head down.

"I never said hello, did I?"

Kavita smiled, thinking of the memory. That cherished thought didn't last long, though, as she remembered she couldn't have any more moments like that with him. She didn't want to be a person whom people continued to die around. Her parents had more life to live. Franklin deserved another chance. Even Dale, as terrible as he was. They had all made mistakes in this life. Maybe Lucky was right. She should join them. She stepped to the edge as the wind flew through her long black locks. The world was silent until she heard a door closing lightly.

It was Mr. Pierre.

He stayed quiet for a long time before speaking.

"You know, Miss Kavita, when I first came to serve your family, I had no one—and I mean, no one. I was once in the same position you are in now. I thought that there was no life left for me to live."

He paused before continuing, and tears flew down his cheeks. Kavita turned to him, stepping down, as she had never seen him cry.

"My whole family drowned."

Kavita immediately defended him.

"That wasn't your fault, Pierre. Father told me the story. I am different. Everything I have done was my fault."

He laughed brokenly. "Oh, my dear, that's where you are wrong. It was my fault. I chose to get belligerently drunk and get behind the wheel with my wife and twin girls . . . The car flew off the bridge, but I only saved myself. I was too drunk even to help my girls. None of them knew how to swim, and if I had been in my right mind that night . . . they would be here right now."

The air grew silent, because Kavita now realized this world was built on lies that were concealed from plain eyes, and it was up to them to pick up the pieces left behind. Kavita had been thrown into a family where each member had come from broken places. Even Mother and Father. Mother had left her family to start a new life in New York City. Father had come from the slums of Pennsylvania in hopes of achieving the American dream. She never knew what she should dream for when everything was served to her on a platter. When she thought she had found an escape, it had been taken from her. Mr. Pierre, a man who she thought had no faults, had done something as heinous as she had. She wept silently when he came and wrapped his arms around her.

"That's why I want you to return home to your family and start over again. Do you hear me?"

"Yes, Mr. Pierre," she said with resolve.

Chapter 32

Adesua Ridley

Adesua sat in Central Park, watching young children play at the Fall Festival. That would have been her, Kavita, and Amelia. Not anymore, though, as the idea she now had of Amelia was not the one she'd grown up with. She couldn't stop thinking of Amelia and who she was now versus who she'd always been. Adesua never would have thought her own sister would murder someone for them. She didn't like the thought that it had gone over her head.

Adesua waved to Joseph, as he was looking for her. They walked and walked until they were entirely out of sight of the large crowd at the festival. As time passed, they ended up in a part of the park she had never before roamed to. Adesua and her sisters would usually rush to get the best picnic spot in the sun on a good day like this. Joseph led her down a winding wooded pathway that made it feel like they were no longer in the city. The trickling sounds of the nearby ponds and fountains made her enjoy the serenity and solitude as she and Joseph walked hand in hand.

Joseph stopped and turned around, gesturing to the natural environment.

"Welcome to the Ramble, where we can ramble until our hearts end." He laughed at his joke before continuing. "Really, Adesua, I wanted to bring you here badly because every place we go, I found the outside world trying to creep in on our every move. This place was my getaway as a young boy. I'd come here and write poems, thoughts, dreams, and my despairs, because everything else was and is a distraction. I could finally hear myself think in a place like this, and I wanted to show you somewhere very special."

Adesua looked up to the sky and was pleased to see not buildings, but instead the sun peeking through every little leaf that offered lovely shade. Even with all the beauty around them, she couldn't help but think of their relationship and ties with Harlem. Years ago, Joseph was the one who'd introduced her to all these powerful people. The politician he had made her get involved with had then stepped away, trying to make his hands clean.

"Joseph, why am I the only one taking the fall for the corrupt things going on in Harlem? When you and I both know what my intention was from the beginning?"

Joseph was taken aback, because not even a calm part of the park could stop her mind from going. He sighed before figuring out an answer.

"Adesua . . . I . . . Well, the shipment you got involved in with the politician ended up being something I had no idea was so corrupt. They just promised me it would help the community and that having you involved would make it untouchable." He knew he had been placing blame on her as well.

The jig was up. If her whole family was put in the spotlight for problems others had created, he should be too.

"I will take the fall, Adesua. If and when it does come out. You have my word."

She started her walk back to Mr. Pierre. Words had no value to her anymore, and what the public thought didn't matter to her. They were still Ridleys above all else. Adesua made it home in time for dinner. Not like they had sat together as a family in a long time. Father and Mother had escaped to God knew where after the press conference.

Once dinner was served, Adesua stood up.

"I would like to kindly ask all staff to close the doors and leave for the rest of dinner."

Omar and Wei looked at each other, confused. Kavita sat there, emotionless. After what had happened to Franklin, there was nothing that could surprise her at this point. Diego stood up and walked over next to her. He knew exactly where she was going with this, and he was going to stand by her side and defend her no matter what.

"Diego and I found out a few weeks ago that Amelia is the one who killed Dale. We didn't want to rush to conclusions without hearing it from her, but she told me herself."

Diego spoke up. "Amelia claimed it was an accident, but we must tread lightly if she is capable of doing this with no remorse. I hate to say this wasn't the worst thing we found out."

Wei pushed his plate across the table. It broke.

"What is it, Adesua?" Wei said with utmost anger.

"She is our father's only *real* child."

Omar stood up, flipping his chair backward.

"I knew it. I knew it. It all makes sense. Father has been using all of us. He never had any plans for us. We were the cover-up after his mistake of having Amelia."

Henrik shrugged, on the brink of tears. He stayed quiet because now he was just as guilty as Amelia.

"None of us had the chance to lead the Ridley Line," Wei concluded.

It was silent in the grand room. What took Mr. Ridley years to orchestrate was a lie they had all been living since being adopted. They were only seen as his spares. Amelia was always the chosen one. Adesua knew this. They all did.

Chapter 33

Amelia Ridley

The drive from the Hamptons was more beautiful than usual. Amelia could sleep at night knowing she would no longer be blackmailed. Mrs. Darla sat next to her quietly, still crying from her actions. As they pulled up the long, winding driveway, she saw every car was lined up there. This meant all her siblings were home. Amelia could finally tell them all the truth. She was dying to. From her being their father's biological child to the blackmailers being people who were close to them. It would all finally be put to rest. At least, that was what she hoped for.

Amelia ran up the stairs to the dining room. She thought she had made it in time to tell them. The staff was whispering in corners as she walked in. Amelia furrowed her eyebrows, thinking how peculiar that was, as they would usually be serving the family dessert and refilling drinks.

"Is there a reason you are not doing your job?" Amelia said it quite curtly.

"Miss Adesua ordered us out," a young girl said with her head bowed.

Adesua? Since when had she ever done that? Something didn't feel right, but she was going to find out. She opened the French doors to an array of angry faces. It was as if she'd stepped into a den of wolves.

They all glared at her in different ways, except Henrik didn't dare lift his head up from his plate.

"Oh, look, it's our beloved queen ready to rule us all, isn't that right, Amelia?" Wei snarked.

"Wei, stop with the antics and tell me what's going on," Amelia replied, annoyed.

Wei laughed, looking at Adesua. "Is this girl really serious?"

He pulled up a chair, straddling it backward and putting his elbows across the top, letting his chin rest on his knuckles.

"Let's start off with the one helluva banger. I didn't think you could top Dale's death. We all knew, deep down, you did that shit! Now for the real kicker: you being Father's bastard child?" Wei slammed the table with the palm of his hand. "You had us all fooled, thinking we were in this together. No, you took the lead just like Father had planned all along. You made us feel like we were unworthy of the position, when truthfully we never had a shot."

Amelia walked over to the table and sat down.

"Father manipulated me since I was a child to never tell a soul to protect our mother. Not only did he do that, but he threatened that if I did tell, he would take all of your shares from the company."

Amelia could see their expressions slowly changing. Wei still had his guard up, not wanting to let it down. Adesua grabbed Amelia's hand. She could finally see her again. Her eyes lit up when she took the time to hear her. They had all been manipulated by Father in some way as the chess pieces in his game. Amelia knew no one else would understand their family in the way they did. She was finally at peace with putting her heart first. No longer putting her Father's expectations first in her vision. No longer would she play this role that Father had wanted for her, and it felt good to let it all go. She could finally exhale.

Was this the speck of time that she needed to finally spill the news of Dale being their Father's child too? How much could their hearts bear?

"I don't want to hide anything anymore from any of you. Yes, I have done some terrible things, but I won't allow Father to ruin our futures. I am willing to do what it takes. Not just for me but for all of us. I need you all to trust me. Whatever it takes to gain your trust back," Amelia said with sorrow. "Over the years, I have seen how Father has treated me differently. I have tried to ignore it, but you're right—I knew. I knew Father was always going to have me lead the company. He probably knew the day I was born, but I can't control him, you all know this," she exclaimed.

She stood from her chair, walking to the window, taking a look at the moon, hoping for a sign. The only thought that came to her mind was to kneel on the ground toward them, and put her head on the floor. It was her way of surrendering the control she subconsciously had over them. Amelia wanted to strip her father's vile ways from her in any way she could.

"Forgive me, my brothers and sisters. As I have asked God for mercy, I ask you and beg you."

The air around them changed heavily. No one wanted to take another breath.

Diego cried out from the pain building up. "I wish we could all go back and remember the day we met. We promised each other that we had each other." He sniffled before continuing. "So let's have each other. I am sorry for joining in on the witch hunt, Amelia. We didn't know what to believe," he said, taking a shuttered look at Adesua.

Adesua walked across the formal dining room, getting Amelia off the ground.

"Get up," she said in a playful manner.

"I love you, Adesua. I am sorry for putting you in an uncomfortable position, making it hard to trust me," Amelia said while hugging her close.

She felt something different than she had in a long time, something that her family had been missing: peace. When that was near, the secrets they shared slowly started to fade away. Wei nodded without showing much emotion, but she knew her kneeling to them was the start. It had changed the power dynamics that her father had pushed on them. Now she would lead with her siblings.

At the nape of her neck, she could feel each hair standing up, pleading with her to tell the truth. Amelia knew that some hurts were unbearable, even for her siblings. Dale was no longer a threat to them, and he surely wasn't one of *them.* They were the Seven Wonders, and he was a mere thought in their past that didn't need any more power. Some secrets were truths that only the dead were meant to carry.

Chapter 34

Kavita Ridley

It was the day of Franklin's funeral. Instead of picking a dress for her wedding, Kavita was wearing a black fur-trimmed dress with a black tulle hat. She tried to conceal her pain. She looked at her reflection in the mirror. She had aged in just a few short months. If she could go back and warn herself, she would never have met Franklin. Because now she mourned his love and loss; she wouldn't be able to have either in this lifetime.

She wept into her black handkerchief. Amelia and Adesua rushed into the room and held her as she broke down. Kavita wouldn't pray this pain on anyone. She craved his touch. She wanted his smell around her once more. Her brothers had begged her not to go in case the Mob made an appearance, but she was going to be there no matter what.

Mr. Pierre drove Kavita and her sisters to St. Patrick's Cathedral. Wei, being the overprotective brother, drove her brothers in his car. She thought one day she would be here for her or Amelia's wedding, but instead of a celebration, it was to mourn the life she could have had. She took down the lace tulle covering her face. The moment her heels touched the ground, the crowd screamed their names. Even in the face of death, they had no sympathy for her. It was another moment when the rich had lost. A moment for them to use in another gossip column.

A time for the rich to be humbled. Kavita let them believe they were winning by allowing them to see her in despair.

Kavita hoped the church would be filled with people, and indeed it was. The large white Gothic arches made it feel like heaven. She hoped Franklin's heaven was like this. Small rainbows were cast from the beautiful stained-glass windows. She did love him, and so did others. She saw the young boys whom he'd gotten out of trouble with the law sitting together, weeping. The elderly lady who lived across the street from him, Mrs. Tamara; he would get her groceries every week as her health had started to fade.

He was more than his past life with Lucky. Even if that was how the press portrayed him, she knew he had done more in this life than most. The smell of incense wafted to her nose. It smelled like sweet honey and lavender. It wasn't Franklin's scent, but she settled for it, as it gave her some peace.

Kavita and her siblings sat in the front row. None of Franklin's family showed up, in fear of retaliation by the new leader after Lucky and Franklin had died. It was seen as an act of disrespect, since Franklin had turned his back on Lucky. Kavita shook her head at how sad it was that even family would turn on him like this at death. She knew that even after all the scandals and secrets, her siblings would be there for her, life or death.

The organ player took his seat and started to play, soft and low. It was a beautiful hymn. The notes reverberated through their lungs. Oh, how she wished it could bring life into Franklin again. As the tempo began to quicken just a tad more, she felt her heart race as the priest came to the pulpit. Father Callaghan gave a head tilt to Kavita in respect of Franklin's passing. He was adorned in green-and-gold vestments.

Father Callaghan had been her favorite priest since she was a young girl. She'd always been fond of him and his stoic Irish ways. She knew he was going to have quite the word to say about Franklin, but she hoped he would spare him.

"Franklin Califero was not a person you'd call a saint, by any means. He was many things: a builder, a person who wanted to create a legacy and a family with Kavita Ridley. He died in pursuit of this and protecting the one he loved."

Whispers and murmurs echoed through the cathedral. They could whisper all they wanted, but she knew every word he said was true. Her head felt heavy as she tried to keep it up. Knowing that Franklin was so close but so far was unimaginable. If he could only have seen the impact he had in one room. Franklin would sometimes find himself insecure that he didn't have the things the Ridleys had, but he had a heart and soul that would have gotten him there. Something her father had lost long ago.

After the service ended, the crowd quickly dispersed, getting out of sight. No one was sure whether the mobsters from Lucky's group would be there. A line of cars waited along Fifth Avenue, with Mr. Pierre in front to escort her. The drive wasn't long, but it was the end of their story. She knew he would have held her hand and said, "This is just a moment in time, my Kavi."

The Woodlawn Cemetery in the Bronx was where he would be laid to rest. He would be beside his father, reunited once again. It pained her that both Franklin and his father had met the same fate. Kavita wished for a moment that she had been pregnant with Franklin's child. She would have had a piece of him in this world. She cradled her stomach, feeling an emptiness that overwhelmed her body.

The priest stood to the side of the open grave near the tombstone. His voice trailed through the heavily blowing wind. He read the final rites. She held a white rose close to her heart, not wanting to release it, as this would be their final thread of love together. She opened up the locket he'd given her with the pressed marigold flowers and a picture of them. She kissed it gently as the rose fell from her hand.

Kavita looked to the sky, hoping he knew she didn't want to leave him. She looked over at a nearby tree. Two men from the funeral were standing far away, wanting to remain unseen. When she made eye contact with them, they turned and walked away. Wei and Henrik stood by Kavita's side as she walked away from the crowd of people. The rest of the siblings followed. Omar brushed his hand on her arm, trying to console her.

"I want to say how proud I am of you, Kavita, for how you are handling this," Wei remarked. "I admit I have been hard on you in the past, but you're doing great, little sis, and we've got you."

Kavita looked up at her siblings. For the first time, they were acknowledging her together. She wasn't being scolded for using her free will to do the things she enjoyed. They saw her as someone who had grown into a woman and who was now mourning death once again, which they had all experienced. She struggled to fight back tears.

"I think it's safe to say we put all of this in the past," Amelia added.

Henrik nodded. "As much as I get tired of cleaning up after your messes, I wouldn't do it for anyone else," he said as he gave Kavita a kiss on the forehead.

"Are we all good now?" Diego asked, taking a look at Adesua.

Adesua approached Kavita, giving her a tight hug and spinning her around.

Adesua chuckled quietly. "I think we are."

The Riverside Park Promenade was golden bright and airy the next morning. Kavita and her sisters walked together hand in hand. After Franklin's death, something had broken in them. The pride in what they should do to protect only themselves faded away. Seeing Franklin dead was different from Dale's death. Franklin was someone who loved Kavita, and they knew it.

The Hudson River was in their view in the early-morning sky. She loved being one with nature. She felt like Franklin was now in the wind that blew past them, ruffling the grand trees. Kavita still wore all black in mourning, but something in her heart felt at peace that the war was over. A ferry slowly chugged along the river. She wanted the same escape.

Kavita saw the glow in Amelia's eyes come back. She had thought she had lost her after Dale's death. The warmth in her was there. The last time they'd sat in silence together was when they were young teenagers. For once, neither one of them had anything to say. They watched the ducks go silently by them. Kavita started humming a song called "Bye Bye Blackbird."

The park wasn't too busy that Friday morning. She expected to see more cars out and about, but the quietness around her was much more prominent as her heels crunched the fall leaves beneath her. Once they made it to the Turtle Pond, there was a handful of people, some feeding the nearby ducks, others reading a book in the shade.

"I don't want us to keep secrets like this from each other anymore," Kavita remarked.

"I think we should go back and burn everything, if I am being honest," Adesua responded.

Kavita had written a letter to each of her siblings, leaving them at their doors. Tonight, on the full moon, they would let everything go. All the pain, the murder, the lies, and the secrets. She was over it, once and for all.

My dearest siblings,

Meet at the lake at 3 am. Tell no one of this. Be discreet, and whatever you do, do not wake Father and Mother.

Yours truly,

Kavita

Chapter 35

Adesua Ridley

It was almost two a.m., but Adesua and Diego rushed to the kitchen as soon as he heard about their night out on the beach. He grabbed a handful of lemons and raspberries, making fresh raspberry lemonade and then cucumber-and-herb-butter finger sandwiches, which were Amelia's favorite. Then, for the boys, he made smoked salmon with a spread of cream cheese and dill. He assembled bowls of fresh fruit, saltwater taffy, and Adesua's favorite, caramel popcorn. He wanted to do more, but an hour had already passed.

He gathered his siblings to help him bring it to the beach. It was the first time in a long time that they didn't need the maids. Amelia grabbed the bowls of fruit and saltwater taffy, heading straight toward the beach. She looked over at Diego while they walked.

"Thank you for thinking of this. I can't think of a better way to end this weekend," Amelia said.

Diego pondered before looking at Amelia with his green doe eyes. "Amelia, thank you so much for being our second mother, even though we never admit to it."

Adesua laughed as she saw Amelia give him a slanted smile. Like Amelia, Adesua knew their siblings had good intentions and tried not to worry her. She saw they had all grown from this in the best way, because most would consider all their ordeals a travesty. She had felt guilty for doubting her family's loyalty, but in the end, they were together and had made it nearly unscathed.

Amelia had forgotten how lovely their private beach was. The beautiful, elegant lanterns cast the perfect amount of soft, warm light, illuminating the sand.

There was just enough light to see because of the bright stars and full moon. She wondered, at that moment, why her parents never came down for small gatherings like this. Unless there was a major event, they were nowhere to be found.

Adesua and a just-awoken Kavita rushed to the cabanas, plopping themselves down on the plush red lounge chairs. Kavita grabbed one of the white pillows and threw it to Amelia to catch. Omar grabbed the volleyball and then threw it to Wei.

"Are you ready for an old game of volleyball together?"

Henrik grabbed his guitar and said, "Well, while you all get rowdy, I'm gonna play some tunes."

It was organized chaos with Henrik playing on his guitar. While Adesua pulled out her paints and blank canvas paper, Kavita found her way to the water. This time, it was her choice. Kavita had never had a fear of the water until seeing Dale's lifeless body in the pond. She used to love splashing water in her sisters' faces at the pool or tossing a glass of water at men's faces when they got too rowdy with her.

Wei and Diego decided to play a match against Amelia and Omar. The siblings looked at each other when Wei started doing his aerobic stretches. He jogged in place, swaying his hands left and right toward each foot. Diego looked at Amelia while laughing.

"Wei, you know this isn't a real competition, right?"

Wei scoffed, pursing his lips in a smile. His two dimples sank in even more by the time he flashed his teeth. "Oh, my dear brother, everything in life is a competition. See this?"

Wei pointed at different things while running in the circle around the net.

"We were the lucky ones. The chosen ones. We could all still be back in our mother country without parents, struggling to eat a piece of bread. But . . ."

He pointed to the heavens.

"We won. Every one of us won in life. Suppose we all chose not to do a single thing else. We have lived lives that other people will never experience. Don't you understand?"

Adesua grabbed her canvas from the lounge chair, moving closer to the beach. "Wei, is this the moment we all sit down in a circle and listen to your plan to take over the world, or are you all going to play volleyball?"

Omar burst out in laughter. Something he rarely did, but it honestly amused him to see someone humble Wei.

"Hey, I was just giving them a chance to warm up, Dusie, hush!"

After two rounds of beach volleyball, Wei and Diego lost to Omar and Amelia. Wei had enough.

"See, I let you all off easy. I had one too many glasses of cold tea." He winked at Omar.

"Ahh, yes, cold tea. I'm sure it was a nice glass of Dom Péri."

Wei waddled to the shore beside Adesua, who was painting Kavita in the water. Adesua had a talent for painting with oils, and her paintings looked so realistic, as if they were photographs. In an hour, she was nearly done with the painting, to Wei's surprise.

"Dusie, you should start showcasing your work again. Why do you insist on filling the house with them? The world should see this."

Adesua looked down, her eyes glassing over in thought. Ever since she'd been embarrassed at the ballet, she hadn't considered she could be anything more than just a Ridley sister. Hearing it from her siblings didn't change that for her. They were at odds, too, but they didn't even realize it. The majority of them, apart from Amelia and Henrik, wouldn't be able to live the lives they had or wanted to have just because of who they were and where they came from. Adesua looked to Wei.

"Wei, I love you, but you know that both you and I have it a little harder, especially since the Chinese Exclusion Act, but you find a way to make it work, don't you."

Wei's eyebrows lifted. "Of course I do, Adesua. You're right, though—we make a way."

He jumped up and headed straight for the table of food Diego had prepared. Adesua realized she may have spoken too brashly, but she knew they had a silent understanding.

Ever since graduating from a Black college, she'd been even more confused about who she was. It had felt like a facade learning about Black history and how they were the generation that could try to make changes in the country. She couldn't remember the last time she'd befriended another Black woman like herself. The closest was when she saw them walking with their already formed groups, while she was walking with her white and Indian sisters.

They'd all looked at them with disgust. She'd felt like she was an ally, in a way, by donating money, but she could never bring herself to go alone to Black communities. In her heart, Adesua felt like a fraud in the Black community.

Amelia looked to the side and saw Kavita walk closer to the sand.

"Well, finally, our mermaid—" Henrik yelled, cutting in. "Or a Siren!"

Kavita rolled her eyes, putting her hair up. "Hilarious, Henrik. How about you be a doll and give your sis a towel," she said with a mischievous smile.

"Hmm, well, it's the least I can do for you, Kavi, since you almost died and all."

Amelia turned her head and sent Henrik a look. "No, no, no, it's too soon, Henrik."

Henrik waved his hand at Amelia.

"What? Everyone knows Kavita has a dry sense of humor."

He rolled his pant legs up to prevent the water from hitting them.

"Here, you little pest—" Kavita dragged Henrik into the water.

He squealed like a child. "Damn you, Kavi!"

They all laughed as Henrik dragged Kavita back to shore. They sat down in a circle near a bonfire. The salty breeze filled their lungs as they passed around the bowl of caramel popcorn and glasses of sweet raspberry lemonade. Henrik strummed a low, lovely melody on his guitar. Kavita warmed up her voice with light humming and began singing over Henrik's notes. They all looked at each other, nearly in tears, as she sang. Adesua looked over to Wei, who was sitting next to Omar. It took a few moments for him to notice her gaze. She mouthed a simple "I'm sorry" to him.

He looked back at the fire, then her, mouthing, "I love you, Dusie."

Adesua smiled at this. If there was one thing the Ridley siblings knew, it was forgiveness. They had no trouble saying they loved each other or giving hugs when someone needed it. On the other hand, Kavita was a little more standoffish, but everyone knew she loved them each uniquely. The stars weren't the only thing shining tonight as the night grew darker. Their love for one another beamed so brightly that Father and Mother could see it from their balcony.

"I never thought I'd see this day again." Caroline wept silently as she laid her head on her husband's shoulder.

"Cherish it, my dear. Cherish it." He rubbed her shoulder as they walked back into their primary suite.

Adesua's eyes blurred at the sight of Mrs. Darla and Jamison walking hand in hand as he helped her hold her balance in the dark. She got closer to the firepit. Jamison carried a bag filled with letters and diaries.

"My little Ridleys." Mrs. Darla chuckled softly. "It's with the greatest regret that I must announce I am leaving. After my betrayal to you, I can't bear to stay another day," she said through tears.

Adesua looked at her, immediately shaking her head. "No, Mrs. Darla, we won't allow it."

"You kids are still too good for your own good." She sighed.

Jamison straightened up as he looked at them. "I am sorry for lying and even thinking of leaking the file for personal gain. I let greed get in the way. To extend my apology, these are all the files and evidence of what you all have done," he said.

"Does anyone else have any apologies or words of confession to offer?" Adesua gave everyone a piercing glance, especially Amelia.

Amelia took a champagne glass and smirked at the thought of grabbing the bottle again—but this time, to pour—then raised her glass. "Here's to a new beginning of us, the Seven Wonders. Let this earth take back the memories and secrets that have besieged us."

Wei looked at Adesua, and seeing the photo of them near the top of the bag, he grabbed it. Amelia and the others made the fire bigger, dumping all the evidence and watching it go ablaze. They all sighed in relief. Their lives could start over now. This time, they would do it the right way. Adesua's eyes started to water as she saw each piece shrivel into oblivion.

While the Ridleys were running around the beach, confessing their dreams and desires to each other, Adesua spoke to Amelia and Kavita about going to Paris when this was all settled. They made a promise to each other as they held hands.

The beloved New York City citizens waited patiently for the Monday news. Young girls brushed their hair, gossiping with their sisters about what could have happened to Dale at the party and about the deaths of mobster Lucky and Kavita's fiancé, Franklin.

The gossip traveled all the way down to middle-class wannabes ready to start rumors in their social circles about what had gone down at the party, knowing well enough that they weren't invited. Oh, how the Ridleys wished this were it. But for now, they all shared one last secret.

Chapter 36

Amelia Ridley

Amelia walked down the hallway, echoing the footsteps of doctors and nurses and the wailing of her mother's tears. Father lay behind closed doors, letting out random outbursts. His grand office that had once been filled with intense meetings was now a room for his recovery. His breath was slowly failing him, and his power was slowly leaving him. Father was no longer the intimidating figure that had made them all go quiet when he entered a room. None of her brothers wanted to see him after what had been exposed about Amelia.

"Mellie, bring me my boy Wei," Father pleaded.

She would nod and say he was coming, but Amelia knew he was never coming. Just like Father's ailing body was failing him, Wei was doing the same, for good reason.

Night and day began to blend together, but this morning, Amelia knew. It was the day of the emergency board meeting. She'd called all the members after Father had persistently failed certain cognitive tests. His mental health was severely declining, alongside his physical health. Mr. Pierre opened the car door for her, as Wei and Omar were driving their own cars to the Ridley headquarters in Midtown.

The sunrays hit the board meeting room, giving her a feeling of hope. Amelia didn't feel nervous, as this was her destiny. She waited for

Wei and Omar to walk through the doors. She adjusted her green skirt and cream blouse before speaking.

"Gentlemen, thank you for coming. It has come time to start this meeting," she said with authority. "As some of you know, my father's health has declined severely. This has caused him to make some unseemly alliances with criminals that I was able to defuse almost immediately before they went to press. I, Amelia Ridley, vote to bring my father, Edward Ridley, out due to a threat to the Ridley Line."

Without hesitation, each man held up his hand one by one. She expected some backlash from Father's longtime friends, but even they had had enough. When money came into play, loyalty was out the door. The motion cleared with flying colors and no conflict. Wei and Omar smiled at their sister. She could see that she'd earned their respect for how she'd handled this.

"As of today, from this point on, we are not here just for greed and to hoard wealth for us all. We are going to correct the wrongs that have been building over the last few years."

The men got a little tight at hearing this. They knew they were sharks and cared only about how to make themselves richer, but hearing it out loud was a different story.

"We will liquidate a vast amount of the Ridley Line's assets and put funds back into Harlem, which was wrongly taken advantage of by our alliance with bootleggers. This affected their livelihood. We can't build if we take away."

Amelia turned to Omar and Wei. She could have sworn she saw Wei's eyes redden. She wasn't going to leave them in the dark like Father had. They had helped Father grow the Ridley Line over the last five years, and she wasn't going to let Father or herself take the credit for it anymore.

"Omar and Wei, from this day forward, will be c0-leading all logistics and strategic control of the Ridley Line's passenger division."

Omar and Wei looked at each other, flashing smiles.

"Every vessel will be of the utmost luxury for our future passengers," Wei said with eagerness.

Omar nodded. "I assure you, there will be no shortcuts with this. We just needed someone to trust us, and this will indeed send the Ridley Line to new heights."

"In light of this, the rest of our siblings will have a fair share of the Ridley Line's future expansions," she said peacefully.

This change was the beginning of a new era. No more tyrant in charge of everything. Amelia had felt a dangerous sense of that control and never wanted to feel that again. This time, it felt right.

Chapter 37

The Press

The New York Times
December 9, 1927
THE RIDLEY EMPIRE HAS NEW HONCHOS IN CHARGE

The health decline of the infamous shipping magnate Edward Ridley has caused a stir at the Ridley Line. This has caused the eldest, Amelia Ridley, Wei Ridley, and Omar Ridley to take over interim control of the Ridley Line. She has announced the liquidation of major assets for philanthropic endeavors. They have invested in Harlem to fix the Mob scandals that have affected the community. The word on Wall Street is that their stock has climbed a staggering seven percent this week alone.

The Chicago Courier
December 12, 1927
THE RIDLEYS' SEASON OF SCANDAL COMES TO AN END?

The Ridleys are no stranger to scandal this year, from a death at their party to their shipping dynasty now changing hands to the younger generation. The eldest siblings are now in control. The police have ruled Dale Caimen's death a tragic accident. The deaths of mobster Lucky Moretti and his nephew, who happened to be Kavita Ridley's fiancé, were a tragic case of kidnapping and Mob ties.

Los Angeles Tribune
February 13, 1928
HOLLYWOOD AND HIGH SOCIETY: STARDUST AND SCANDAL

The Ridleys have everything. Death, power, talent, and bingo, INHERITANCE. Rumor has it that Kavita Ridley has been seen in the studios for her talent. Omar and Wei Ridley have been rumored to be talking to a luxury cruise designer from our great sunny state of California. The Rockefellers can move out of the way and learn a lesson from the Ridleys on fixing a ruined reputation!

The Ridleys had gone quiet for the first time in over a decade. The world was talking, not just the people of New York. The press waited for their next move, but even the Ridleys didn't know what it would be.

Epilogue

Amelia nodded to herself while tears flowed. Adesua hugged her tightly, and each of her brothers bid a silent farewell. Kavita stood there for a moment, observing the goodbyes. They could each feel their hearts getting lighter with every word that brought them closer to walking away from the life they once knew. There was a certain beauty in the ignorance of not knowing what would happen next. Each of them had had calendars planned out for their lives since the moment they'd set foot on the estate. Now the only thing that was dragging them away from their desires was no longer a factor.

"I am lucky to share a name with you all. I always wanted a family, and my heart is breaking at the thought of us separating, but I know God will somehow bring us back together," Kavita said with haste, gasping and in tears. They circled for one last group hug.

Wei kissed Adesua on the forehead, then bumped her arm with his fist, a little roughhousing after everything they had been through together.

"To the Seven Wonders," he whispered confidently as they all brought their fists together in one circle, then broke away solemnly. They all had a role to play in this new hand life had dealt them.

Kavita and Adesua held hands in the back seat as Amelia looked out the window. The estate seemed so much smaller to her now as they drove away. Her brothers all waving goodbye felt so *final* to her. She was terrified of having made this decision, sure it was out of desperation and would leave her feeling a little empty. But for the first time, she could feel the fear escaping her lungs, a release of the pressure of what her life was no longer.

The sun started to rise as they approached New York Harbor. The SS *Paris* stood in the water as a haven for the girls. Adesua and Kavita squealed excitedly as they looked at Amelia.

"We are doing this!" Kavita yelped in joy, looking in awe at the magnificent ship.

Adesua smiled. The stars were aligning for the Ridley sisters. The gangway was filled to the brim with crew and passengers, but the sisters felt like they were finally on the right path. All their fears melted away with each step they took as they got closer to the inside of the ship. As the ship set sail, Amelia smiled in wonder, taking in the views of New York getting smaller and smaller through the grand windows as she walked the promenade.

Seven Days Later
Paris, France

The days blurred together as they sailed across the Atlantic Ocean. The ship came to a stop, to the Ridley sisters' surprise. They had made it to the Port of Le Havre. Amelia got a taxi for the girls, and they made their way to the Transatlantique Express. Paris was one step closer, and so were their new lives.

Adesua had imagined what the streets of Paris would be like in contrast to New York. She hoped that maybe she, too, would find her family here in artists. Adesua silently thanked Joseph as she watched the small fishing villages and large cliffs go by. The Normandy countryside seemed so full of life, which was so different from New York's vast skyscrapers. She caught a glance of Kavita resting with a serenity she hadn't seen since they were children.

Kavita slept for the first time in weeks. Adesua and Amelia smiled at the fact that their little sister had found some peace. Amelia thought momentarily about how her plan had turned out to be bigger than she'd expected—in a good way. Having her sisters by her side made it all feel complete. The train began to slow, but her body pulsated with anticipation. She was home.

Amelia walked hand in hand with her siblings into the Paris she had once known. They marched with excitement, uncertainty, but most of all, freedom. Something they hadn't tasted in too long.

The sisters gawked at their surroundings. Adesua noticed a woman with bright-red lips painting to her heart's desire. Amelia pulled a slip of folded paper out of her pocket. It was the last thing holding her back from this new world. It was her confession that she was Dale's murderer. At one point, she was going to release it and deal with the consequences of her choices. Instead, she was able to help her sisters, and especially brothers, start anew one last time before she focused on becoming a better version of herself.

This was a goodbye to New York, a goodbye to upholding her family's reputation. A goodbye to the kind of control that had choked their lives of any magic.

Le Monde Parisian Lundi, 23 Janvier 1928

RIDLEY EMPIRE IN SHAMBLES: HEIRESSES FLEE AS NEW SCANDALS EMERGE

Allegations of corruption rattle the Ridley Line, while Edward Ridley's three young daughters have gone missing from New York.

The difference between New York and Paris was that the secrets were sweeter and *deadlier*. Amelia tore up the paper and released the pieces to the wind, watching as the wind carried them along the Seine until they gracefully vanished like the secrets of their past.

Well, at least that was what the Seven Wonders hoped for.

Acknowledgments

Wow, we really are just on a floating rock in the middle of space, and somehow or another, my book landed in your hands. In all seriousness, life is truly beautiful and filled with endless opportunities that I must thank God for. I could have continued to give up on this story when I got married at twenty or after becoming a divorced military wife, oh, and a single mother! Society would have told me to give up a long time ago, but I persisted because I come from a lineage of badass, beautiful, powerful Black women.

Which leads me to thanking my beautiful family, the Colley Clan, as we recently named our humble abode Castle Colley. Natalie Colley, my inspirational and loving mother, is a force to be reckoned with. When I close my eyes and think of the word "power," a picture of my mother comes to mind. Granny, Aurelia Colley, who is still the best English teacher in the world, molded me into the quirky and eclectic being I am today. Thank you for forcing me to watch Turner Classic Movies, which I grew to love, and being the foundation of what every author should be, and that is genuine. Cardiss Colley, my crazy and fun auntie, you are a glowing light in my life, and I wouldn't know what to do without you. My sweet princess and beautiful daughter, Aurora Cain, you are the main reason I keep going and growing every day. With your love and joy, I am complete.

To my lovely agent, Ashley Hong: Words can't compare to the gratitude I have for you. It was divine timing that I was blessed enough to have you from the beginning. Thank you for going through the many drafts of *TRR*, which were around ten or more! You went through the trenches with me and motivated me to be the author I am today. At every step of the process, you were there for me, and I thank God for you!

To the amazing editors, Liz and Lindsey: I appreciate your watchful eye in making sure *TRR* was molded in the way it needed to be. Elizabeth Agyemang, how blessed am I to have an amazing editor who championed my book and heard me. You saw the potential of how beautiful this story will be, and for that I am incredibly grateful. Each revision brought *TRR* to where it is today, and I am blessed to have you as an editor and a friend.

Ruth Hervies, you dynamite rock star of a woman, for over fifteen years of friendship from beauty pageant auditions to us both finding our way in the publishing industry. I appreciate you for supporting me, always.

To Nicholas G. Sims, my fellow Mobile family, I thank you for helping me visualize the greatness of *TRR*.

To my close friends Dayla Rae Trest, Floriane Gorosin, Nicole Collins, and Paloma: Where would I be without our conversations and hangouts? I mean, seriously, talking me down from the verge of a breakdown or making me dinner when I was in the middle of a deadline. It takes a tribe, and I am so very thankful.

Thank you to my other families: the Youngs from Terrance; Adrian Tolliver; and especially Janie Tolliver, for keeping me inspired in my writing over the years and for being an amazing teacher.

To Aunt Margarette and Uncle Joe Joe: Love you always for supporting me!

Thank you to Marvin, for always funding my crazed young adult book days.

Thank you, Charles and the Yelding family, for being there to show me the ways of up north and always giving a lending hand if I was ever in need.

Where do I begin with my lovely and amazing author friends who have kept me sane through all the dealings and fiascos of debut life? I appreciate each of you: Hannah Grace, Nekesa Afia, Charlene Wang, and Kristin Offiler!

Shout-out to my favorite Delco family, the Bellews, for showing this Southern belle the beauty of Pennsylvania, especially Philly and Lancaster, and informing me that water is indeed pronounced *wooder*.

To the teachers who changed my life. Miss Shannon Deas: I love you, and I hate that you aren't here to see this book come to life. I just want to thank you for staying after school when my mom was working two jobs and letting me watch a movie with you or read a book.

Thank you, Mrs. Patterson, for being there and encouraging me to be a better reader even from the first grade!

Thank you, Mrs. Waite, for being the best English teacher to me in middle school. Although you were hard on me, it made me into the writer I am today. I thank you so much for that.

To my 2012 Duke University summer camp people, you know who you are! I am so glad that I had roommates like the each of you from China, South Korea, India, Venezuela, France, Canada, and more. This was a summer that changed my life by learning about each other's cultures and slang. I can't wait to see you all again!

A major shout-out of love and gratitude is for you. Yes, *you*! The reader, the visionary, the other wonder. Wow, I am honored to have you reading this. For the ones who have been here for the last five years to the ones who just found me, you made this possible. I pray love and blessings in your life and that you see the wonders of the world around you.

Finally, to New York. I became a woman here. I am sure you are wondering, *What do you mean by that?* New York City was the first place I visited alone at the age of twenty-three. I never traveled without my family, in fear of being by myself. Here, I never felt alone. As every soul walked by, I realized how every face I saw had a story. No one cared what I did. No one cared how I dressed. I felt at home here. Which is why I set *TRR* in this great city filled with chance, love, and new beginnings. Now I truly understand that if you can make it here, you can make it anywhere.

Here's to us all being the next wonder.

Dramatis Personae

THE RIDLEY HEIRS

Amelia Ridley – Eldest Ridley daughter; the calm, cool, and collected responsible sibling

Adesua Ridley – The artistic sister who finds her way into the world of Harlem

Kavita Ridley – Wild child; youngest daughter who lives for the thrill of finer things

Wei Ridley – Eldest Ridley brother, who takes the spotlight any chance he gets

Omar Ridley – The stoic mediator, an empathetic elder brother

Diego Ridley – The jovial younger brother, an inspiring chef who is stuck at Columbia University

Henrik Ridley – Youngest Ridley brother, musically talented, and wit to boot

FAMILY AND RIVALS

Edward Ridley – Father, who ensures the perfect family image and line of succession

Caroline Ridley – Mother, philanthropist who is polished and protective of the Ridley heirs

Jamison Grant – Amelia's first love and heir of the rival family

Ella and Garrison Grant – Jamison and Elion's parents, the Ridleys' rivals

Elion Grant – The unpredictable, reckless younger brother of Jamison

Dale Caimen – Gossip columnist who sees only red, revealing society's darkest secrets

Franklin – Kavita's brooding fiancé, who doesn't fit the usual mold of the upper class

Lucky Moretti – A mobster whose goal is to wreak havoc in high society

Sebastien – The flamboyant cousin who is the life of the party

Theo Montgomery – Adesua's childhood friend

Fred Remington – Caroline Ridley's brother who stays out of the limelight

HOUSEHOLD AND SOCIETY

Mr. Jenkins – Head butler

Mrs. Darla – Head maid

Mr. Pierre – Chauffeur

Chef Laurent – Household cook

Joseph – Adesua's boyfriend

Lila, Nicole, Pam, and Ellie – Kavita's close friends

Kai Zhang – Wei's new friend

Shuye Zhang – Wei's love interest

Nathaniel and Gregory – Wei's college friends

Iman Gerielli – Ballet patron

Elena Fontaine – Manhattan Ballet director

HISTORICAL FIGURES

Harlem Renaissance

Ann Lowe – Black fashion designer who created gowns for the Ridley sisters

Aaron Douglas – Harlem Renaissance artist whom Adesua Ridley admired

Josephine Baker – Famous dancer, singer, and actress who is fond of Kavita

A'Lelia Walker – Harlem socialite who introduces Adesua Ridley to the Dark Tower

Zora Neale Hurston – A novelist whom Adesua runs into at the Dark Tower

Duke Ellington – Jazz bandleader, opens up the Ridley gala with his music

Bessie Smith – Singer who performs at the Ridley gala

Society and Industry

William E. Harmon – A patron of the Harlem arts whom Adesua briefly sees at the Foundation party

Daniel Ludwig – Young shipping prodigy seen at the same convention as Amelia Ridley

Commodore Harold S. Vanderbilt – Commodore of the New York Yacht Club, where Amelia sees him

Vice Commodore Vincent Astor – Vice Commodore of the New York Yacht Club, where Amelia sees him

Rear Commodore Winthrop W. Aldrich – An American banker who isn't fond of the Ridleys

The Astors – Family who has centuries of prestige and old money compared to the Ridleys

The Vanderbilts – Shipping tycoon family who also see the Ridleys as competition

About the Author

Photo © 2025 Jimena Lopez Fate

K.M. Colley writes thrillers, contemporary mysteries, and cinematic stories that explore legacy and ambition. Her work often centers around powerful families, glamorous settings, and complex characters. Born in Mobile, Alabama, she's currently based in Tampa and Philadelphia. When not writing or reading, K.M. enjoys traveling, learning new languages, and building a creative legacy. She's also passionate about raising her autistic daughter, who dreams of creating her own comic book one day.